*Sovereign Power. Eternal Pleasure.*

## The Secret History of Elizabeth Tudor, Vampire Slayer

"A spellbinding book, at once lush and intensely compelling . . . passionately crafted. . . . I found *The Secret History of Elizabeth Tudor, Vampire Slayer* to be one among that rare breed of fictional works: the lavish page turner—a book of elegant prose that you can't put down."

> —Kresley Cole, #1 *New York Times* bestselling and
> award-winning author of the *Immortals After Dark* series

"Get ready to know a shocking new side of the great Elizabeth I. Clever and surprising, Weston's tale of this regal young queen sparkles with intrigue, unfolding in graceful layers to reveal a previously hidden history of timeless, supernatural love and well-buried secrets."

> —Shana Abé, *New York Times* bestselling author
> of the *Drákon* series

"A fascinating blend of paranormal and historical, starring Elizabeth Tudor as a sixteenth-century kick-ass heroine—what a great concept!"

> —Kate Emerson, award-winning author of
> the *Secrets of the Tudor Court* series

"Breathtaking! Rich with passion and otherworldly intrigue, a bold new account of Elizabeth Tudor's vigilance and daring."

> —Sherri Browning Erwin, author of *Jane Slayre*

**This title is also available as an eBook**

# *The*
# SECRET HISTORY
## *of*
# ELIZABETH TUDOR,
# *Vampire Slayer*

---

# LUCY WESTON

**G**

*Gallery Books*

NEW YORK   LONDON   TORONTO   SYDNEY

Gallery Books
A Division of Simon & Schuster, Inc.
1230 Avenue of the Americas
New York, NY 10020

First Gallery Books trade paperback edition January 2011

GALLERY BOOKS and colophon are trademarks of Simon & Schuster, Inc.

For information about special discounts for bulk purchases, please contact Simon & Schuster Special Sales at 1-866-506-1949 or business@simonandschuster.com.

The Simon & Schuster Speakers Bureau can bring authors to your live event. For more information or to book an event contact the Simon & Schuster Speakers Bureau at 1-866-248-3049 or visit our website at www.simonspeakers.com.

Designed by Jaime Putorti

Manufactured in the United States of America

10  9  8  7  6  5  4  3  2  1

Library of Congress Cataloging-in-Publication Data is available.

ISBN 978-1-4391-9033-3
ISBN 978-1-4391-9039-5 (ebook)

*Acknowledgments*

_____

My deepest appreciation to all those who have steadfastly as-sisted me in my efforts to bring *The Secret History of Elizabeth Tudor, Vampire Slayer* to the attention of the public. A sensible regard for their safety prevents me from thanking each by name but I trust that they know who they are. I also wish to thank Mister Bram Stoker—posthumously, of course—for setting me on a path that, though not of my own choosing, is at last of my own making.

# The
# SECRET HISTORY
## of
# ELIZABETH TUDOR,
*Vampire Slayer*

*Midnight, 15 January 1559*

---

In the moonlight, the scaffold appears to be made of bleached bones from one of the leviathans that wash up on our shores from time to time to general alarm, for what godly world encompasses such creatures? The platform is raised high above the crowd of gray shadows gathered around its base. A woman climbs slowly, carrying the weight of her anguish and fear. She holds her hands clutched in front of her, as though in prayer. Stepping out onto the platform, she steps into the beast's gaping maw and is devoured.

Sometimes the woman in my vision is my mother; other times she is I.

For most of my youth, I have expected to die on that spectral scaffold, sacrificed to the same great beast that took my mother. That I have not met such a fate by this, my twenty-fifth year, is no doubt due to the mercy of Almighty God, although Doctor Dee credits my survival to the alignment of the stars at the moment of my birth, which suggests that my life rests on a cosmic whim.

However I came to be, I am not male. For that sin—whether hers or mine—Anne Boleyn died. My mother went to her crowning with me in her belly, through sullen crowds that called her a witch and conjured her death. I have done somewhat better. This day, the gray shadows have spewed into the streets of London, where, imbued with the ruddy cheer of winter under a chill blue sky, they have hailed me with such vigor that, for a little time, I have let myself bask in the false glow of their approbation. Still I do not forget.

My ladies have no notion of what I see as I sit gazing out onto the Tower Green, seemingly glad to rest in the aftermath of the tumultuous welcome into my capital. They see only the empty, moon-washed lawn agleam with winter frost behind the cheery, reflected glow of the fire that warms my bedchamber. Pretty girls mostly of my own age, they bustle about under the watchful eye of Kat Ashley—my former nurse and as close to a mother as I have ever known—folding my clothes, chatting among themselves, excited for the coming day.

As am I. Truly, I look forward to the moment when the holy oil will touch my brow and breast, and I will be transformed into the anointed of God, chosen by Him to rule over my father's kingdom. The irony does not escape me. Child of the despised queen whose head had to be cut off to save the king's manhood, I have Henry's red hair and his name. Since Mary's autumn death, I have his throne. Somewhere, I like to think that my mother is laughing.

It is dark but clear, with moon shadows sharpening all the angles of the ancient White Tower—the Conqueror's pride—which looms over the fortress added onto by so many monarchs down through the centuries. Nothing moves on the river beyond, save for the fast-running tide. Peering through the leaded glass of the royal apartments set snug against the inner curtain wall, I feel a surge of affection for ancient London. I will have to be as a Gypsy rope walker in the years to come to have any hope of balancing between the city's puffed-up merchants and rapacious barons, its sullen Catholics and fire-breathing Reformers, all amid the babble that rises from its docks and spills over into ever-rancorous Parliament. But I am good at balancing. I was born with a light step and an instinct for how and when to stretch out my arms to embrace what I need most. Nothing so surely marks me as a changeling, for neither of my parents possessed that skill.

In my bed gown and cap, wrapped in a lace-edged wool shawl against the dampness that penetrates the old stone walls, I am ready to slip into the high, four-poster bed curtained with embroidered silk. I long to stretch out beneath the ermine blanket and dream my queenly dreams.

There is a knock at the door.

My ladies turn as one, rapt. Do they truly believe that my Robin would be so bold as to call on me in my private chambers the night before my coronation? My dearest friend and, so far as I will allow it, my secret lover, he has known from the darkest days when malign men sought to prevent me from ever becoming queen that only the utmost discretion stands between us and disaster. I cannot believe that he would put us both at risk at so crucial a moment.

But then who comes at this, the midnight, hour?

A maid opens the door. Two men stand revealed. Doctor John Dee, just past thirty years of age, is the younger, although he manages nonetheless to convey an impression of great sagacity. I met him for the first time two years ago when Robin brought him to my notice. The scholar and magician rightly called by the honored title of magus had risked his life to counsel me, having barely survived arrest and interrogation at the order of my sister, Mary, who feared him greatly. She had reason to do so, for it was Dee who cast the horoscope that foresaw the time of her death, an act that, had it been discovered, would have sent him to the stake. Armed with that knowledge, I was able to outlast the plotting of my enemies. They browbeat my sister to order my execution, virtually to the moment of her final breath.

In the aftermath of Mary's demise, Dee determined the most auspicious date for my coronation, now scant hours away.

The magus is tall, possessed of piercing brown eyes, with a pale beard halfway down his chest. Wisdom and gravity adorn him as much as do his scholar's robes. Beside him, William Cecil looks smaller and of less consequence. That impression is almost comically misleading. Cecil is my closest adviser, the man I call my "Spirit" and whom I trust above all others, who in the dark years of my sister's reign kept the light of hope alive in me. In his late thirties, already burdened by gout despite his avoidance of all excess, he is as virtuous in his private life as he is ruthless in matters of state. Both qualities make him invaluable to me.

"Majesty," the two murmur in unison as they enter and incline their heads.

"If we might speak alone," Cecil adds. He glances at my ladies, who hover close together like so many bright-hued canaries suddenly sensing the presence of a cat.

I dismiss them with a wave of my hand. They go, trailing backward glances of concern. Before the door closes behind them, I hear their anxious murmurs.

Only Kat remains, dear Kat, who came to me as my nurse when I was scarcely four years old and has remained at my side ever since save for those dark times when she suffered imprisonment for my sake. I have said and it is true that I received life from Anne but love from Kat. I love her in return. Virtually my first act upon learning of Mary's death and my own ascension to the throne was to name her First Lady of the Royal Bedchamber. She takes her responsibilities seriously, sometimes too much so.

"You, too," I say to her, but gently for she is old now, well nigh on to seventy years, and I would not hurt her for the world. All the same, she must recognize that I am no longer the lonely, frightened child she cosseted. I am a woman now and Queen.

"Majesty—," she begins.

I cut her off with a smile. "I worry for your health, dearest, for how could I ever manage without you? Please me and go to your rest."

She obeys but not without a frown that creases her withered-apple face and would have shriveled men less intent upon their business.

"What has happened?" I ask at once when we are alone, for something grave must have occurred to explain their presence in the dead of night.

"We come on a matter touching on the security of the realm," Dee replies. "If Your Majesty would be so good as to accompany us . . ." He gestures in the direction of the door.

I am, to put it plainly, dumbfounded. The procession into London and the reception afterward for the city's dignitaries, each vying with all the others for my notice, ran late. The coming day promises to be both glorious and fraught in the extreme. By what right does anyone lay claim not merely to my attention at such a time but that I should actually go with them for some unnamed purpose? Even such good servants as Dee and Cecil must need explain themselves.

"What matter touching on the security of the realm?" I demand. "Do not speak in riddles but state your purpose clearly."

Cecil is accustomed to my sometimes querulous nature, Dee far less so. Both pale slightly.

"Majesty," Cecil says. "The threat to your realm is so strange and sinister, so defying of all mortal reason, that upon the advice of good Doctor Dee, it was determined that it could only be revealed to you now."

"The conjunction of the planets was not favorable before this hour," the magus endeavors to explain. "But it will remain so for only a short time. You must come with us."

Had I not known both men so well and had they not served me with such devotion through perilous times, I would have ordered them from my chamber at once. As it was, I still seriously consider doing so.

"Please, Majesty," Dee entreats. "Time is fleeting and there is much to accomplish."

Before I can reply, Cecil lifts the heavy fur cloak I wore earlier in the day and drapes it over my shoulders in a gesture at once protective and insistent.

"We are your most loyal servants, Majesty," he says simply. "I would lay down my life for you and so would Doctor Dee. I beg you to find it in your heart to trust us for just a little while and I promise that all will be made clear."

In all fairness, Cecil has earned my forbearance, as has Dee. Though I remain reluctant to engage in so odd an enterprise, I acquiesce. Wrapped in the fur cloak, I remove my silk chamber slippers and allow Cecil to help me don a pair of leather pattens. That done, I suffer to be led from my rooms and down the stone corridor to the winding steps that give out onto the Tower Green.

At once, my breath freezes in the chill air but I scarcely notice, so glorious is the sight I behold. The sky, shorn of clouds after the leaden storms of recent days, is a riot of stars. Orion hunts in the west but I have little time to contemplate him before Dee draws my attention elsewhere.

"Look there, Majesty, Jupiter rises in Aquarius as Mars does the same in Scorpio. Both augur well for your rule. As you are the lion, so shall you command the powers of war and wisdom throughout your long reign."

"God willing it will be long," Cecil says fervently. He is shivering already. "It may not be if Her Majesty takes a chill."

"Then let us go on," I say, suddenly more cheerful in the face of this strange adventure.

We turn in the direction of the Chapel of St. Peter ad Vincula. When Mary held me captive in the Tower, where I dwelled in daily expectation of my death, I was allowed to pray only in my rooms. That suited me well enough for I had no desire to enter the place where my mother is buried, having been carried there directly from her execution mere yards away and deposited in her grave with scant ceremony.

Nor is she alone. Catherine Howard, my father's other slain queen, lies beside her along with poor Lady Jane Grey, the brilliant child who my dear Robin's treacherous father tried to foist on the realm, thereby bringing ruin to his own family. The Nine-Day Queen died in the same manner as my mother and Catherine Howard, whose final resting place she shares.

Dee must sense my reluctance for he touches my arm lightly and says, "Pray forgive us, Majesty, but the signs are unmistakable. Only in this place at this time can we achieve what must be done."

Having gone so far, I tell myself that it would be cowardly to turn back. Even so, I enter the chapel slowly and stand for several moments staring down the short nave toward the altar. There, just to the left near the chapel's north wall, is the simple flagstone slab beneath which my mother lies. Nothing else marks her presence or that of the others. Yet I know where she is all the same. Several years ago, I pestered poor Kat, who surely deserves better from me than I have ever given her, to tell me what she knew. She complied, if reluctantly. From her, I learned the details of my mother's death and interment as recorded by eyewitnesses. I have never spoken of it with anyone else, not even Robin.

"Hurry, Majesty," Dee says, and urges me forward.

I still do not comprehend what he and Cecil intend, yet I obey all the same. Something about the nearness of my mother's grave draws me on. Clutching the fur robe tightly, I walk toward it, unable to take my eyes from the cold gray slab that holds her earthbound.

But that is absurd. My mother's soul, which I privately accord to be as pure as anyone else's, has long since flown to its reward. Nothing lies beneath the slab save her mortal remains. And yet—

"Majesty?" As though from a great distance, I hear Cecil speak. He sounds uncertain, but that cannot be right. The most trusted of my counselors is a man of extraordinary competency never at a loss in any situation.

Until now. I turn and see him just behind me, pale in the faint glow of the lamps kept burning in the chapel all night, some say to hold at bay the vengeful ghosts who dwell there. By contrast, Dee seems in his element, his eyes alight with excitement.

I turn my head again toward the grave. A faint but unmistakable mist rises from it, illuminated by the starlight pouring through the high windows above the altar. Scarcely aware of what I am doing, I move closer. The mist grows, expands, thickens, until I am engulfed within it. Oddly devoid of fear, I stand as though observing all from outside myself, able only to marvel at what is happening.

The silence is so profound that I can hear my own measured heartbeat. Apart from that, there is only a great hush, as though the world beyond has ceased to exist. I can no longer feel the floor beneath my feet; it is as though I have become detached, floating free of earthly strictures. The mist has a quality of warmth and softness that I would not have expected. Additionally, I imagine that I smell roses. Far in the back of my mind, a memory stirs: my mother, twirling me in her arms, in a garden filled with white and crimson blossoms.

And my father looking on, weighing us both through slitted eyes.

I breathe and with each breath the mist enters into me, becomes part of me, filling me. The barriers between what is myself and what is not begin to shimmer and grow transparent until they melt away altogether. I am the mist and it is I. Looking down the length of my body, I discover that I am shimmering as though lit from within by a bright, white light. Still, I am not afraid. My mother is there with me. I hear her speak, not in words as we know them, but in the deepest recesses of my heart.

"My daughter," Anne says, "do not fear your duty. Embrace it that this realm may be preserved against the scourge of evil that has come upon it."

She speaks, and my heart, so long steeled against the cruelties of the world, cries out in yearning for her. Without hesitation, I take the final steps and kneel beside my mother's grave.

How to describe what happens next when I scarcely understand it myself? It is as though a great wall within me suddenly cracks and the light pours through it. I am blinded, and yet I see for the very first time. See my beloved kingdom unfolding beneath skies across which sun and storm alike speed in an instant. See night and day flow in quick succession as ages pass, armies clash, and fortresses rise and fall. See myself rising above my city, above my realm, a queen regnant clothed in majesty, armed with power unlike any I have ever glimpsed while all around legions of red-fanged, black-winged enemies soar across the moon.

I bear it so long as I can before my mind reels away to find surcease in blessed darkness. Dee and Cecil together catch me as I slump unconscious to the chapel floor.

Drifting over the city, following the pewter ribbon of the river, I, Mordred, king of the dark realm, came to the ancient hill where once Gog and Magog were worshipped by wiser folk than are to be found there now. The temples of the old ones are buried under the timber of the Saxons, interred in turn beneath the stones the Normans raised, foundation for the abode of kings, the place of execution for queens. I smelled the earth, well sated with blood. It warmed me.

She was sitting at a tower window behind a curtain of frost that ran like a web of frozen ferns across the leaded panes. Fire-haired, pale-skinned Elizabeth, child of Anne, the one for whom I have waited so long. I confess to a certain excitement upon seeing her finally.

She was not conventionally beautiful, being both too slender and too tightly strung like a fine thoroughbred mare that resists mounting. No matter; she was everything I desired, everything I needed. Or she might be. The coming hours would tell the tale.

Little men with little minds would do their utmost to make her my enemy. I, who would give her immortality if only she had the wit to take it! I remember being human, if only barely, as a dream that dissolves upon waking. It is a mayfly's existence, here today, gone today. Surely, she would recognize better when it is offered to her. If not—

Her throat was white and slim. I could just make out the thin blue tracing of her life's blood coursing beneath her skin. Could feel on my tongue the hint of how she would taste. Hunger stirred in me but I could wait, if only for a little while.

*Separated by mere inches but invisible to her, I observed Elizabeth at my leisure, watching the steady rise and fall of her breath beneath breasts round and ripe as young apples. She appeared absorbed in her own thoughts, with no sense of me, not then, nor any awareness that she sat not on the edge of a throne but perched on the hinge of fate. Swing one way and I would open the eternal vistas of the night to her and place her by my side in golden halls where death can never rule. Swing the other . . . I would drain her to the final carmine drop and throw regret away along with her hollowed husk.*

*Surely it would not come to that.*

*A flicker of motion on the Tower Green drew my eye. Bustling in their importance, the men of the hour hurried along with their cloaks clutched close against winter's chill and their own fear. No doubt they had a plan to manage Elizabeth if she balked, but they looked anxious all the same, as well they should for they involved themselves in matters vastly beyond their ken. Balanced on the air, hovering over my ancient and eternal kingdom, I watched them come. They paused at the foot of the stairs leading to the royal apartment to exchange a final, anxious glance.*

*And up they went.*

*I followed when they emerged again with her in tow. I watched them enter the chapel that holds so much pain. I witnessed all that transpired from my perch on the far side of the high window above the altar.*

*That light . . . the roses—oh, yes, I smelled them. Dear, dead Anne still couldn't resist meddling, scant good it would do her.*

*It was too much for my poor Elizabeth, of course. When it was done, she lay on the slate floor, hovered over by her fretful gentlemen, so pale and still, scarcely breathing. I could restore her with a touch, but this was not the time. She had chosen her path; now she had to follow it to me.*

*It was as well that the centuries had taught me patience for I* swear, were that not the case, I would have claimed her there and then. How tempting to do so beside her mother's grave. How exquisitely just.

They lifted her, only just managing between them despite her being wand slim. Her head fell back against the magus's arm, her face turned up to the altar windows through which I gazed. A strange yet hauntingly familiar sensation overtook me, and for a moment I saw another face, so similar, so implacably different. Morgaine, my love. My betrayer.

Away then, from memory and shadow into night made bright by the certainty that victory, so long awaited, would not now be long denied.

*Before dawn, 15 January 1559*

———

*I* return to my senses with no thought but to remove myself from the chapel at once. With Cecil and Dee on my heels, I flee across the moon-washed sward, past several startled guards, and up the stairs to my privy chamber.

"What magic do you conjure?" I demand of the magus the moment the door closes behind us. My heart beats so fiercely that I fear it will spring from my chest, my breath is labored, and dizziness threatens to overcome me. I sag into my chair, gripping the carved arms, and glare at Dee.

"You know I forbid sorcery in my realm! Do not imagine that because you have been of use to me I will make an exception for you."

For a man just accused of engaging in the black arts—an offense for which he can burn—the good doctor seems oddly unconcerned. Indeed, he appears to be in the grip of a strange elation that similarly afflicts Cecil. My Spirit's cheeks are flushed, and for once the gouty pain in his legs does not seem to trouble him at all.

"It worked!" the magus exclaims. He clasps his hands in glee, looking at me as a parent might gaze upon a child who has performed vastly beyond expectation.

"It may have worked," Cecil corrects, precise even in his excitement. "We cannot know for sure until—"

"But you saw!" Dee protests. "The mist, the light, there can be no question. Her Majesty has awakened!"

I am tempted to regard all this as gibberish, for so it surely sounds. Yet in the manner of both men is a seriousness that I cannot dismiss. Beyond that, the word Dee used—*awakened*—fits too perfectly with what I have only just begun to notice.

The world, even wrapped in hushed night, has acquired clarity unlike any I have known before. Every object in my chamber seems to shine with a faint but unmistakable inner light hitherto unseen by me. And there is more. I hear all manner of things with new awareness—the crackle of the fire, the snap of frost outside my window, the surge of the tide against the piers of London Bridge, and beyond an exhalation all around and within, as though the world itself is breathing. I feel beneath my fingers the carving of the chair in which I sit in all its intricate detail. And I smell . . . smoke, wool, leather, the silk bed hangings imbued with the delicate aroma of lost cocoons, my own skin and the musk perfume adorning me, and beneath it all, the fetid stirrings of the Tower moat and the river, mercifully held in check by the blanket of frost.

"What is happening to me?" I ask, more to myself than to either of my counselors, yet they endeavor to answer.

"Your Majesty," Dee says, "you are experiencing the result of a confluence of heavenly alignments occurring only once in each millennium that in combination with the unique qualities of your own nature and in the presence of your late mother's mortal remains, from whose bloodline your calling comes, has awakened in you certain hitherto latent powers."

This pretty speech leaves me entirely confused. I turn to my Spirit. As always, Cecil strives to provide clarity.

"Majesty, at your birth, your mother arranged secretly for the casting of your horoscope. It revealed signs sufficient to convince her that you are the one whose coming had been long predicted in certain arcane circles. To shield you until you could come into your own, this information was concealed from all save a small group sworn to your protection. I have the honor to be a member of that group, as does Doctor Dee."

This makes only slightly more sense to me than what the magus said. All the same, it has the ring of truth. My father, in his lethal disappointment at my failure to be the male heir he so desired, would never have bothered to have my horoscope cast. But neither would he have allowed anyone else to do so lest it be used for treachery. My mother would have had to act in secret even as she feared for her own life. Had she sought some reassurance that the terrible sacrifice she had made in bearing me might somehow be redeemed?

"What arcane circles?" I demand. "Damn you both, speak! I will have no more mystification!"

The two exchange a glance. Dee clears his throat and, throwing off some of his usual gravity, blurts, "Majesty, our realm is under threat from a dread enemy more terrible than any you can imagine. It can only be defeated by the most extraordinary powers, which, grace to God, we believe you now possess."

"Of what enemy do you speak?" I demand.

Does he mean the Pope, who threatens to excommunicate me if I do not return my realm to the rule of Rome? The Spaniards, who, unless I agree to marry their king, my late sister's despicable husband, will turn all their might to my destruction? The French, dedicated intriguers and worse? The Irish, intent on outdoing the French in every manner of mischief? The Scots . . . the Welsh . . . I can go on and on for truly I am beset by enemies of every stripe. Yet none are more terrible than I can imagine. What else then lurks within my realm?

*Scourge of evil.*

My mother's words spring into my mind, bringing with them

a sudden sensation of cold that sweeps over me despite the warmth of the nearby fire and the fur cloak I still wear.

"An ancient foe," Cecil says somberly. "Come to this kingdom in the distant past during the time of Arthur. They were very nearly defeated then but not entirely. A remnant remained, which, grown stronger down through the centuries, now threatens to overwhelm this land. You are our only hope of stopping them."

"What enemy?" I ask. "By what name are they called?"

"They go by several names," Dee says. "The Babylonians called them demons and sacrificed their children to placate them. The Hebrews warned of them, calling them beings that lived by drinking the blood of innocents. The Greeks worshipped and feared them. The Romans did the same. For centuries, they have been known in this kingdom as *revenant*, arising out of death. But they are also known by another name, one we believe they use for themselves: vampire."

My breath catches. He is speaking of a foe from beyond the mortal realm, creatures of the dark, vile beings capable of making the skin crawl and the mind cringe in horror.

"How can this be?" I protest. "Surely, God would not allow—"

"The Almighty in His infinite wisdom sends us challenges we cannot always understand," Dee says. "But He never leaves us unequipped to meet them. Your existence is proof of that."

My existence? I am the child of a despised mother who died because she bore me. I have lived all my life under the shadow of death. Even now, staring out the window into the depths of night, I swear that I can still see the spectral scaffold waiting for me.

"Arthur fell to them," Cecil says. "But his kingdom prevailed. Your kingdom now, my lady, yours to protect."

My mind reels at the thought and, in so doing, snatches at what passes for reason. "Arthur fell to his bastard son, Mordred, who was a man like any other for all that he was evil—"

"No, Majesty," Dee says grimly. "Mordred was born a man but he chose the path of darkness, becoming a vampire in order to gain the power to defeat his royal father. He sought to rule this realm for all eternity, but he was stopped by the first of the great vampire slayers from whom you descend directly."

"I know my lineage. There is nothing such as you—"

"Morgaine Le Fey, called enchantress by those who do not understand what she truly was," Cecil says implacably. "You are of her blood, as was your mother. A thousand years have passed since Morgaine defeated Mordred, leaving him with only a withered remnant of his kind from which, unfortunately, he has rebuilt his revenant kingdom. Now it falls to you to complete her work."

Am I expected to battle beings from the nether reaches of Hell? Creatures who suck the blood of innocents and threaten to destroy my realm? And to do so because of—what? An alleged legacy from a rumored sorceress who may or may not have truly existed?

"What are you saying?" I demand. "Are you suggesting that Mordred still lives?"

My counselors exchange a look. Several moments pass. Finally, with obvious reluctance, Cecil says, "We believe he does, Majesty, and that he intends to challenge you for rulership of this realm."

How to express my shock and incredulity? Of everything that has happened in this strange night, this news surpasses all.

"A thousand-year-old—what did you call him?—vampire, the son of Arthur, challenges my right to rule?"

"You see," Dee attempts to explain, "therein lies the problem. He *is* the son of Arthur, the first and arguably—forgive me, Majesty—the greatest ruler of this land. It is our understanding that he feels entitled to what he regards as his rightful inheritance."

"Then he is mad . . . or you are. Or the world is. It is all madness."

Real dangers I understand only too well—the Pope, the Spaniards, and the like. Ghosts may be real, or at least enough people think they are to deserve serious consideration. But this—blood-sucking vampires, a thousand years, Morgaine Le Fey, for pity's sake!

Madness. And far too much for my poor addled brain to comprehend.

"Leave me," I order with a wave of my hand that I have to hope is suitably regal even in my shaken state.

They stand frozen, two statues staring at me in dismay.

"Leave me!"

I cannot endure their presence a moment longer. Fear and, worse, a sick feeling of despair claw at me. I survived my father's rage, my mother's death, my sister's vengeance—for this? To plunge into a macabre conspiracy of evil and dark magic in which I cannot trust even my own reason, subject as it is to strange visions and perceptions?

Would that I were a simple girl in Robin's arms with no thought but for life and love!

Instead, I fumble my way to my lonely bed, finding there only fitful dreams and the chill dampness of my tears.

A king cannot afford to show weakness. I learned that from my father, who learned it too late to save himself. I was his weakness, as it happens. Arthur loved me despite my failings, so he claimed, when all I wanted was to be loved for them.

Tant pis, *as the French say. Too bad.*

The night was still young as I alit on the far side of the high wall surrounding my manor. I smelled frost and woodsmoke, a felicitous combination even to the "scourge of evil." Anne again, always so dramatic, except, oddly enough, at the very end when a preternatural calm possessed her. A doe raised her head from the lichen she nibbled and stared at me. I passed on by her and turned toward the path leading to the house.

Lights shone in the high windows of the hall. Those of my subjects not out and about were gathered there, amusing themselves. I encouraged them to do so. Away from my presence, without the subtle but constant reminder of my power, some few among the kindred might have been tempted to challenge me. I do so hate to slay my own kind, if only because it is a reminder that nothing, not even immortality, is forever.

The thrall on watch opened the double doors and skittered back a few steps, standing with head bowed beneath the hood of its robe that concealed all. They resemble monks a little, the thralls, as they creep about in reverent silence, appearing when needed, disappearing as readily. Some have served me for centuries; others are more recent

THE SECRET HISTORY OF ELIZABETH TUDOR, VAMPIRE SLAYER     21

additions to the household. Male or female, they all look the same, when one bothers to look at them at all. I could wish they didn't shuffle quite so much but their devotion is not to be faulted.

My private quarters commanded the high tower above the sprawling mansion built decades past by Henry and given by his daughter Mary to the Archbishop of York, from whom I bought it. He had no idea whom he was selling to, of course, although I am not entirely sure that would have made a difference. I did, after all, pay handsomely.

My library boasted a sweeping view over the river toward the city proper. I did not expect the chamber to be unoccupied and I was not disappointed. The most faithful and ambitious of my courtiers, the Lady Blanche, stood at the windows, looking out. Her hair, dark as midnight silvered by the moon, tumbled down her back. She was garbed in white—her constant affectation—and did not turn until I entered and closed the door behind me.

In the flickering light of the lamps, her lips looked very red. Clearly, she had been feeding. Her smile was, I assumed, deliberately provocative.

"Did you try her?" she asked. "How does she taste?"

My cloak, damp with melting snow, landed on the high-backed, carved chair where I tossed it. I loosened the ruff at my throat while walking toward her. "Don't be tiresome. You know nothing of her."

"She is the Queen. What else is there to know?"

I had been reading Dante, always a favorite of mine. A copy of La Divina Commedia, the edition with Botticelli's marvelous illustrations of Hell, lay open on a chair in front of the fire. I set it aside, poked the flames a bit, and sat down.

Always so good about anticipating my needs, Blanche brought me cognac in a crystal snifter. She perched lightly on the arm of my chair and trailed her hand down my arm.

"Is she as pretty as people say or are they merely flattering her?"

"Her father was handsome in his youth. She resembles him."

"Not her mother?"

In fact, Elizabeth did favor Anne in the sharpness of her chin and the catlike slant of her eyes. I wondered if she knew that.

"It doesn't matter." The cognac burned pleasantly as I swallowed it in a single draft, then wrapped a hand around the nape of her neck and drew Blanche to me. "She could be a crone so long as she serves her purpose."

I smelled the blood through her skin. My hunger stirred. Blanche knew nothing of my plans for Elizabeth and I saw no reason to change that. Particularly not while I still had uses for her taut, urgent body pressed against me.

When my fangs pierced her throat, she moaned faintly. The fire leapt higher, burning hotter. Tomorrow crept toward us, eclipsing all the yesterdays.

*15 January 1559*

———

The world looks no better by morning despite sporting a bright blue sky. I rise, weary and tense, to face my ladies, all of them consumed with excitement for the coming day. As they buzz about, seeing to my toilette, I struggle to convince myself that the events of the previous night were no more than a fever dream.

But I have no fever and, worse, the pattens I wore to venture out to the chapel are still beside my bed, lying where I had kicked them off, mute evidence that what I remember truly did occur. I stare at them as I am laced into my corset and hoop-skirted farthingale. Two of the most trusted men in my service believe that my kingdom is under demonic threat. I myself experienced a strange transformation that I can still barely credit. No amount of hoping on my part changes any of that.

Inevitably, my ladies sense my distraction and, mistaking it for nerves, strive to soothe me, twittering about with urgings of small beer and conversation. With an effort, I mouth pleasantries that I am far from feeling. Kat is not fooled by them; I can tell. She directs all without ever taking her eyes from me. I know that she wants to ask what has happened and am glad that there is no opportunity for her to do so.

Finally the gown of gold and silver tissue that a dozen seamstresses have labored over for weeks is lowered over my head, the crimson velvet cape lined with ermine is placed on

my shoulders, and we are away at last. Out on the green, spar-
kling in morning sun, I pause to receive the cheers of the
Tower guard before going out into my city across the Lion
Tower drawbridge, where I am greeted by an exuberant
crowd, more than a few of whom have waited since before
dawn to see me.

Merchants, traders, peddlers, and goodwives line the bankside along with, I am sure, a full measure of the thieves, whores,
and actors who make up London's hidden world. I want to
think only of them, my people, but I find myself wondering if
Mordred and others of his kind are lurking in the shadows even
then, watching and plotting.

To distract myself, I look out over the great river that is the
lifeblood of my city. Beneath the clear blue sky, the Thames is
thronged with boats of every description that are, in turn, reflected in it. Anything that can float is on the water with every
wherryman blessed with a full load, all eager to escort my royal
barge upriver to Westminster Abbey. I step on board, taking my
seat on a platform raised so that those onshore can easily see
me, and give the order to set off.

The bridge looms before us, no less than twenty stone arches
framed on both sides with houses and shops that teeter so high
as to seem about to topple over. Between them lies the only
span across which all carts, wagons, horses, and flocks coming
from the south can enter London. Truly, nature and the industry of man have made my tax collectors' duty as easy as possible.

My good people are hanging from every window to cheer me
on. Banners are flying, trumpets blaring; it is a day to gladden
every heart. Despite the dark shadow hovering over me, I smile
and wave in good cheer. We negotiate the stone piers without
incident. At high tide and with a swift current, even the wariest
boatman can have his craft smashed asunder in the mill race

that forms between the bridge supports. It is a reminder that strikes me as apt for the day.

Picking up speed, we pass crowded close to the long, timbered warehouses that stand cheek by jowl, with the ships' chandlers, seamen's inns, and the two- and three-story houses of prosperous merchants. Behind them, narrow streets and lanes are tightly packed with squat, daub-and-wattle houses, some admittedly squalid, set among a sea of church spires. In the distance, I see the great tower of St. Paul's and the even more splendid spire and cross of St. Mary Overie.

Musicians accompany us, playing sprightly airs, yet not even my favorite music can dispel the ominous pall that clings to me. I have looked forward to this day for so long, often fearing that I would never live to see it, yet now it has taken on a weight and meaning that I cannot still fully grasp.

Through the press of people on the royal barge, I glimpse Robin and beckon him forward. He looks very fine in a doublet of burgundy velvet with a jerkin over it of black silk and cloth of silver. His mustache and beard are finely oiled and combed. His legs, which are uniformly acknowledged to be excellent, are well turned out in black hose. He wears a short cloak, I suspect because he does not wish to conceal those fine legs, and a hat strewn with gold bangles and a jaunty feather, which he sweeps off as he approaches me.

We are of an age, Robin and I, and are both survivors of turbulent, dangerous childhoods. He understands me better than any other can. We share a love of drama and poetry, hunting and hawking. He makes me laugh, and he makes me happy. Anyone who thinks ill of that can hie off to Hades.

I smile and hold out my hand to him. He comes through the crowd, tall and limber with the grace of a natural horseman, takes my fingers, and brushes them with his lips. Without releasing me, he steps closer. I feel the warmth of his breath as a caress against my neck as he murmurs, "You look tired. Is something wrong, Your Majesty?"

The wind lifts a curl of his black hair. He is deeply tanned, his skin drinking in the sun even in our northern clime. His brown eyes are, as almost always, irresistible to me. I fancy they are windows into his soul.

"I am . . . distracted," I say, careful to keep smiling. Let the avid audience watching our every move believe we are engaged in no more than light repartee.

Joining in my masquerade, Robin laughs as though I have said something witty. Under his breath, he asks, "What has happened?"

"Not here." My face is growing stiff for grinning. "We will speak later. Find me before the banquet."

He nods and sweeps a bow. Loudly he says, "As Your Majesty commands."

I turn away, dismissing him even as I promise myself that I will not have to do so much longer. Once I am anointed queen, I will be bolder in putting forward my friends and chastising my enemies. But for the moment, the habit of discretion still clings to me.

Robin withdraws, leaving me to pretend interest in the passing scene. Farther along the river, the wharves give way to manor houses surrounded by broad lawns and gardens running down to the river. The long roof of Westminster Hall and the adjacent Palace of Whitehall come into view. Finally, I spy the vast transepts and apse of the Abbey, built by blessed Saint Edward the Confessor, where, shortly now, I will be crowned.

The narrow streets from the Whitehall water steps to the Abbey are packed so tightly that I wonder how anyone can breathe, the crowd held in check by yeoman guards holding steel-edged halberds at the ready. No one seems to mind as men, women, and children alike cheer me mightily. I smile and wave, wave and smile, all despite the apprehension that makes me stare uneasily into the crowd, wondering who might be concealed there. As I pause to accept a bouquet of flowers from a little girl who gazes at me with awe, a cloud moves over the sun, casting us all into shadow. I shiver but keep smiling, always smiling. A little farther on, I stop again to listen to a grizzled old man perform a poem recalling his witness of my father's coronation. The sun has come out again, filling the street with silvered winter light, yet still the shadow clings to me. I thank the old man kindly and move on, passing finally beneath the entrance to the Abbey. There I pause for a moment to catch my breath and further compose myself for the ordeal ahead.

As I step inside the Abbey, lit by a thousand candles and lamps, onto a bright blue carpet that runs the length of the nave, a thousand and more pairs of eyes turn in my direction. Virtually all the peerage has crammed inside for the ancient rite by which a sovereign is consecrated. Every one of them—every duke, earl, baron, knight, and all their ladies, perhaps most particularly the ladies—scrutinize me for any sign of weakness. Were I to show the slightest hint, I have no doubt that a goodly number would turn against me at once with the rest following quickly enough.

But anyone who hopes to see evidence of failing on my part is destined for disappointment. Since tenderest childhood, I have been forced to conceal my emotions even under the most turbulent circumstances. That mask has become second nature to me, though at times it seems more prison than protection.

The high, pure voices of the boys' choir ring out as the ancient ceremony begins. After the opening prayers, a canopy is raised over and around me to shield me from the eyes of all but

the attending prelates. I am anointed with holy oil on my
hands, breast, and head. I had wondered if, at that moment, I
would truly feel myself transformed. The reality is not disap-
pointing, precisely, but my experience of the night before ren-
ders it inconsequential. Seated on my throne, I receive the
symbols of my royal estate, including the ring wedding me forever to my people, the only spouse I truly want, although I will
never be so impolitic as to say so. No one needs to know that
the mere thought of giving any man the power of husband over
me fills me with visions of the scaffold.

At long last, the royal crown of England—seven pounds of
gold and gems—is placed on my head. I take my sacred oath on
a Bible held aloft by William Cecil, whom I have chosen for
that honor in recognition of his service to me. The assembled
peerage cheers lustily amid the blare of trumpets, then one by
one each lord comes to kneel at my feet and pledge himself in
God's name to be my faithful servant. Some of them may even
mean it. The hard truth is that I do not doubt most of them
would just as readily kneel before anyone else who they believed would preserve their power and privileges.

In the aftermath of the ceremony, a great banquet is laid out
in Westminster Hall. A privy chamber has been readied to
allow me a brief respite. There Robin finds me. He slides in past
Kat's frown and my ladies, who pretend to be busy chatting
among themselves so that we can have a modicum of privacy.

"May I tell you how beautiful you are, Majesty?" he asks as he
slips onto a stool beside me and takes my hands. "Your radiance
blinds us all. As I watched the crown being put upon your head,
I—"

"You cannot be both blind and watching," I say, cutting him
short. Ordinarily I enjoy flattery, but just then I have no patience for it.

With a quick glance to be sure my ladies are out of earshot, I say, "Robin, the most extraordinary thing has happened."

His brief look of petulance at my tart response vanishes. At once he turns serious. "I knew you were troubled when I saw you on the barge. What is it?"

I am trying to decide how to begin when I remember that Robin is of a family of mingled Norman and Saxon blood significantly older in lineage than my own. It occurs to me suddenly that if Cecil and Dee are right, he might not be entirely ignorant of what they have revealed to me.

"Have you ever heard of a danger to my kingdom from beyond the mortal realm? One so perverse and deadly as to defy belief?"

Even as I speak, I hope that Robin will not only disavow any knowledge but will persuade me that the very idea is absurd. Cecil and Dee are mistaken, my fears are overwrought, and what I think I experienced at my mother's grave is no more than an illusion born of too little sleep and too much worry.

Instead, Robin sighs deeply. His shoulders sag and suddenly he will not meet my eyes.

Slowly he says, "I told myself that it couldn't be true—and that even if it is, it is all in the past and would have no effect on you. But now you seem to be saying that—"

Incredulity fills me. He knew and did not tell me? How is that possible?

"You knew? And you said nothing to me?"

"You cannot blame me for this," he insists swiftly. "I could no more credit what I heard than you seem able to do. And I certainly did not want to give you reason for yet more dread and worry when you already are far too afflicted with both."

"But even so, if I had been given some warning—"

"Would you have done anything differently? For that matter, what have you done? What has happened?"

Kat turns her head just then and peers in our direction.

I touch Robin's hand in warning. "Not here. Come to me to-night."

At once he leans closer and presses my fingers. "Beloved—" he whispers.

"To talk," I say hastily, though my senses surge and a wave of heat washes through me. Until Robin took me into his arms for the first time, I was half-convinced that I was not as other women, being so distrustful of passion as to deny it any part in my nature. How mistaken I was—but that is a matter for another time.

At length the day I had so joyfully anticipated, only to endure so impatiently, nears its close. As I progress to White-hall, my favorite of the royal residences, where I will remain for the full ten days of celebration following my crowning, Cecil squeezes his way through the crowd of nobles to my side.

"Majesty," he says, "if I might have a moment—"

My head feels encircled by a band of iron, this despite that before leaving the Abbey, I replaced the heavy crown of my father with the far daintier diadem of gold studded with sapphires, rubies, and pearls that was made for my mother to wear at her own coronation. Officially, I did so for comfort, but in fact I cannot let the day pass without commemorating my mother. The more astute among my nobles recognize the diadem for what it is, a bold assertion of loyalty to her. Those whose families helped to bring about her ruin are put on notice that her daughter will be far more dangerous prey.

"Tomorrow," I tell Cecil. "Come in the morning. We will breakfast together and speak privately."

He deserves that for all his good counsel, but he is displeased all the same.

"There are urgent matters touching on the events of last night—," he begins.

"No one knows that better than I, but we will accomplish nothing while I am so weary."

When Cecil tries to press me, I gesture to my ladies, who swiftly surround me, cutting him off. Within that feminine cocoon, I go directly to my apartment, through the privy gallery, clogged by courtiers who wait in hopes that I will give them audience; past my library, wherein my beloved books await such leisure hours as I am able to wrest from duty's demands; past my dining and dressing rooms; through the withdrawing room, which I share with my ladies; until at last, I come to my bedchamber.

A royal residence has stood beside the Thames since the time of Edward, the saintly king who built Westminster Abbey. But my father put his stamp on the palace that is now my own. Given his taste for intrigue, it should come as no surprise that the royal apartment is well equipped with discreet passages allowing for hidden comings and goings. One such passage grants the most private access to my chamber.

Knowing that Robin will soon come and eager to speak with him, I allow my ladies to strip me of my regalia, peeling away the layers until I am left in nothing at all. With my feet blessedly bare, I wiggle my toes and feel the blood return to them. When the last pin is removed from my hair and my fiery tresses fall free, I groan with pleasure. Kat laughs and rubs my scalp as one of my ladies holds my bed gown near the fire to warm it before dropping it over my head. Wrapped in a robe, I sit with my feet propped up on a stool and sip a posset. Too soon I am fighting to keep my eyes open.

"To bed, Majesty?" Kat asks. She looks as exhausted as the

rest of my ladies after the eventful day. Taking pity on them, I
wave a hand.

"Off with you all. I'll sit awhile, then retire."

They protest that they will keep me company until I am
ready to sleep, but go all the same with only a little more
urging. When they are gone, I sigh in relief. Having set aside
the posset, I rise to open the leaded window a crack, just
enough to admit a reviving draft of cold air. I am staring out
over the river, silvered by moonlight, when a faint prickling
lifts the hairs on the back of my neck.

I watched the coronation from a perch in the deep shadows beneath the rafters of Westminster Abbey, my unfettered presence there further proof, if yet more was needed, that no god favors mortals over us, for surely any such deity would bar us from his holy places.

Elizabeth looked lovely, for all that she was obviously under considerable strain. She could hardly be blamed for that, given the gauntlet of scrutiny she had to walk to reach her throne. The Spanish and Portuguese were at that time rumored to have discovered in the darkest reaches of the equatorial regions cannibals who, I am certain, would not have fallen on her more ravenously than would her own nobles had they been given the slightest encouragement to do so. At least her mother, walking to the scaffold, knew she was about to die. Elizabeth could only wonder when and how the sword would fall on her.

The ceremony was interminable, saved only by the excellence of the music. The banquet afterward was the usual excess of overly rich meats, florid sauces, and a waste of good wine squandered on poor palates. The insufferable Dudley was there, of course. I marveled that she could not see him for what he was. He pretended to love her while seeking nothing other than the restoration of his traitorous family, whereas I . . . I confess, I was developing a tendresse for Elizabeth. The thought of her touch and scent . . . the smooth skin of her supple neck . . . and most particularly of her taste quite overwhelmed me at times. Call me foolish, but I have always believed in love.

The ever-intrusive Cecil sidled up to her as the banquet was ending. I was glad to see that she sent him on his way with short shrift. I had considered removing her Spirit but had left him alive, judging that he could be useful to me in years to come.

At length and at last, she withdrew. I watched her maids strip her of her raiment, garment by garment until at last her pale skin was revealed in all its glory. Her legs were long and tapered, the thighs sleek with muscle. The soft nest of fire between them drew my gaze. I imagined touching her, feeling her respond, feeding from her. Passion warred with amusement as I watched her wiggle her toes in the thick carpet. Still, I was not fooled. Her eyes were shadowed with fatigue. She was living on her nerves. When her ladies had gone, she opened the window and looked out toward the river. Her expression was pensive and, I thought, filled with yearning.

As was I. The time had come; I would wait no longer.

"Elizabeth," I breathed, and sent her name as a prayer out into the night.

*Night, 15 January 1559*

---

*I* turn, expecting to see Robin emerging from the hidden passage, but there is no sign of him. Nonetheless, the sensation that I am not alone grows stronger, becoming impossible to ignore. Slowly, I move toward the concealed door set in the paneled wall. At the touch of a hidden lever, the door swings open on hinges that are always kept well oiled. Beyond lies only darkness. I wait, scarcely breathing, thinking to see the flicker of light heralding Robin's approach, but there is nothing.

I resist for several minutes as the lure grows stronger. Finally, telling myself that I am merely curious, I take a lamp from a nearby table and step into the passage. At once, I am engulfed in darkness just beyond the small circle of light in which I move. The passage leads deep within the south wing of the palace. There are, so far as I know, only three entrances—one in my own rooms, another in the apartment I have arranged to be given to Robin, and a third to be found down a flight of steps, along another, older passage that may date from the time of Edward or even earlier, and finally through an iron gate concealed behind a false wall that leads out into an ancient, walled garden near the river.

It is madness to go as I do, clad only in slippers, a nightgown, and robe. Worse yet, I am without a single guard despite the constant threat to my life from innumerable sources. Never in my wildest imaginings would I have behaved in such a way. Yet

I proceed along the passage, through the gate, and out into the winter garden.

I can smell the river—chill but dank, moving sluggishly at that late hour—vying with the pall of smoke hanging over the city. In honor of my coronation, and to induce my people to love me, a generous measure of wood and coal has been provided to every household. Even the poorest tenement dweller is warm that night, but not their queen. The cold ripples up from my feet, causing my muscles to clench. My breath frosts in the chill air. I shiver and, determined to cast off the madness that has seized me, turn to go back inside.

A shadow moves at the edge of the garden, shifting out of darkness, devoid of light, blacker than night. I stand frozen, observing it take form. Too swiftly for my mind to grasp, it resolves into the shape of a man—tall, broad-shouldered, cloaked. My throat closes, preventing me from making the slightest sound, far less a cry for help. I can only watch helplessly as he strides toward me, no sound of his footfall on the gravel path interrupting the silence. As he nears, the lamp I hold flickers and goes out.

No matter, I can still see him clearly, his pale skin luminous as the moon, radiating light. His eyes beneath sweeping brows are wide, dark, aglow with fierce intelligence. His forehead is high, his nose a straight blade leading to a chiseled mouth, his chin square and firm. Terror grips me. I hear his name in my mind but I would have known him under any circumstances—*Mordred*. Yet he fits nothing of what I have been told. This scourge of evil whose very existence violates the natural order appears to be the creation of a master sculptor intent on evoking nothing less than perfection in form and manner. He is, quite simply, the most beautiful being I have ever seen. I, poor fool, can only gape at him as he steadily closes the distance between us.

The unrelieved blackness of his garb shimmers with his inner light. He smells of wind and night, and something deeper, imbued with power that I cannot identify but which I yearn for as iron filings will lean toward a lodestone. His voice, when I hear it at last, is deep and compelling.

"Elizabeth. How glad I am that you have come to me."

He holds out his hands, the palms turned up in invitation. A fierce need to feel his skin against mine sweeps over me. The lamp begins to slide from my fingers.

*Evil.*

Absurd! No such word can describe this being of vivid life and beauty, this dark prince who waits, smiling, silently bidding me to take the few steps necessary to put myself within his reach. My feet, no longer frozen, feel light as air. I have only to move the slightest distance—

An hour and more ago, my mother's diadem was removed from my brow, tucked carefully away back into its velvet case, and returned to the lead chest where my jewels are kept. Yet just now I could swear that I feel its weight upon my head. So vivid is the sensation that I almost reach up to confirm its presence.

Instead, I tighten my grip on the lamp. Just as I do so, it springs back to light.

"Mordred." At the sound of his name, terror flickers again at the edges of my mind. But at the center, where all my attention focuses, is my own will, honed in the years of danger and death, warring with the strange, inescapable attraction to him that seems to grow with every passing moment.

"Whatever magic you think to work on me," I say, "it will avail you nothing."

Or so I tell myself. Mordred appears less convinced. He frowns and drops his hands.

"Elizabeth," he chides, "you should not listen to your supposed confidants, Dee and Cecil. They are small men who
would make you small as well."

The familiarity with which he speaks of my counselors
makes me frown in turn. How can he know what passed between us?

"Let me guess," he says. His gaze flicks over me, lingering as
though he sees straight through my garb to bare flesh. I fight a
blush, schooling myself to stillness, and watch him unflinch-
ingly.

"They told you that I am evil incarnate, a deadly danger to
you and your realm. They claim that you and I are fated to be
enemies, and they at least implied that you can win the struggle
between us. In every particular they have lied to you."

"My counselors do not lie." Cecil and Dee might be mistaken
from time to time, but neither man has a mendacious bone in
his body. Moreover, if Mordred believes that I will take his word
for anything, he truly does think me a fool.

"Men consumed by fear cannot recognize truth," he says.
"They are weak, unlike us. I can feel the strength in you. It
is . . . seductive."

He steps closer, and I feel in turn the strange attraction drawing me to him. But I resist, determined as I am to stand my
ground.

Boldly, I raise the lantern. "Stay where you are."

He stops, but he also smiles, as though being patient with a
child. "I am no threat to you, Elizabeth, to the contrary. I am
here to help you become what you are truly meant to be."

"I am Queen by grace of God and all that is holy."

"You are indeed, much good may it do you. Queen of a realm
surrounded by enemies. The only question is, who will win the
race to dethrone you?"

That suggestion stings, coming as it does too close to the truth of my fears. But he is not yet done.

"You are as stubborn as your mother."

"You knew her?"

I speak before I can stop myself. Dozens, probably hundreds, of people are still alive who once knew my mother, to some degree at least. But only Kat has ever been willing to speak of her to me and then only reluctantly. For the rest, Anne Bolyen might never have existed.

"I knew her very well," he says, "but that is for another time. I want to show you something."

He reaches out a hand, and to my horror I move toward him. Not because I choose to do so; I do not. I slide across the frozen ground as though I have no control over myself. The lamp falls from my hand; vaguely, I am aware of it smashing on the ground. The thin fabric of my bed gown and robe press against my legs as I am mysteriously pulled toward him. The moonlight falling across the garden begins to whirl as though the whole world has gone mad. Horror fills me as I realize that I am help-less to stop him, perhaps at least in part because I do not wish to do so.

Mordred's arm closes hard around my waist. Breath rushes from me. I am engulfed in his touch and scent, his strength, and most alarmingly of all in the stunning sense of recognition that floods through me, as though I have been waiting, yearning for this moment, through unfathomable eons. Every nerve in my body is vividly alive. I feel him as I have never dreamt that it is possible to feel, as though the barriers between us are dissolv-ing. A pulse leaps suddenly in my throat. I arch my neck and moan softly.

"Elizabeth," he murmurs with unconcealed satisfaction, then adds, "Hold on."

To my astonishment, we rise suddenly into the night sky. Terror and exaltation surge in me in equal measure as the ground falls away beneath me. I am ashamed to say that I cling to him as I feel against my breasts the deep rumble of his laughter.

"Look at our city," he says. "Exquisite, isn't it? I have seen it in so many ages, so many guises, but never like this. It is about to burst free and become a true city of the world like old Rome or Byzantium. London is destined to be the capital of all the world."

I steel myself and peer down, only to be instantly entranced by the vision I behold: London, slumbering in moonlight beside the ancient river, steals my breath. I stare in fascination at the vista of the city spread out before me, from the spires of Westminster Abbey past dwellings noble and humble, over the great roads leading into and through the city, coming finally eastward to the Tower, standing sentinel over all. My beloved city and yet not—for laid so gently upon it, as though through a veil, I glimpse a sight I can scarcely credit, a city of vastly greater size and power in which alabaster buildings gleam and darkness itself seems banished.

"See what is possible," Mordred says seductively. "Think of the pride and courage that has made this land, the trials that have been endured, the tribulations over which we have triumphed. Think of what that can mean not just here but everywhere."

And I do, seeing before me a vision of honor, boldness, and, coming as the sun itself, a golden age that would transform the world.

All drenched in blood.

I stiffen against him, struggling to be free.

"Don't," he warns, and tightens his hold. "If you fall from me, you will die."

No dream, then. No charmed phantasm of my disordered senses but cold reality instead. As much as my poor mind can barely encompass what is happening, I do truly soar over my island kingdom in the arms of the vampire king. It is beyond belief yet I must endure it all the same. Nor is he yet done. To my stunned eyes, the dark expanse of the channel preserving us from the chaos that is Europe appears and vanishes behind us in a heartbeat. We drift over slumbering France, following the silver ribbon of the Seine, climb higher over snow-draped mountains, all in an instant as though time and space have no meaning, until we come at last to the city bathed in gold where rats scurry out of every sewer and into every palace.

"How is this possible?" I ask when I can speak at all.

Mordred smiles. "A topic for another time. Suffice to say that time and space are nothing at all as you experience them and no obstacles of any kind to me."

Even as I struggle to grasp his meaning, I cling to him, awed by what he lays bare.

"Rome," Mordred says, gesturing below, and I, no longer able to muster a challenge to him even in my mind, can only accept what I see before my dazzled eyes.

We hover near the great dome of St. Peter's before drifting toward the nearby Apostolic Palace, entering through a high window that flies open at our approach. Down a long corridor lit by torches, past guards who stir uneasily but seem unable to see us, through a gilded door, and into the inner sanctum of God's Vicar on Earth, Pope Paul IV.

"I will smash the bitch!" the old prelate cries in Latin, which I understand all too well. "That spawn of a whore who dares to take England's crown! I will send her to the furthest reaches of Hell and reclaim her benighted land for Christ's own!"

"He is drunk," Mordred whispers in my ear. "And regretting his belatedly acquired chastity. But he does mean what he says. He wants you dead in the worst way possible."

"What harm have I done him?" I protest. "I will burn no Catholics, I swear, if only they are loyal to me."

"How can they be?" Mordred says. "Not once His Holiness orders them to overthrow you. They will be caught between you on one side and Rome on the other. No man or woman can live so divided."

Mordred leans back a little, looking at me. "Neither can any realm survive in such a state."

My throat tightens so that I can scarcely breathe, so great is my fear. What he says is true. Pitted against the Pope himself, how can I hope for the peace and prosperity my country needs so desperately?

But Mordred is not yet done. "You have not seen the worst," he says, and we are gone, out of the palace, away from the Eternal City, faster than the wind that parts at our passing so that we fly within a tunnel of night and sky, burrowing through it at what speed I cannot guess. We emerge over the ancient city of Valladolid, where the Spanish have their capital at present, though rumors are that King Philip means to move it to Madrid. The Moors created Valladolid, the City of Walid as they called it, though no one wants to remember that now that the heathens are gone from the land. Its winding streets, gracious buildings, and hidden gardens remain, reflections of the dreams of its lost masters.

"Look there." Mordred points through the high, leaded windows of the palace, through which I glimpse, as though in a dream, my late sister's husband, the despicable Philip, kneeling at prayer in his gilded chamber. A slight man, round-faced with pale blue eyes, he has the usual jutting lower lip and chin of the blighted Hapsburgs. His acolytes praise him as endlessly courteous and gracious. I have a different impression of him. Before my sister, who had the misfortune to truly love him, was even dead, Philip was angling to make me his wife. Truly, I would leap from the nearest cliff before embracing such a loathsome fate.

Mordred laughs at the fierceness of my expression. "Have a little pity for him, won't you? He could hardly bring himself to touch Mary, but he lusts after you. You appear regularly in his dreams that, to his great distress, invariably conclude with *nocturnus ejaculatio*. He considers himself shamed by you."

"Enough!" I am dismayed to discover that Philip thinks of me in such terms, even more to learn that he would hold me responsible for the wayward passion of his own body.

"For that sin," Mordred continues relentlessly, "he contemplates burning you. Indeed, he tells his closest counselors that nothing less than your death in the flames will please God and purify England."

Horror clutches at me. I stammer, "But he still claims to want to marry me."

Mordred cast me a chiding look. "And that will prevent him from killing you? . . . How exactly?"

I have no answer. The vision Mordred casts before me goes beyond even my worst nightmare. My mother was, at least, spared the fire. My father, in a show of mercy conditioned on her saying nothing against him in the final moments of her life, sent to France for an expert swordsman, who struck her head off her slender neck with a single blow. Presumably, she felt nothing. Yet her executioner was also ordered to do as tradition dictates: he lifted her severed head, not to show it to the avid crowd as some assume, but to show my mother in the final moments of her consciousness her own headless body. So much for mercy.

Mordred tightens his arm around me and says nothing more. We climb toward the moon, emerging out of clouds to bathe in its radiance.

"It is not my purpose to distress you, Elizabeth," he says as the white cliffs of home slip beneath us. "I only want to be certain that you understand who your enemies really are. Do not be misled by Cecil and Dee. They have no real understanding of what they're dealing with."

We are drifting downward. The chimney pots of London rise beneath my feet. An instant later, we land softly on the frozen ground of the walled garden beside the Thames.

Still holding me close, Mordred bends his head. I feel his breath against the ultrasensitive skin of my neck. "Their ignorance comes from fear," he says. "For the sake of this realm, I beg you not to succumb to it."

Confusion fills me, born in no small measure from the hunger growing in me for his touch, his scent, and more . . . for the very taste of him. Worse yet, I cannot reconcile my faith in my counselors and what they have told me with Mordred's seemingly heartfelt concern for England. But beyond even that, I confess that his demonstration of power leaves me stunned and, God help me, envious.

With him, all limitations seem to fall away and all things become possible.

"What do you want of me?" I ask.

He straightens and steps away from me. At once I am bereft. Only with the greatest effort do I stop myself from reaching out. The black night of his cloak drifts around him. Through it, I seem to see the faint outline of the wall, as though he grows ethereal.

"I want you to be the queen you are meant to be. Not merely England's but mine. Join with me, Elizabeth. You will have all the power you need to defeat your enemies and you will never know fear again."

"What are you saying . . . ?"

"Become one of us, but not only one among many. Become our queen and mine. Together, we will rule over this realm and keep it safe from all enemies now and forever."

Become what he is? A creature of the dark . . . a being destined to never stand in the light of God? How could I even consider such a thing?

And yet . . . how he looks glowing in the moonlight, all strength and majesty, the deep timbre of his voice a caress I have no wish to deny. This being who carried me to such heights, revealed to me the scheming of my enemies, and who claims only to want to help me defeat them. Is it so unthinkable that we should be allies and even more?

Treacherous temptation rises within me, blocking out for the moment all rational thought. It would be so very easy to say yes, to take what he offers and, in the taking, set down the terrible burden of fear and dread that have haunted me all my life.

So very easy . . .

But why then had my mother warned against him as I knelt at her grave? Why had Morgaine Le Fey battled him? If Mordred wanted only to preserve England, why had he slain Arthur, his own father and the greatest king this land has ever known?

I back away from him, my arm thrust out as though that could somehow ward him off. "I cannot . . . the price is too high. My humanity, *my very soul*, and for what? I am sworn before Almighty God to care for those He has placed under my rule. I cannot make them subject to a creature so far outside the natural order."

A flash of anger passes across his face and is quickly gone. He shrugs as though he expected my refusal and is not deterred by it.

"As you will, Elizabeth, at least for now. But I ask you this: You say I am outside the natural order, yet here I am. What does that say of your Almighty God? If He really is all-powerful and all-knowing as your priests claim, then I and those like me can only exist because He wills it. But if we truly are here despite him, he is a poor, weak godling who cannot help you. Who then will you turn to in your hour of need?"

Having presented me with the puzzle that has occupied the greatest theological minds for centuries—how can evil exist within the creation of a loving God?—Mordred vanishes. To be more precise, he dissolves into the air. I am left staring at the bloodred moon.

Impatience drove me from Elizabeth. That and the fact that in providing so dramatic a demonstration of my power, I had temporarily exhausted it. I needed to rest and think. I had not expected her to be an easy conquest; indeed, I would not have wanted her to fall into my arms too readily. I reveled in her courage and her will. Truly, she was a queen for the ages.

Even so, I was surprised by the stubbornness of her resistance. I confess I found her pride made her even more alluring. She seemed inclined to regard our union as a matter of conscience when her every thought should have been focused on her own survival. Her father had never made that mistake; Henry's conscience was ever the slave to his power, bending this way and that according to whatever he thought most expedient. But her mother . . .

Dear, dead Anne was a different matter. She chose conscience over the life I would have given her. I had to hope that her daughter would not be so foolish.

Soon enough, Elizabeth would have an opportunity to decide. The lesson she was about to learn would serve as a reminder of just how fragile her hold on her throne—and her life—truly was.

Through the fog of exhaustion I decided that I would let her plead a little before forgiving her. Magnanimity, correctly displayed, becomes a king. That, too, I learned from my father. Of late, Arthur was in my thoughts more than ever; with the prize about to fall into my grasp, I felt his presence more vividly than I had in centuries.

Indeed, as weary as I was, I caught myself glancing over my shoulder, as though I expected to find him watching me.

The King of the Vampires afraid of a ghost? The notion was absurd enough to wring a laugh that rasped in my throat. Despite what the credulous believed, Arthur was not remotely "the once and future king." He was, in plain fact, a few fragments of yellowed bone, if even that, and a memory. But the latter had more power by far than I wished to admit.

Dank mist rose to cloak the river. In it, I saw the contours of an ancient battlefield—Camlan—and relived the moment when my mortal father discovered the bargain his son had struck to become immortal. It was the last moment of his life yet long enough for him to gaze upon me with pity.

The fool! I am Mordred, king now and forever! No flame-haired wisp of a girl would stand between me and the destiny to which I was bade from the first hour that ever I drew breath.

Elizabeth would surrender or she would perish. As I alit on the far bank, stumbling just a little, I told myself that she had enough of Henry in her to make the right choice.

Why then did I imagine that not only Arthur hovered over me but Anne as well, the two conspiring across the centuries to thwart my victory over both Elizabeth and the kingdom that should long since have been mine?

*Midnight, 16 January 1559*

---

R obin found me standing stock-still and shivering in the garden. He said later that I looked like a ghost, my skin as cold as ice and my eyes so vacant that he feared my soul had fled into a realm where he could not follow.

Unable to rouse me, he flung his cloak around me, scooped me into his arms, and hastened down the passage back to my bedchamber. There he sat me in my chair nearest the fire and knelt, chaffing my hands and feet until warmth returned to them. Having bundled every blanket that he could find on top and around me, he poured brandy for us both and made certain that I swallowed a fair measure before taking a sip of his own.

Only when the color finally began returning to my cheeks did he take a deep, shuddering breath and pull up a stool to sit beside me.

"For the love of Heaven, Elizabeth, what happened?"

I look at him—dear, familiar Robin, the only man in whose arms I have ever wanted to be—and feel so wrenching a sense of betrayal as to scarcely be borne. Compared to Mordred, Robin looks . . . ordinary. Not unappealing, certainly, but no match for the compelling seduction of the vampire king.

Yet Robin loves me; not for a moment do I doubt that or his true faithfulness. Never would he wish me to do anything ill to myself, much less urge me to sacrifice my immortal soul to live as one of the scourge of evil, ruling over England for all eternity.

Never growing old. Never dying. Remaining young and beautiful and a queen forever.

Out over the city, circling the moon, beneath a dark star, I swear that I hear Mordred laughing.

Of course, I can say nothing of that to Robin. All I can tell him is that I was drawn into an encounter with Mordred that left no doubt as to either the vampire's existence or his power.

"You actually spoke to him?" Robin asks when he has absorbed the full import of my revelation. When I nod, he all but bursts with curiosity. "What is his manner? What does he seek? Did he dare to threaten you? By God, if he did, I will—"

I lean forward and take his mouth with mine, sealing away whatever ill-advised vow he was about to make. Deliberately, I make the kiss long and deep and am relieved to feel my passion stir. I still desire Robin, grace to God. I am not yet Mordred's creature nor, I vow, will I ever be.

"He looks like a man," I say, though that is not strictly true. No man possesses the inner brilliance that shines from the vampire, and no mere man can claim his beauty. "As for what he wants, that is very simple. He wants to rule England."

Robin does not seem to hear me. He clasps me close, his hand closing over my breast, and seeks to kiss me again.

"Beloved . . . ," he croons in that voice I know means he wants us abed, about such sport as we allow ourselves given that I cannot risk conceiving.

"Do you not hear me?" I demand, shoving him away. "Mordred wants England, and he has conceived a brilliant plan to get it."

Disgruntled, Robin regains his balance and pretends interest in the brandy. Scion of the great house of Northumberland, which had itself thrown the dice to win the throne and lost, he has no illusions about how power is gained and kept.

"Does he intend to attack you?"

"I don't know. Cecil and Dee think that he does, but it's clearly not his preference. He claims to want only to help me defeat our enemies both foreign and domestic. Of course, there is a price for his help."

"And that would be?"

Winter wind whistles round my father's palace. In my heightened state, it sounds like the moaning of lost souls. I shiver despite the many blankets around me and look into the fire.

"He wants me to become what he is and for the two of us to rule England together."

Robin pales. His hand, still holding the brandy snifter, shakes. He sets the crystal goblet down carefully on a nearby table and stares at me.

"You can't mean that."

"I do and, much more importantly, so does he." I turn to him, driven to explain the trap in which I fear to find myself. "Think of it, Robin. Everyone is pressing me to marry. Some favor a foreign prince, others think I should choose an English lord, but they all assume that I must wed. Mordred's claim is that alone among my suitors, only he can bring me the power I need to keep England safe forever. If I announced that a high lord of British lineage, newly returned from some distant portion of the Continent bearing with him vast wealth, which I have no doubt Mordred can command, was my choice as husband, certainly there would be great curiosity. But there would also be tremendous relief that I was marrying, and quickly enough my nobles would accept him."

"This is madness," Robin exclaims. "Do you not understand what he is? What he would do to this land if he ever got control of it?"

I finish my brandy in a single swallow. My throat burns and I have to blink back tears before I can answer.

"I did not say that I accept his claim. For pity's sake, have more faith in me than that. But the truth is that I know too little and I must know everything, not just what Dee and Cecil say but what has been passed down secretly over the ages."

When Robin does not immediately respond, I catch his hand in both of mine. "For the love of God, Robin, I have no one else to ask. My father's line is not so ancient as to know of this, and besides, what is left of the Tudors but me? As for my mother's family . . ." I do not have to tell him how badly the Boleyns have fared in the shadow of the scaffold.

He sighs deeply but relents, as I knew he would, and takes his place again at my side. "I can't vouch for what I have heard. It is all just rumor and legend. Some of it may be true, some not."

"Tell me all the same. Leave nothing out." Later, I will sort the wheat from the chaff, but for the moment, I need to discover as much about Mordred as I possibly can.

Robin thinks for a moment, then speaks slowly as he struggles to recapture a distant memory. "I heard the story when I was seven, the year before you and I met. My brother John told me one night when we were sitting up late by the fire. He meant to frighten the wits out of me and he succeeded, what with his tale of unholy creatures who drink the blood of innocents so that they can live forever and gain extraordinary powers beyond the ken of mortal men. I'd have thought that he was making it all up except that he was very precise about certain things."

"What things?" I prompt.

"He claimed to have the tale from our father himself, who had it from his father and so on back as far as anyone could remember. John was the eldest, so I believed that our father would have told him and no one else."

Poor John Dudley, dead these many years. So, too, his other

brother, Henry. Only Robin was left in the aftermath of his family's treason, alone and friendless in this world except for an equally solitary and threatened princess.

"Go on," I urge. "Tell me exactly what your brother related."

He takes a breath, clasps my hand tighter, and says, "The story that has been passed down is that an ancestor of the Dudleys fought with King Arthur and was with him right to the end when Arthur fell at Camlan. Supposedly, this Dudley actually saw the great king killed by his son, Mordred. The experience made such an impression on him—I gather he thought that he had witnessed something truly unholy—that he told his own sons of it so that they would tell their sons and so on down through time in order that it never be forgotten."

"But Mordred also is said to have died at Camlan," I remind him.

Robin nods. "According to my ancestor, the claim that Mordred died was concocted to conceal what had actually happened, namely that Arthur's bastard son had forged an alliance with the vampires. By becoming one of them, he acquired extraordinary powers that enabled him to slay his father, who, as we all know, was the greatest warrior England has ever seen and could not be killed by any mere man."

"And he did all that in order to become king in his father's place?"

Robin nodded. "Arthur had refused to make Mordred his heir because he sensed his attraction to evil. He wasn't willing to trust his kingdom to a man he believed to be ungodly, not even his own son."

I repressed any thought of what Mordred must have made of his father's rejection of him and pushed on.

"But nothing worked out as Mordred expected," Robin continued. "After King Arthur fell at Camlan, Morgaine Le Fey sought out Mordred. She had some sort of power. My ancestor did not know exactly what it was, but with it, she managed to kill many vampires. She wounded Mordred himself grievously, but he was able to escape and go into hiding. Since then, he has bided his time, waiting until he could grow strong enough to return and take the throne. In the aftermath of Arthur's death, the Saxons overran the kingdom and darkness reigned over all."

The wind had become louder as Robin spoke. It seemed to batter against the palace walls as though determined to find some chink, some weakness through which it could gain entry.

"It isn't just a matter of being strong enough," I say, almost to myself. Since my encounter with Mordred, my thoughts have been scattered and incoherent, but they are slowly coming to-gether. "He has a better route to the throne now. Instead of having to kill to take it, all he has to do is wed."

Robin pales. "He cannot think . . . it would be an abomina-tion! Every lord in the land would rise up against him at the first hint of what he truly is—"

"Would they? Would they really, Robin? What if he not only promised them wealth and glory beyond any they had ever dreamt of but actually produced it? What if he laid waste to our enemies and set England above all the nations of the world, as he claims is this land's rightful destiny? Do you truly believe that our lords—our rapacious, greedy lords who unfailingly have put their power and privileges above all else—would reject what he offered?"

Robin knows the nobility as well as I do; he cannot deny what I say. But there is far more to England than its nobles, as he reminds me.

"What of ordinary folk? Do you think for a moment that the decent men and women of this realm will bow their heads to a demon king?"

"No," I say, for truly I did not. "They will huddle down and pray for relief from the one person who is supposed to protect them above all others—their anointed queen. Me! And therein lies the flaw in Mordred's plan. By God, he has misjudged me. While there is breath in my body, I never can—I never will—condemn my people to such a fate."

I speak quietly, but with such steely certainty that I know Robin will understand. Mordred could have made his offer to my sister, Mary, but her whole life was a testament to her faith in God, preserved for good or ill through much suffering and despair. He must have realized that she would never accede to what he wanted. Had he merely been waiting for her death to bring me to the throne—the young and frightened princess through whom he thought to rule?

If so, Mordred is in for a terrible shock.

"Morgaine Le Fey's power did not end with her," I say. "It exists still."

"How can you know that?" Robin asks.

I reply with far more confidence than I feel. "Because it has passed to me. I possess it now and I will not hesitate to use it." As I speak, the memory of what I experienced the night before rushes through me. For an instant, I am kneeling again on the floor of the chapel, seeing the light pouring from me and feeling the world become at once more vivid and less real, as though I have come to glimpse a far vaster reality beyond.

Even so, my bold claim is sheer bravado. I do not know that any such power exists, much less that it is now mine alone. I have only Cecil's and Dee's word for the strange vision I experienced at my mother's grave. Face-to-face with Mordred, I was helpless to resist him in any way.

That will have to change, and soon.

"What do you mean, it has passed to you?" Robin demands. He is on his feet again, staring at me.

I hold out my goblet to be refilled. The brandy gives me strength and banishes the lingering effects of my otherworldly encounter with Mordred. "Apparently, I am not only my father's heir. I am also Morgaine Le Fey's through my mother's lineage."

Startled, Robin lets the bottle linger too long. Amber liquid sloshes over the top of my glass. I lick my fingers and take a sip of courage.

"Sit down, and I will tell you all about it," I say.

He is, after all, my dearest friend, my confidant, and—given certain necessary limitations—my lover. I would withhold nothing from him. Nothing save my heart, which has been locked away since the day my mother died. Sometimes I imagine it nestled like her diadem in a velvet chest, brought out to be displayed only on the rarest occasions before being hidden again, safe and inviolate.

Far beyond the reach of Mordred.

Grace of God, let that be so.

*16 January 1559*

———

*R*obin slips away before dawn. We had lain on the bed together but chastely, spooning for comfort as we talked far into the night He had a thousand questions for me; I had few answers. At length I slept, but raggedly. Alone now, I await my ladies, harbingers of the new day, my first as anointed Queen.

They come all in a flutter, bright with excitement, restrained only by Kat's watchful eye. She finds a moment when they are occupied to frown and whisper, "Is something amiss, my lady?"

I should have known that she would sense the change in me, this woman who knows me longest and best. But who also sees me through the eyes of maternal love, of which I take shameless advantage whenever I feel the need to mislead her.

"How could anything be other than exactly as it should be?" I answer with a smile. "It is a new day, a new reign, and I am Queen. Everything is perfect."

She smiles in turn but her gaze remains watchful.

With relief, I dip a toe in my bath and sink into the sea of girlish conversation. Had I seen what Lady Letticia wore to the banquet? Did she imagine that color favored her? Is it true that impecunious Lord Heverton is wooing a wealthy widow from Brighton with nary a title to her name? Had the Duke of Sussex really been caught in flagrante with the sister of the Earl of Camden, with the lady refusing to display a flicker of remorse? Such are the doings of the royal court, but let them not be mis-

taken for idle chatter. To the contrary, the lives of my nobles
are of keen interest to me, touching as they always do on matters of loyalty.

I dress and go to meet with Cecil, as promised, my way pre-
ceded by the usual shouts of warning by my guard: "The Queen
comes! The Queen comes!"

My courtiers, avid for sight of me, scatter to either side that I
may pass. The ladies sink into deep curtsies as the men bow low,
each managing these elegant maneuvers without ever taking
their eyes from me. I acknowledge a favored few but do not
slow. Let them make of my haste what they will. Perhaps they
will merely think me eager to be about my queenly duties, or
more likely, they will concoct a dozen and more rumors of plots,
counterplots, intrigues, and the like before I have scarcely left
their sight. It is a sovereign's duty, like it or not, to provide grist
for the vast gossip mill that is the royal court.

Cecil is pacing the floor in my withdrawing room, but halts
abruptly as I enter and turns in my direction. His usual air of
confidence is missing. He appears gray and worn. A stab of guilt
darts through me, buried quickly beneath stark practicality.
Cecil knows that I will always be unsparing in the demands I
put on him. It is the bargain we struck years before when he offered his services on the chance that I would, despite all odds,
rise to the throne and carry him also to great heights.

"Majesty," he says, inclining his head.

I do not stand on ceremony but go to him and touch his face
gently. "My poor Spirit, you are sorely used."

For a moment, I fear that he will crumble before such unaccustomed kindness, but he rallies and even manages a faint
smile.

"A poor night's rest, nothing more. I am ready at your service, as always."

"Well and good but sit." I gesture to the servants, who hurry to pull out our chairs and bring dishes to the small, round table near the windows where I typically eat alone or with, at most, one or two intimates.

When I am seated, Cecil takes his chair. He waits until our cups are filled with stout and a platter of sliced beef is set before us. That, with a hearty mustard and a good white bread, makes a more than ample breakfast, in my opinion. I eat sparingly, as always, and Cecil seems too distracted to eat at all.

He takes a sip of stout, delicately pats the foam mustache from above his lips, and says, "I regret to tell you, Majesty, that the body of a young man was recovered from near the Thames this morning. He has not been identified yet, but his garb suggests that he was a member of the gentry. He bears ritual marks that Dee tells me are associated with Mordred and his kind."

My hand freezes while spearing a slice of beef on the point of my knife. "What marks?"

"Twin piercings in the vicinity of his throat, from which apparently his life's blood was drained."

I drop my knife and sit back, staring at Cecil. "It is true then, they drink blood?"

He nods. "They depend on it for what they know as life. There have been other such occurrences of late. I regret to say that they are becoming more common. The conclusion appears unmistakable that the vampires are increasing both in number and boldness."

"I can certainly vouch for the latter."

Cecil raises a brow. "Majesty?"

Briefly, I tell him of my encounter with Mordred. Certain details I omit as irrelevant to our discussion. Cecil has no need to know of the vampire king's otherworldly beauty or how easily I had been seduced into offering him such scant resistance. But my Spirit does need to understand my deep concern in the face of my helplessness.

"This power you and Dee claim I have acquired was in no way evident, not for a moment. I had no sense of it at all. The plain truth is that Mordred could have killed me, had he chosen, and I would have been helpless to stop him."

Cecil reddens as I speak, but with my final words, the color drains from his face. He places both his hands flat on the table as though to steady himself and takes a deep, shuddering breath.

"Majesty . . . I do not know what to say. If this monster had—"

He does not have to continue. I understand all too well what would follow hard on my death. Rival factions warring for the throne—presumably including the vampires themselves—would tear the realm apart. Foreign enemies would not hesitate to take advantage of the opportunity provided by the resulting chaos. Before they were all done, my beloved land would be little more than a carcass picked clean.

"What matters," I say quickly, "is that he did not. But before I even consider confronting him again, I must know if there is any truth to the powers that you and Dee claim I have."

Regaining control of himself, Cecil says, "I know what we witnessed, Majesty. The radiance that surrounded you can only be termed otherworldly. I have never seen such a sight in all my life, and I cannot believe that it heralded anything less than a momentous transformation."

Would that I shared his confidence, but until I have real evidence that he and the magus are right, I nurture grave doubts about my ability to deal with Mordred. That worry hangs over me as Cecil and I conclude our breakfast and he accompanies me to the presentation room, where I am scheduled to receive various foreign ambassadors.

I enter to the blare of trumpets, which even for so newly minted a queen as me sound oddly natural to my ears. How closely they all crowd round, my courtiers, foreign visitors, and the like. How avidly they watch me. The foreigners take my measure for their masters, to whom no doubt they will send reports on the next tide. But what I must manage most adroitly is the assessment of my own people, for my success as queen will rest as much on their trust and faith as on my will.

Sunlight streaming through the high windows gilds the oak paneling. I glance up at the banners hanging from the iron braces set all around the room. Some frayed and faded, others still fresh, they are the bold reminders of the struggles my ancestors waged to claim and hold the throne that is now my own. I look from that proud lineage to the avid crowd so gloriously arrayed and muster a bold smile.

"Good lords and ladies," I say, "you are all welcome here. It is my duty but also my delight to receive you. We stand together at the beginning of a new age, on the cusp of a new world, and I say to you all that England shall play the noblest part in shaping what is to come. We are a nation and a people who have never shied from accepting the sternest challenges, and under my rule so shall we remain. Let the world know that this realm is and will always be free, strong, indomitable, and, above all, English!"

My nobles cheer heartily for they have a sensible fear of foreign entanglements. Too well they remember how the Spanish strutted through court while Mary ruled and how more than one Spaniard cast covetous eyes on English lands. So, too, they remember when the writ of Rome held sway over this land. Some no doubt miss that, but the clear-eyed, ambitious men and women of my court know which side of their bread holds the butter. They will not fail me, nor I them.

As for the foreign ambassadors, I see their sober gazes and understand that my words will resonate in their masters' ears. I have thrown down a gauntlet, daring any to defy my rule and England's freedom together. In time, some enemy or another will pick it up. But for the moment, frowns give way quickly to professional smiles and practiced congratulations.

Then there are the gifts, presented with flowery protestations of respect and friendship on behalf of monarchs I am quite certain bear me neither. Even so, gold, pearls, fine silks, and exotic porcelains will always find a home with me. I make a pretty speech thanking each ambassador and send them all on their ways having committed myself to precisely nothing. And I manage all that despite my mind being constantly on Mordred and the danger he presents.

At length, I am free to withdraw to my rooms to prepare for the afternoon's tournament to be held in my honor. Robin is riding in the lists carrying my colors, of course. I am confident that he, always the most skilled of horsemen, will acquit himself nobly. I have a special purple gown for the occasion that I am looking forward to wearing. Purple may seem a risk with my fiery hair, but it looks uncommonly good on me, so my ladies say.

In Cecil's company, I am returning to my apartment, making my way through the eager members of my court, who bow low at my passing while trying their best to gain my notice. Several attempt to advance petitions, but I merely smile and keep on. They can work a little harder for my favor.

Cecil and I are speaking of my need to meet with Doctor Dee as we pass through the gallery leading to my rooms. My Spirit is assuring me that the magus will be able to answer all my doubts when a man springs suddenly from the crowd. I have only the most fleeting glimpse of him—young, dark-haired, wide-eyed—

before he shouts, "Death to the usurper!" and flings himself at me.

The world seems to move out of kilter—or perhaps I do so. Whichever, we no longer fit together. Time slows and all else with it save myself. I am set apart, observing all that happens as the young man draws a knife from beneath his doublet and comes ever so slowly toward me. Cecil raises an arm—slowly, so slowly. Guardsmen move toward us, but they may as well crawl through quicksand. Every action and reaction that should happen in the blink of an eye plays out instead across a vastly longer horizon of time. Only I appear to be unaffected.

A shadow moves on the edge of this strangely stilted scene. With it comes a frisson of sensual awareness. The caress of air against my skin, the rhythm of my own heart, the sudden warmth rising in my body, all threaten to fill me with languor I can ill afford. I glance to the side just as Mordred appears. He looks much the same as he did in the garden, even to his chiding smile. Once again, the rush of attraction that overwhelmed me before in his presence threatens to take command. The realization of how powerfully I am drawn to him at once excites me and fills me with dread.

"Really, Elizabeth, you should take greater care. Or at least insist that those you entrust with your safety do so."

I draw breath, remind myself that I am Queen, and face him squarely. "What do you know of this?"

"I? Only that this fellow—he was sent by the Pope, but you have so many enemies that scarcely matters—reached our fair shores a fortnight ago and has been making his way toward this moment ever since. None of your protectors discovered him, no one prevented him from entering into the very heart of your palace, and—if not for my interference—no one would have stopped him from killing you."

He points at the young man, who stands now with his right arm raised, the knife gleaming in the rays of winter sun streaming through the high windows of the gallery. The hatred that contorts his face chills my blood.

"This is where you die, Elizabeth. Cut down a single day after your crowning. Your people will have scant time to mourn you before they can think of nothing but their own survival."

This cannot be happening—I think. Having lived in the shadow of death for so long, I would have thought myself accustomed to the possibility that I can die at any moment. But face-to-face, quite literally, with my own mortality, I can scarcely grasp it. I stand frozen, staring with unwilling fascination at the final moments of my life.

Mordred shakes his head at my folly. He takes my arm and draws me off to the side of the gallery. "Consider this an illustration of our partnership, Elizabeth. When we reign together, you will be invulnerable. But until then—"

The supreme note of certainty in his voice returns me to myself, the realization that he considers it a foregone conclusion that I—poor, weak creature that he assumes me to be, for I have given him no reason to think otherwise—will fall in with his designs without demur. Pride can be a stumbling block, but it can also be a great source of strength in the darkest times.

I take a breath, another, and feel the veil of fear and disbelief that has paralyzed me dissolve.

Feel something else as well. Rising within me, a sense of light and strength that sings as it comes, as though all of Creation reverberates to a single, irresistible note. On the crest of that ethereal music, I strike.

"Never!" I exclaim. "I will never become as you! Slayer of your own father! Consorter with evil!"

I raise my arm and the light sings. I have my father's crown but truly it is my mother's blood that drives me in that moment. Blood that poured out on the scaffold, soaking into the land, nurturing my realm with all the love and care she would have given her own child had she been allowed to live.

Power gathers within me, shoots down my arm, and leaps across the small distance separating me from Mordred. A beam of silvered light strikes him full in the chest.

He reels back, staring at me in astonishment. With a snarl, he raises his own arm and sends at me a suffocating black cloud that would surely have snuffed the life from me did not I manage just then to block it with another bolt of light.

Neither one of us moves. We stand, staring at each other, light and dark, mortal and immortal, locked in combat, until finally Mordred says, "As you will, Elizabeth. But know this—I have had a thousand years to refine my powers. You will never be a match for me; I could kill you now, if I wished. I will give you time to discover that, to realize that you truly have no choice but to give me what I want."

And with that he is gone, vanished into the black cloud, which disappears with him. I have no chance to think of what has happened or what it means, for at the same instant, time speeds up again, resuming its accustomed course.

I hear and see, in quick succession, Cecil cry out and—bless that dear man—charge directly at the attacker with his head down to butt him in the chest. At the same moment, the guards, no longer mired in quicksand, surge forward to seize the villain. Various people scream, one or two ladies affect to faint, but it is all over in moments. The man is on the ground, his hands secured behind him, the knife in the grip of one of my guards.

Everyone turns to me.

At once, I see their bewilderment. An instant before, I was walking beside Cecil, well within range of the attacker. But now I stand several yards away near a wall of the gallery.

I must act quickly before awkward questions can be asked.

"What a poor fellow this is," I declare loudly as, smiling, I come forward. "To manage his business so ineptly. I swear I could have strolled to Greenwich and back before he remembered what he was about."

"Majesty—," Cecil begins but I silence him with a glance. My Spirit knows me well enough to realize that I have my reasons for making light of the situation.

"As you say," he declares. Gesturing to the guards, he adds, "Secure this bumbling fool that he may be questioned at the Queen's pleasure."

Taking Cecil's arm, I go on at equal volume, "I declare this must all be a farce. No doubt the poor dolt is an actor seeking attention for some group of players. Perhaps we should have them all to court. What do you think, good lords and ladies? Shall we allow them to entertain us?"

It is all nonsense, of course, and everyone knows that, but it is the best that I can do to sow confusion about exactly what happened and why. People will know what they saw, but as the evidence of their own eyes makes no sense, they will quickly come to doubt it. With a little adroit managing, the assault on me can at the least be minimized, if not made to vanish from memory altogether, or so I hope.

I move on down the gallery, but with each step my limbs feel weighted with lead. I am all but sagging against poor Cecil by the time we finally step inside my apartment. My ladies cluster round, unsure whether to cluck over me in distress or make light of the matter as I am doing. Kat is white with distress. I

manage a wan smile for her and wave the others aside. With my
Spirit's help, I continue into my privy chamber, where I only
just manage to reach my chair before collapsing.

"Yesterday's festivities have left me wearier than I realized." I
have so little strength after the struggle with Mordred that I can
scarcely hold up my head. This does not bode well for any
future confrontations between us, but I cannot think of that
just now. Indeed, I can scarcely think of anything.

Once again, dear Cecil intervenes. "I fear Your Majesty has
caught a chill."

Taking the hint, I sneeze. "Yes, you are right."

At once, Kat musters my ladies into action. She seems considerably cheered for being given something to do. A posset is
prepared, a night robe warmed. Cecil is banished until I can be
bustled into bed, by which time I am deploying what little
energy I have left to keep sneezing while dapping at my nose in
what I hope is a convincing manner.

"The tournament—," I say weakly.

"Will have to be postponed," Kat declares. "Her Majesty
must have complete rest, after which, no doubt, she will be perfectly fine."

Cecil, who has only just then been readmitted, bends close
to me and whispers, "Was it Mordred in the gallery? Was that
what happened?"

I nod and grip his hand. "Tell Dee he is not wrong, Morgaine's power is real, but it has left me sorely drained."

A flash of relief darts across Cecil's face but hard on it falls
the shadow of dread. Truly, we both know that the power of
which I speak is beyond the ken of mortal men and women.

"Then rest," my faithful Spirit says, "and do not fear, I will
see that no one makes too much of this. As soon as you are
able, send word and I will bring Dee to you."

"And Robin, as well. He knows more of this than any of us realized."

Clearly, Cecil is not pleased. I know that he considers my feelings for Robin a bar to the royal marriage that everyone, including my Spirit, assumes I will have to make. But he acquiesces all the same, rightly judging that he has no choice.

"As you say, Majesty. There is also someone else I would like you to meet, a man I believe can be useful to us. I will bring him as well, with your permission."

I nod but weakly for I am scarcely awake. Cecil's voice fades as I drift into a dreamworld at once hauntingly familiar and unknown. Gilded rooms form and shift around me, filled with mist concealing whatever is occurring within. Shapes move but darkly, without sufficient form for me to recognize them. I hear voices but only one is familiar—my mother's, Anne's. I cannot make out her words no matter how I strain to do so but I sense urgency in her tone.

I am still trying to listen to her when a light tapping at my door returns me to this world.

The scheming, ungrateful creature! How dare she pit herself against me! I, who offered her the world? So great was my disappointment that I could think of nothing save to regain the manor and hide myself away in the chamber beyond the library where not even Blanche was permitted to enter. Too frustrated to even consider feeding, I lay on my velvet-draped bier, contemplating what had happened.

Anne would never have been able to attack me so boldly. What power she had from Morgaine's line was only enough to make her of potential use to me, nothing more. I had assumed it would be the same with Elizabeth, but now seemingly disconnected events compelled me to consider a far different possibility.

A queen choosing to die by the sword when she could have saved herself by allying with me. The arcane signs and symbols protecting her motherless daughter. Dee's prattling about a conjunction of the stars that comes only once in a millennium. The light rising from the grave. The smell of roses.

Anne loved roses. But so did Morgaine, who wore them as her emblem. Her power surpassed any that I had managed to acquire over all the centuries, even to the extent of granting her glimpses of the future. Had she seen where three slain queens would be buried? Where they could serve as a conduit for her own power to return into the world with the coming of her one, true heir?

Did she lie there, too, all this time? Waiting?

If my fevered musings had any foundation at all, I faced a vastly more serious danger than I could have imagined, yet with it came the chance to undo at last the loss that still haunted me.

Morgaine, alive again in Elizabeth! My love returned to me, but this time as my true companion and ally. I must win her to my side. Enraged though I was by her effrontery, the potential rewards of forbearance proved too great a temptation to resist. I would wait, giving her time and opportunity to see the error of her ways. When she did—

I imagined her in my arms, beneath my touch, her taste forever on my lips, the sweetness of her surrender made all the more piercing by the challenge she presented. The sensation filled me with almost unbearable longing, yet I was still able to draw upon the deep reserves of patience and fortitude that the centuries had instilled in me. Only a little time more, I told myself, and all my desires would be fulfilled now and for eternity.

Floating on moonlight, adrift in memories, I succumbed to that most treacherous of mistresses—hope.

*Evening, 16 January 1559*

———

L amps have been lit in my chamber. As I slept, darkness has crept over the city. I sit up with a start. How could I have let so many hours slip by while I idled uselessly? That is the act of a weak woman, not of a queen. Swinging my legs over the side of the bed, I am about to rise when Kat inches the door open and peers in. Seeing me, she hurries to my side.

"Please, dearest, let me help you. Are you feeling better? May I fetch you some ale or perhaps cider? Will you eat?"

"Enough of that," I say briskly. "I must dress. Is Cecil here?"

She frowns, clearly prepared to cosset me for far longer than I will allow. "He is, just outside and growing a bit impatient, if I may say. He is not alone."

I am relieved to hear it. "Quickly, there is no time for anything elaborate. Decent will have to do."

Kat helps me into chemise and petticoat, and drops a simple skirt of embroidered ivory damask over my head. I fidget impatiently as she laces me into a matching boned bodice and attaches the separate sleeves. When she tries to put up my hair, I swat her hands away.

"Leave it; he will have to take me as I am." I pinch what color I can into my cheeks and muster a smile.

"Dear Cecil," I say when he all but hurtles into the room, scowling in anticipation of whatever it is that he expects to find. Myself still incapacitated, perhaps? Too exhausted and weak to be of any use? I hope that my Spirit knows me better, but if he does not, he is about to learn.

Robin is hard on his heels. He comes to me at once and clasps my hands in his. "Are you all right? What happened? I would have come sooner but I thought—"

I press his hands in turn and say softly, "It is as well that you did not. I am merely tired, nothing more. As for that fool who attacked me—"

"He is dead."

I pull back a little, staring at him. "What? Who is dead?"

"The man who tried to kill you. He had poison hidden on his person. As soon as he was thrown into a cell, he took it. The guards found him dead mere minutes later."

My breath hisses through my teeth. "Who knows of this?"

"Almost no one. Cecil warned the guards on pain of death to say nothing. But this leaves no doubt that it was a serious attempt to assassinate you."

"I never thought it was anything else," I reply, still keeping my voice low. "Very well then, we must determine what is to be done."

With good cheer that I am far from feeling, I bid Kat leave me with Cecil and Robin. A third man, unknown to me, steps forward. He sketches a passable bow, a little stiffly, but what else is to be expected from those not born to the skill? He is all in black but for a modest flash of white at his throat, the uniform of the self-made man. I am surrounded by such men, another legacy of my father's. He saw them as useful and perhaps they were, but I wonder if at the end of his days, Henry did not quail at the upheaval he had unleashed. Has any man so conservative in his nature ever more grandly overturned the world?

"This is Francis Walsingham," Cecil says by way of introduction. "Lately returned from the Continent, where he has proved his worth in various challenging situations. He has certain skills that I thought might prove useful to Your Majesty."

I incline my head in acknowledgment of the somber, long-faced man, who does not take his gaze from me. He looks like a young schoolmaster but his eyes appear far older than his years. I know of Cecil's habit of trying out new men on missions abroad before deciding whether to bring them into his service. My Spirit is rigorous in his vetting of such men, and never more so than with one he is introducing to me directly. Apparently, this one has impressed him.

"What sort of skills would that be, Mister Walsingham?" I inquire.

His smile is fleeting and so filled with sweet sorrow that I can only wonder at the view of humanity he harbors. "I am a ferreter out of truth, Majesty. I seek it in the dark places where others prefer not to go. I smell it out, as it were, and when I see it, I know it infallibly for what it is . . . or is not."

"Infallibly?"

"So much as any man may. I thank Your Majesty for the opportunity to serve you."

"As to that, we shall see." I sit and bid them do the same. Cecil takes the chair that I always insist he use because of the pain his gout causes. Robin and Walsingham make do with stools.

"It is my understanding that Doctor Dee would be joining us." Surely I made it clear that I expected him to do so. Great though my respect is for the magus, he will need a better than average excuse for his absence.

"I have sent word to his lodgings, Majesty," Cecil says. "He is only slightly delayed, having been occupied with a matter of great importance."

"What would that be?" Robin has moved his stool so that he

is close beside me. I watch Walsingham watching him and wonder how much the ferreter out of truth already grasps.

"Something to do with an astral configuration that he believes portends great events," Cecil explains. "In the meantime, Majesty, might I ask you to hear what Mister Walsingham can tell us?"

I incline my head in permission, curious to learn why Cecil favors him.

"Majesty," Walsingham begins, "as Sir William indicated, I returned recently from the Continent, where I have been pursuing inquiries touching on your security."

"What inquiries? Be precise, man, Cecil should have told you that I have little patience for dithering."

Robin chuckles but his humor fades quickly when Walsingham, who appears unaffected by my tartness, replies, "I have been looking into the activities of those known as vampires. Much remains to be discovered about them but I have had some success in penetrating their dens."

His matter-of-fact manner startles me, all the more so because of the shock I still feel at confronting the existence of such beings. At the same time, I realize what has happened here. Cecil, knowing that the time of my awakening was close at hand, must have set out to discover all he could about the vampires, the better to equip me to fight them. As much as I appreciate his foresight, his failure to inform me rankles.

"Then you know that they are real?"

"Indisputably, Majesty. I encountered references to them on the Continent, including claims that they had come to England in distant times and are still present here. At first, I dismissed the story, but I have since concluded that it is true."

"And why," Robin asks, "have you done so?"

"Because since my return I have sought and found them here. They frequent particular areas of London, always at night and either singly or in small groups. They maintain a certain discretion—"

"How many of them are there?" I ask abruptly.

"It is impossible to say, Majesty. They are adroit at concealing themselves. However, if one could be captured, questioning could yield useful information."

Cecil shoots Walsingham a hard look, making it clear that any such suggestion has not been cleared with him in advance, as it should have been. Walsingham will be reprimanded for such a lapse, I am sure, but whether it will matter to him remains in doubt. Even on short acquaintance, I perceive that he is guided by his inner urges rather than concern for what others think. That could make his advancement in life difficult but for the fact that his thinking seems to run alongside mine.

"Do you have any idea how such a capture could be accomplished?" I ask.

"The vampire must be rendered insensible long enough for him—or her—to be bound with chains of silver. My inquiries indicate that the metal has a considerable dampening effect on their strength. Prolonged exposure may even bring about death, but that would not be our immediate objective."

"You actually believe that you could hold one of them long enough to force him to talk?" Robin inquires.

Walsingham nods. "I do."

Reluctantly I disagree, "From what I have seen of Mordred, that is unlikely. His strength is far too great."

"But the others are not as strong as their king," Walsingham counters. "He permits no one to achieve a level of power that could challenge his own authority. It is probable that only a very few of them possess strength even remotely approaching his." He pauses, glancing at Cecil, then adds, "Or yours, Majesty."

I raise a brow. "Or mine? Are you that well informed, Mister Walsingham?" Willing as I am to accept my Spirit's confidence in the man, this surprises me.

Before the schoolmaster can respond, Cecil interjects, "It may interest Your Majesty to know that Francis's stepfather, Sir John Carey, was related to your mother by marriage and stood high in her confidence. She relied on Sir John for certain sensitive matters pertaining to your safety. Francis has been preparing for the task of protecting you since he was a tender youth."

A memory stirs. I recall Kat mentioning that my mother did not much care for William Carey, who had wed her sister, Mary, but made her a poor husband. However, my mother thought far better of his brother, John. In her extremis, might she have turned to him for help in keeping me safe?

"Then you are most welcome in my service, Mister Walsingham," I say.

That he knows of my awakening simplifies matters greatly. What he proposes makes good sense, but to capture a vampire of any sort will be a daunting task. I am considering the implications of that when a page knocks on the door to inform us that Doctor Dee has arrived. The magus comes with an air of preoccupation, as though his mind still lingers on whatever great matter delayed him.

Dee sketches a quick bow. "Forgive me, Majesty. I would have been here sooner, but I thought it best to confirm my findings without delay."

Without standing on ceremony, he draws from within his robes a scroll and lays it out on a nearby table. We all peer at what proves to be an astrological chart, showing the planets and constellations as we know them.

"For some time now," Dee says, "I have been watching a traveler who appeared first within the house of Cancer, but is now resident within Leo. Although indistinct at first, I am certain now that the traveler is a comet, and that, if it continues on its appointed course, it will enter Virgo very shortly, perhaps this night."

My hands grip the arms of my chair. As everyone knows, comets are harbingers of great events, particularly concerning royalty. My own affinity to Virgo is obvious, but I am uncertain what to make of the presence of a comet in that constellation at such a time. Fortunately, Doctor Dee is able to enlighten me.

He rolls up the scroll as he says, "This transit of the constellations, combined with other signs, heralds the coming of a decisive moment in Your Majesty's queenship. You have an opportunity to demonstrate your power or, contrarily, to bow before the blow that is being struck at you. The choice is yours."

So far as I am concerned, that concludes the matter. The heavens give me warning that if I do nothing, I will be signaling my weakness, which will surely embolden Mordred even more.

"Tell the court that in order to assure my swift recovery from what ails me, I will remain in my chambers tonight."

The revelries surrounding my coronation will have to go on without me. I have other matters to attend to.

"If Your Majesty needs more rest—," Cecil begins, but breaks off when I rise from my chair.

"Mister Walsingham, you will show me these places that are frequented by vampires."

"Absolutely not!" Robin declares, but he is all but drowned out by Cecil's swift protestations.

"Unthinkable!" my Spirit exclaims. "Your Majesty's safety—"

"Does not exist!" I declare, on my feet, determination surging through me. I am Queen! I will not be controlled by anyone—man or vampire. Nor will I take refuge in lies and deceit that can, however well-intentioned, only harm me.

"Mordred came right into this palace! No barrier could stop him and I was barely able to compel him to leave. In truth, he claimed to do so only because he still believes that I will yield to him. God forbid that he be proved right! I must learn how to use this power of mine, otherwise I will fall to him as Arthur did, and where will my kingdom be then?"

I assume my case to be persuasive beyond all questioning, but more than that, I assume that I will be obeyed. Unfortunately, I am wrong on both counts.

"This is madness," Robin insists. He, too, is on his feet, glaring at me with no pretense of deference to my will or respect for my authority. "You only just survived an assassination attempt. Now you want to put yourself directly in the path of one or more of those unholy beings?"

Cecil shoots him a grateful look so out of keeping with the usual tension between them that it catches me off guard. "Your Majesty's person is far too precious. We will seek out an appropriate target, and when every measure for your protection has been taken, then you can—"

"Do not think to direct me so!" I interrupt, raising a hand to cut him off. "You and Doctor Dee arranged for me to acquire this power. You, least of all, can caution against its use. I will not sit here, behind walls that offer no protection, while my people are stalked by evil and the very soul of my realm is at risk."

As I speak, the reasonable enough fear that I feel at confronting Mordred again falls away. Once more, I sense the singing light rise within me. Nor am I alone. The faces of the men change markedly at the same moment, and I realize that they are seeing me transformed.

Driven by curiosity I cannot resist, I look beyond them to the tall, gold-framed mirror set on its own stand near the fireplace. Since my ascension to the throne, I have seen myself in that glass many times, usually garbed as a queen to meet my people, which is to say as an icon of hope and faith. But never have I seen myself like this. My body is wreathed in light; only my face and the fiery glory of my hair are visible. I appear an otherworldly creature of eerie beauty.

The light ebbs slowly but a faint halo of luminescence remains all around me.

Robin is breathing hard as though he has received a great shock. I can scarcely blame him. Dee has paled but his eyes glitter with exhilaration. Walsingham smiles as though pleased by this affirmation of my power.

"At least allow me to summon guards to accompany us," Cecil says finally. He cannot take his eyes from me.

With an effort, I wrench my gaze from the mirror. "No guards. We cannot risk anyone else finding out about this. Cecil, you will remain here at court to deflect curiosity. I will tell my ladies that I am not to be disturbed by any but you. Let it be known that I am recovering well."

"Majesty—" Cecil looks so anguished by my decision that I cannot help but regret causing him such distress. But queens are made of sterner stuff than ordinary folk. No amount of concern for him or anyone else will sway me from my course.

"This is not a matter for debate, Sir William. Mister Walsingham, are you prepared to guide me?"

"I am, of course, Majesty—"

"Not without me," Robin says. "If you will allow no other guard, you will at least accept my protection."

"And my own," Doctor Dee adds quietly. It does not escape my notice that he has made no effort to dissuade me. Nor has Walsingham. Either they value my life less than do Robin and Cecil or they are less blinded by sentiment.

"I have no skill with a sword," Dee adds, "but I do have certain other means available to me should we encounter any difficulty."

So it is settled—Cecil will remain behind to conceal my absence while Robin, Dee, Walsingham, and I take to the streets of London, hunting a vampire who might be persuaded—by whatever means necessary—to yield useful information. I confess to a surge of excitement as I contemplate so daring a quest.

Robin is considerably less enthusiastic. As he secures the silver chains he has sent for in a pouch fastened around his waist, he murmurs for my ears only, "I still say this is madness, but if you must do it, then at least promise you will stay close to me?"

I toss a nod that I hope he takes for assent as I fasten my boots and throw a long, black wool cloak over my shoulders, securing it to conceal my garb fully. With the hood pulled up to cover my hair, I fancy that no one will recognize me.

Walsingham dons his own cloak, as does Dee. Robin makes do with a short cape that will not interfere with his sword arm. Together, we four make ready to venture into the hidden passage.

Just before we go, I clasp Cecil's hand. "Do not torment yourself with worry. We will be back before dawn."

White-faced and clearly beyond such facile reassurances, my Spirit nods nonetheless. "If you are not, you understand that I will be unable to conceal your absence much beyond then?"

"You will do as you must." We share a look, a tacit reminder of the plans we have made in the event of my death. I have, contrary to what most of my advisers believe, named an heir, but I have done so secretly for I am not such a fool as to raise a rival to my rule. I will say only that my Scottish cousin should make no plans to come to England, for not even death will drive me to settle her posterior upon my throne.

But enough of that; the topic displeases me mightily.

Robin opens the door to the passage and we go, I in the lead with the others following close behind. Shortly, we come out into the walled garden where I encountered Mordred the previous night. From there, it is only a few yards to the concealed ironbound door hidden amid the fall of ivy. Robin opens it with a key.

Silently, we slip out, securing the door behind us. I stand for a moment, breathing in the night scents of my city as it occurs to me that I have never before gone among my people unheralded and unrecognized. All my life has been spent within the precincts of palaces and great houses, sealed off from the world beyond. I am at once excited and afraid of what I will discover as I set off after Walsingham into the narrow, twisting streets of London.

Walsingham must have arranged to have a boat waiting at the bottom of the Whitehall water steps, whether to whisk him away quickly if his meeting with me did not go well or in anticipation of his plan's being accepted I cannot say. We step into it quickly, the four of us taking our seats on the rough wood planks. The night is cold but there is no wind to claw through our cloaks and chill us to the bone. Instead, an unnatural stillness hangs over us, broken only by the thrust of the oars as the wherryman glides us out onto the dark river. Looking back over my shoulder, I see the tall windows of my palace aglow against the darkness. The court will be at supper, after which there is to be a masque. Banquets bore me, but I adore a good masque and I regret missing it. Never mind; far more serious matters beckon.

The tide is running with us and we make good speed down-river around the bend from Westminster and from there to the opposite shore of the river. Our little group steps out onto the shingle ledge. Water laps against stone steps slick with moss. Robin goes first. He reaches down to take my hand and help me up the steps. We move carefully onto the road that runs along the bankside. Directly ahead of us is the High Street rising to St. Margaret's Hill, where the bullrings and bear-baiting rings are. I can see the distant glow of torches and hear the blood cheers of the crowd. To our right looms the far quieter precincts of St. Savior's Church, the site of heresy trials during my sister's reign. Some claim they can still hear the wailing of the doomed, but to my ears nothing disturbs the silence save my own measured breath. Far more lively are the timber-and-daub taverns all along the High Street that cater to travelers en route to and from the south. Light and laughter spill from them, and in the near distance, I catch a snatch of song.

Rats scatter at our approach. I pull my skirts up several inches above my ankles and advance cautiously. At this late hour, most Londoners are home or already in their beds, but here the streets remain as full as in broad day. More than a few of those we pass appear drunk, lurching as they walk, while up ahead a pair engage in clumsy fisticuffs. Women, some little more than girls, hover in the cast-off light of tavern windows. Despite the chill, most have pulled down their bodices to expose their breasts, their nipples pale and puckered, surrounded by cold flesh that looks not unlike that of a plucked chicken. I wonder that any man can find such a display alluring as we move quickly on. An older woman—in her thirties with a toothless smile—clutches a babe to her breast. She stretches out an arm beseechingly toward us. Several more children, all of tender years, are crumbled at her side, shivering under rags.

"What is this?" I demand. "I have been generous in relief for the poor. There are places for them."

Not as many as in my father's time, when the churches and priories offered basic food and shelter to the neediest. "Creative destruction," Cecil calls it, opining that out of the waste laid across this land, a greater good will arise. Yet in fairness to him, he spends his days and far too many of his nights struggling with the damage that was done when my father shattered the system that had sustained the poor for so long. I am one more result of that great rending and therefore bound by conscience to repair it.

"A matter for another time, Majesty." Dee urges me onward.

I will confess to a great curiosity regarding the Bankside. The mayor of London and its aldermen complain incessantly that because they have no authority there, Southwark, the Clink, and Paris Gardens—to name the most colorful neighborhoods—are riotous places given over to masterless men, thieves, whoremongers, and the like. There is some truth to that, however they must be cautious in their criticism for it is my writ as queen that runs in the Bankside. I have always believed that a certain amount of liberty makes people less inclined to rebel, therefore I am prepared to tolerate it—up to a point.

Walsingham pauses for a moment to get his bearings, then leads us along the High Street. Shadows lurk near the entrances to alleys, but none bestir themselves to trouble us. We continue on until we reach an inn popular with seamen and foreign merchants, as evinced by the babble of languages that breaks over us as we step beneath the low lintel.

The floor, covered in rough paving stones, slopes downward. The interior is dark and hazy with smoke. A pair of long, rough-hewn tables set with benches fills most of the space between the walls stained with soot amid patches of dampness. I catch the pungent smell of malt mingling with that of meat pies of dubious provenance. Clusters of men, most in leather jerkins and homespun trousers, are hunched over their mugs, intent on the nine-men's morris boards carved into the surface of the tables or on the dartboards hung on the back walls. Betting appears to be fast and serious.

Until, that is, we enter. Then all eyes swing in our direction, only to slip away as quickly. Conversation dies along with the sprightly tune a fiddler had been playing. My companions form a circle around me with Robin in the front, shielding me from scrutiny. I peer round them as best I can.

The barkeep is big, large-bellied, and ruddy-skinned with a

no-nonsense air befitting his trade. He wipes his hands on his leather apron and nods in our direction.

"You'll be wanting the White Hart, three doors up, sirs. Fair custom there for you and the lady."

Without so much as a blink of the eye, Walsingham shoots out a hand, grasps the man by the throat, and in a perfectly pleasant tone says, "We'll be wanting your back room. You've no problem with that, have you?"

The barkeep outweighs Walsingham by several stone and tops him by half a foot. In a contest between them, the outcome should be a foregone conclusion. Moreover, we have an attentive audience. Patrons shift in their seats as one or two appear to consider involving themselves. Robin is about to intercede when I put a hand on his arm, stopping him.

I have seen the look in Walsingham's eyes, as has the barkeep. Cecil's new man may appear to be a mild, thoughtful sort, but he possesses the temperament of a true fanatic—cold, implacable, and utterly without conscience. Ordinarily, I distrust such men, but I can make an exception when they are deployed in my service.

The barkeep having managed a strangled assent, Walsingham releases him, nods cordially, and leads the way toward the back. What interest we have managed to arouse evaporates like water on a hot stone. At first, we appear to be approaching a solid brick wall. Only as we near it do I see the dark curtain covering the entrance to a private room. We step through to discover far more gracious surroundings—polished tables set with comfortable, high-backed chairs such as would not be amiss in my own chambers, fresh rushes on the floor, the warm glow of beeswax candles, and—most startling of all—several alcoves containing low platforms heaped with pillows that to my eye appear garishly foreign.

"Keep your hood up," Robin murmurs, and I see why. Several of the faces I glimpse are at least vaguely familiar. It takes me a moment to realize that members of my own court are present, as are several wealthy merchants also known to me and one or two foreign ambassadors.

Robin turns up the collar of his cape, mindful that he, too, may be recognized. Dee and Walsingham have no such concern. The latter being newly returned to my realm, he has no need of circumspection. As for Dee, no one would account it in the least strange that he appears in odd surroundings or amid dubious company.

We arrange ourselves around a table. A boy dressed entirely in black, his face schooled to blankness, approaches and inquires as to what we will have. The men order but I am distracted, watching the other occupants of the room. I can pretend no familiarity with what goes on in taverns, but in the revelry of the court there is always good cheer, whether real or manufactured. I am not accustomed to the quiet pervading this room or the strange placidity of its occupants. Surely they should be playing cards, gambling, groping barmaids, or some such? Instead they sit or lie stretched out on the pillowed platforms as though lost in dreams. I am bewildered.

The boy returns bearing a carafe of Rhenish wine, several tankards of ale, a serving of sausages, and something I have never seen before, a small, crystal vial set alone on a pewter plate. Walsingham pays, startling me with the amount of coin that changes hands. I do not pretend to know the price of everything, but I have a decent enough sense of how to run a household to realize that the outlay is extravagant.

"Why so dear?" I ask, hoping he will infer that I do not reimburse unnecessary expenses.

He gestures at the little vial. "Do you know what that is, Majesty?"

When I reluctantly confess that I do not, he explains, "It is the most prized creation of the alchemist Paracelsus, a tincture of milk of poppy combined with alcohol and various other substances, crushed pearls, amber, musk, and the like. It is called laudanum."

"From the Latin *laudare*, to praise?"

"Indeed. Paracelsus praised its ability to relieve pain of every sort while exalting the spirit. It has become the fashion in certain quarters on the Continent, and now it has appeared here."

"Paracelsus," Dee snorts, making of the name his own comment on the matter.

I suppose a degree of professional jealousy is understandable. Dee is a great man in many ways, although perhaps not so great as he assumes. But Paracelsus . . . dead only a handful of years, the brilliant Swiss alchemist is heralded as a genius for the ages. His name attached to any substance would make it instantly appealing. And if it actually does what is claimed—

"It is what draws people to this place?"

Walsingham nods. "Up until a few months ago this was no more than an ordinary tavern popular with the sort of men you saw in front. But recently, this back room was added on, exclusively for the use of laudanum takers." A bit abashed, he adds, "I apologize for the expense, but if we did not purchase at least one vial, our presence here would be instantly suspect."

I nod and, from beneath my hood, look more closely at our fellow patrons. A man of middle years, his dark beard sporting a few strands of silver, lolls back in his chair with an expression of utter contentment on his face. Nearby, another, younger man hums quietly to himself while studying his own hand with apparent fascination. They are by no means exceptional. Everywhere I look, men of substance and means appear transformed into creatures of blissful self-absorption. Their state might be considered enviable were it not so unnatural.

"All laudanum users?" I ask.

The schoolmaster nods. "Cast into such a state, I believe, at the design of those who would prey on them. If I am right, laudanum has reached our shores through the vampires themselves. They are using it as a lure."

The idea horrifies me but it is not without logic. If the tincture does as it is said to, it must render any intended victim docile in the extreme.

"Then you expect them to appear here?" I ask.

Silently, Walsingham inclines his head once more.

Robin, who has been listening intently, takes a long swallow of his ale. Under the table, he clasps my hand. I allow Dee to tempt me with the Rhenish wine, which proves surprisingly drinkable. Walsingham, who seems most in his element, goes so far as to try the sausage but puts it down after a couple of bites. We wait. I am thinking that we should move on and try another place when a solitary man pale in complexion strolls into the back room. He glances at us but only in passing before he takes a seat in the shadows.

I am reminded at once of Mordred; though the new arrival is not so beautiful, he possesses the same ethereal beauty that attracts me viscerally. He wears the garb of a gentleman, but I have never seen him before—for surely I would remember. If I did not recognize him to be a vampire, I would guess that he was in his early twenties. As it is, I wonder how old he truly is, how much of life he has seen if his can be called life, and what he will do if he realizes who I am.

What I am.

Morgaine Le Fey slew many vampires, so Dee claims. Mordred escaped her but how many others fell? Can those of the same kind sense the danger I represent, if danger I truly am to them? That remains to be determined.

"Watch," Walsingham murmurs, following my gaze.

The boy approaches the vampire with obvious reluctance, remaining several feet from the table and keeping his gaze averted. The moment the order is completed, he darts away.

I lean closer to Walsingham. "Do they eat and drink as we do?"

"I have observed them to do so but I cannot say whether they derive sustenance or merely pleasure from it."

The curtain to the front room parts. A trio of young men enter, all outfitted in the particolor hose and garishly lined short cloaks that were the style a year or two ago. They have the look of second and third sons such as the country gentry send up to London in hope that they will find advancement in the mercantile houses or the law courts. Judging by their wide-eyed stares and vapid expressions, I surmise that all three will be back whence they came in short order, assuming they survive their brush with debauchery.

They take their seats amid much nervous glancing about and murmuring to one another. The boy in black approaches. A small debate ensues that I gather has to do with finances, but eventually two of the crystal vials are set before them.

Debauched and bankrupt. Truly, their families will be proud.

We wait, pretending interest in our refreshments, in each other, in anything other than the pale man and the hapless youths. I watch him watching them and my stomach churns. Having partaken of the contents of the vials, they slump in their chairs, empty smiles plastered on their faces, eyes rolling

here, there, and everywhere. One of them expounds some gar-
bled point of philosophy as though it contains all of revealed
wisdom, while another giggles and the third pays no attention
at all, being occupied in studying his fingers, which he flutters
before his face.

I wonder how much longer I can keep my scantily padded
rump on the hard wood seat. My newfound power stirs rest-
lessly.

"Perhaps we should look elsewhere," I say, but just then Dee
flicks a finger, drawing my notice back to the trio. The philoso-
pher has risen to announce that he needs to take a piss. He
staggers over to the back door and disappears out it.

Unnoticed by his companions but not by us, the pale man
also stands and slips away after him.

"Now." I rise from my seat, filled with urgency, resolute and, I
hope, indomitable.

The back door gives onto a narrow, fetid alley framed by the
tavern on one side and a high wall on the other. Even in winter's chill, the alley reeks of urine and refuse. Heedless of the
stench, I look in both directions at once but see no one. The
drugged youth has vanished, as has his pursuer.

I pick a direction on instinct alone and turn in it. "They
can't have gone far." Please God let that be so. If Mordred's
ability to bend time is common among the vampires—

But it seems that it is not for scarcely do I get beyond the
alley than I see, on a small path leading down to the river, the
shapes of two men. Or a man and something that masquerades
as one.

"There!"

I trust that the others are following me but I do not wait to
be sure. Skirts flapping, I run as the light takes flight within me.

My cloak having flown open, my ivory skirt and bodice glow like the moon, my pulse keeps time with a wild, feral tune.

I will have him, I will! And he will tell me all I need to know. All of Mordred and the rest. What I must do to defeat them so that I will prevail. Will live. Will rule. Queen regnant until in the fullness of mortal time, as it please God, I die.

Does my step falter? Surely not for my resolve is firm. There is no question of what I must do. The temptation Mordred poses, vastly greater than any the crystal vials can provide, is no temptation at all. So I tell myself. I know my purpose, I will not shirk it. For the sake of my immortal soul, I cannot.

What good really is an immortal soul when an immortal body is to be preferred? Young, strong, and beautiful forever.

No! By God, I will not be tempted! The man is limp in the other's arms. The pale one bends over him, the tender flesh of his victim's neck exposed, and I . . .

I leap, through air and time, the light pouring through me, out of me, ready in an instant to strike.

He who I suspect of being all manner of unholy things lifts his head, and in that instant, I see, in the light I am suddenly made from, the carmine stain of blood on his bared teeth, his stretched lips, his furious, beastly beauty.

This vampire snarls and, raising both arms to shield his eyes, drops the hapless youth. Power coils within me. I take a breath, gathering all my will, and hurl a lance of blinding white light directly at the creature. My only intent is to render him sufficiently insensible to secure him in the silver chains that Robin carries. I have no notion of what power I yet command, no thought at all that I could actually kill him.

A wild howl rends the night. His back arches, his head thrown up to the sky, as the light pierces him. I only just manage to skitter to a stop scant yards away, staring at what I have wrought.

For a moment, the vampire appears to glow more brightly than any moon. The light is so intense that I am forced to look away. When I manage to glance back, this creature stands transformed. A web of dark fractures appears in the center of his chest, near where the lance of light struck, and spreads quickly, expanding into a mosaic of tiny pieces that for a heartbeat hang together, then fly apart and vanish like so much dust into the night.

Before I can begin to grasp what has happened, a clamor from the road above alerts me that we are not alone.

"You there, halt! In the name of the Queen!"

For pity's sake, the watch, so often libeled as lazy and ineffectual, or worse, has stumbled upon us. Not one man but two armed with cudgels have spotted us from the High Street and are sprinting toward the footpath. In another moment, they will be upon us.

"We must go," Robin says as he seizes my arm.

"Indeed," Walsingham agrees, and turns to lead the way back to where we must hope that the wherryman, well bribed, awaits.

But it is too late. My stalwart servants, determined to do their civic duty, are almost close enough to make out our features. I am frantically calculating if they can be bribed into silence or will have to be executed when Dee steps forward, draws from beneath his cloak a small, dark object, and tosses it toward the oncoming men.

It lands with a soft thump and instantly explodes. Incandescent white light, almost as intense as my own, flares strongly enough to temporarily blind the pair. Robin seizes my hand and together we flee into the mist rising from the river. My heart is pounding, my breath coming in gasps, when we near the bridge and—thanks be to God—find the well-bought wherryman just where we left him.

"Draw oar!" Walsingham shouts as we tumble into the boat. "Put your back to it, man!"

Robin pushes me down against him so that no one pursuing us will see my face. The warmth and strength of his dear, familiar body provide me with some comfort, but I can still feel running through me the fierce energy like summer lightning that consumed me at the moment I took the vampire's life. In its wake, a dark yearning stirs within me. I have a sudden urge to press my mouth to Robin's throat and savor there the hot beat of his life's blood. The very notion freezes me. I remain motionless against him until we are in the midst of the river. Only then do I trust myself enough to stir. Raising my head, I look back from whence we have come, seeing through the tendrils of mist the watchmen standing, defeated, on the shore. Their curses reach me faintly on the still night air.

Not until we reach the Whitehall water steps do I allow myself to acknowledge that I have taken an irrevocable step in slaying a vampire. In some way I cannot yet understand, the act has changed me utterly.

I felt it happen, although I had no notion at first what it was, so long had it been since a vampire had died by any hand but mine. Yet experience it I did for all my kind are linked to me, who made them. The death shocked me from the sea of dreams in which I floated. I sat up abruptly and howled.

At once, the door to the chamber flew open and Blanche appeared beside my bier. She flung her arms around me as she cried out in alarm.

"What has happened, my lord? What is wrong?"

Her eyes were wide with fear but with excitement, too. She relished anything she thought would make me need her more.

"Get away!" Truly, I could not abide her touch or that of any other. I knew, even then, what Elizabeth had done and what the consequences of it would be. In killing, she had grown stronger. How long before she realized that? How long before she sought out more of us to slay?

Snarling, I turned away from Blanche, but she was not dissuaded. Again, she approached me.

"It's her, isn't it, the Queen? She's done something."

I cupped moonlight in my hands and rubbed my face, struggling to regain my senses. The chamber, spacious though it was, seemed to constrict around me. I could not bear to remain there any longer.

"I hope you weren't too fond of Ambrose," I said on my way to the door. "He's dead."

Blanche frowned and smoothed the gown that clung to her like a second skin. "I don't understand. Why would you—?"

"Kill him? I didn't."

"But then who—?"

I did not bother to answer but went out quickly, knowing what needed to be done and anxious to get to it. Behind me, I heard her fearful whisper.

"The Slayer has come."

----

All conversation ceased the moment I strode into the great hall. Beneath the wide, arched ceiling so high that it faded away into shadows, a hundred and more of the kindred were gathered, garbed in velvet and silk, bestrewn with jewels, as glorious a court as any monarch could wish. Here and there, a few strummed lutes or fingered a virginal, but most were occupied with dice and cards. How they loved to gamble, my children! How it invigorated the tedium of endless life.

As one they turned to me. I looked at their pale faces, all so beautiful, felt their eager strength, and threw wide my arms.

"My beloved," I said, for I did truly love each and every one of them. "Why do you tarry here? The moon summons you to feed! Sate yourselves that you may better serve me in the great struggle upon which we are embarked. Go forth without restraint!"

They rose as one, cheering me, and spread themselves upon the night. In moments, the great hall was empty save for the thralls, who huddled in the shadows.

I slumped in a chair beside the fire, aware of Blanche hovering nearby but unwilling to call her to me. All my thoughts were of Elizabeth—her beauty, her pride, the longing I felt for her that grew more intense with each encounter. Incredibly, she was beginning to eclipse Morgaine in my thoughts, something I would never have thought possible. *Was my hunger for her obscuring my reason? Should I kill her there and then before her power could grow any greater? But to do that would cost me my surest route to the throne . . . not to mention Elizabeth herself.*

*I told myself that I would exact a price for her arrogance so high that she would quake from ever paying it again. After this night, she would come to me on bended knee and grant my every desire.*

*Yet, truth be told, it was I who quaked deep within as memories crept over me of the last time a Slayer had walked this earth.*

*Against a landscape of death and ruin, I thought I caught the scent of roses.*

*Before dawn, 17 January 1559*

_____

"Your power is growing, Majesty." Dee's satisfaction at this development is unmistakable. The magus regards me with the scrutiny he might afford a successful experiment.

Not so Walsingham, who understands what my impulsive act has cost us. "Better we took him alive," the schoolmaster says, "that he might be questioned."

I agree but silently, for I am still struggling to come to terms with the extraordinary fact that I have killed an otherworldly creature who under other circumstances might have lived forever. My power is real . . . and as Dee rightly perceives, it is growing.

We are back in my chambers, having reached there through the passage. Cecil receives us with unalloyed relief, but as he learns what happened, he turns grim.

"We are dealing with powers far beyond the ken of mortal man," my Spirit says. "Let us be grateful that Her Majesty was not harmed."

The others murmur their agreement but I scarcely hear them. I am lost in my own thoughts, seeing over and over again the moment when the vampire, an immortal being of great power, flew apart like so much chaff upon the wind. What has come into me that I am capable of such a feat?

Having poured me a generous measure of brandy, Robin returns to where I sit near the fire and places the goblet in my hand, closing my fingers around it.

"Drink," he urges. "You are pale as a ghost."

That may be, but oddly the fatigue that gripped me after the first use of my power is absent. Instead, I feel alive in a way that I have never before experienced. Unbidden, the thought rises in me that in killing the vampire, I have absorbed his strength.

But there is no comparison between me and creatures who take sustenance from the blood of innocents. None at all.

My hand shaking, I raise the goblet and drain it to the dregs. From the corner of my eye, I see Dee and Cecil exchange a glance.

"There will be other opportunities," the magus ventures. "It is early days yet."

I all but choke on the last of the brandy and resist the impulse to hurl the goblet at him. Rising from my chair, driven by the energy that threatens to burst my skin, I exclaim, "Mordred has bided his time for a thousand years, growing in power, becoming something unimaginable, and you tell me it is *early* yet?"

Forcing myself to breathe deeply, I struggle for calm. "We must try again and quickly."

Walsingham hesitates. Clearly he does not want to provoke me, but he is troubled. "Majesty, I have had only a fortnight to discover the vampires' whereabouts. While I was able to determine that they frequent the tavern, there is much more I am not yet certain of."

"We could try there again," Robin suggests.

I am tempted but my better sense warns against it. "Word will spread about what was seen. The area will be too closely watched."

The schoolmaster nods reluctantly. "I fear Your Majesty may be correct. But there is another possibility."

"Out with it."

"I have heard rumors about the presence of vampires at Southwark Manor."

The possibility shocks me. Southwark Manor belonged to my father before it passed to Mary, who gave it, if memory serves, to the Archbishop of York. I had heard that he sold it, but I realize now that I have no idea to whom.

"How certain are you of this?"

"Not enough to suggest going there this night, Majesty," Walsingham says quickly as though to forestall any such notion. "But I will investigate further without delay."

"It will be dawn in a few hours," Robin points out. "Her Majesty needs to rest. Come back when you have something useful to tell her."

Ordinarily, I dislike Robin giving orders on my behalf, but this time I let it pass. The full import of what has happened threatens to overwhelm me. I wrap my arms around myself in a weak stab at comfort and make no demur as Robin ushers the men out.

He shuts the door behind them, shoots the bolt to secure our privacy, and comes to me with swift strides that leave no doubt as to his intent.

"For God's sake, Elizabeth, this is madness."

I start to laugh but catch myself, afraid that I will cry instead. "Perhaps it is a dream and in another moment we will wake."

"More likely a nightmare." He pulls me hard against him and I feel his strength all along the length of me. My breath eases, and slowly I let loose my arms and twine them around his neck. His skin is so smooth and tender there. I can smell the essence of his life beckoning me. A fleeting thought of Mordred speeds across my mind. I do my best to ignore it.

"Stay with me," I murmur.

Robin exhales deeply and nods. The tension eases from me,

to be replaced by another sort of urgency. Robin must feel it, too, for he smiles against the curve of my cheek. He bends slightly, lifting me in a smooth and easy motion. He is strong, this master of my horse, made so by years in the saddle and in the training for war that is pursued by all true gentlemen willing to lay down their lives for their sovereign. Or better yet share in a great victory to the wealth and glory of their houses. He carries me to the bed and sets me down gently, turning me on my side so that he can reach the laces of my gown. When they are loosened, he touches his mouth to the nape of my neck and begins slowly, exquisitely, to work his way down. I have known this sweet torment before and he knows full well what effect it has on me. I am moaning long before he reaches the base of my spine. Robin, curse him, is chuckling. He slips his hands beneath the loosened folds of my gown and cups my breasts.

"I adore you, Elizabeth. You know that, don't you?"

"Hmmm . . . of course . . . oh, yes . . . like that . . . more . . ."

He does my bidding, stroking between my thighs until I am rigid with pleasure and swiftly thereafter limp with welcome release. I lie against him, panting softly, until he rises to remove his clothes. By candlelight, I savor his body, yet in the back of my mind is the gnawing, intrusive thought that he is not so beautiful as I imagine Mordred would be in similar circumstances.

Appalled to be thinking of my enemy at such a time, I push the treacherous notion aside and welcome my own dear love back into my arms, eager to give him the pleasure he has given me, but only in the same way for we can risk nothing more.

Despite Robin's protestations that the "French gloves" he has acquired prevent conception, I can never grant him the full liberty of my body. It is not that I disbelieve him, only that I believe too well that his ambition is greater than his sense. I will not be trapped into marriage by any man nor ordered into it by any counselor.

Nor compelled into it by powers that, when compared now to what I feel growing within me, may not be so daunting after all.

On the cusp of such thoughts, I nestle closer against Robin, who is already asleep. He will have to wake soon enough and creep away, but for a few precious hours we lie entwined as though the world and all its cares do not exist.

Yet I feel it all the same, there in the night, close beside him. Something stirring in my city, something unholy that leaves me wide-eyed and tense, unable to do more than drift on the surface of sleep, until at last gray dawn comes.

I wake alone and lie without moving, staring at the high canopy above my bed. It is an old habit from tenderest childhood. If I remain still, scarcely breathing, nothing can hurt me. Would that were true.

My ladies come, throwing open the bed curtains, filling the room with their chatter. I smile and rise, wash my hands and face, drying them on the soft cloth Kat proffers. I clean my teeth with a soft twig, spit into a cup. I suffer my hair to be brushed and rubbed with a length of silk until it gleams.

All the while, I can scarcely breathe. A heavy, ominous presence lumbers toward me. I can feel it coming, sense its contours, but I have no sense of how terrible it truly is until Cecil appears.

He stands just on the far side of the opened door, a silent and pale presence, rocking back and forth on his heels as he does only when he is particularly anxious. Despite being half-dressed, wearing only my bed robe, I send my ladies away, throw a wrap around my shoulders, and bid him sit. Further, I serve him ale with my own hands and do not let him speak until he has taken a long draft.

I cannot lose Cecil. Without him, how will I find my way through the web of threats and treachery that are the swaddling clothes of my newborn reign?

I sit across from him and put my hand over his. "Whatever has happened, together we will find a way to deal with it."

He smiles weakly, as he must, for I have used the same words he has spoken so often to me in darkest times. In this moment, the pupil has become the teacher, which puts me in mind of Walsingham, but only briefly. Before I can wonder what progress the schoolmaster has made, if any, since we last spoke, my Spirit says, "I regret to tell you, Majesty, that a series of attacks took place in the city last night. A dozen or more poor souls are dead, and an unknown number, likely very high, are injured."

A wave of coldness washes through me. My hand goes from his hand to my throat, where I feel an unaccustomed pressure. "What attacks? Who was responsible?"

"Mordred, without doubt. The dead all bear the signs of having been fed on by vampires, as do the injured. Such incidents have been growing in number, as you know, but never have we seen anything like this. The watch has managed to keep the matter quiet thus far, but if another wave of attacks occurs . . ."

He does not have to continue; I know too well what will happen. My people, so lately thronging the streets to celebrate my coronation, will reel in terror. Quickly, talk will spread that I have brought this calamity on them. They will remember that my mother was condemned as a witch, among other things, and that my father declared me a bastard before reversing himself only for necessity's sake. How long will it take until they decide that I am unfit to rule?

"We must stop this now," I declare, "before it goes any further. I will send soldiers to Southwark Manor. Anyone found there will be arrested and—"

Cecil holds up a hand, forestalling me. "Majesty, your pardon, but you cannot do any such thing. Above all else, this conflict must be concealed, not only from our own people but from the foreign ambassadors and merchants in the city. Imagine the result if word of what is happening here were to spread beyond our borders."

He is right, of course. Nothing would so embolden the legions of my enemies as the knowledge that England lies under demonic threat. The Pope would call for holy war and the Christian kings of Europe would respond, led, no doubt, by perfidious Spain. No force that I could raise would have any hope of withstanding them. It would fall to Mordred to save England, if he could, an eventuality that it occurs to me he might well desire and even be working to attain.

"Forgive me," I say, startling my poor Spirit, who is not accustomed to such humility on my part. "I spoke in haste. Even if I could send soldiers against Mordred and his kind, there is no reason to believe that they would prevail."

"Alas, Majesty, there is every reason to believe that they would not. Our realm lies under mortal threat such as has not been seen in a thousand years. Only you can save us."

For a moment, panic rises in me. I cannot possibly be equal to so great a task. All my life I have been told that I am a mere female, lacking the courage and heart of a true king. A realm ruled by a woman is an aberration. My people wait in expectation of my marriage so that they may have the comfort of a man's steady hand on me and on my throne.

Fie on that! I am Elizabeth, daughter of Anne. I have survived the effort of my enemies to destroy me from the day of my birth. They are as dust whereas I am Queen. But I am also just beginning to realize that I am more; I am heiress to Morgaine and as such the Slayer so long awaited. Mordred thinks to stop me by harming my people. Better he think how to save himself when I come against him!

"Majesty?"

Cecil is looking at me peculiarly. I have not spoken but something in my expression gives him pause.

"We must not act impulsively," he cautions.

My resolve is as steel within me, molten hot and ready to be poured into the vessel of my will. Yet I see the wisdom of what he says. Rising, I extend my hand. "Nor can we delay. I count on you to confer with Doctor Dee and to discover whatever Walsingham has learned. Then we must prepare. I will not suffer my people to be under such threat another night. Do you understand me?"

He clambers to his feet, bows over my hand, and nods. "As you wish, Majesty, but—"

"Do as I bid." I soften the dictate with a smile. "Now go, dear friend. I must dress and show myself to the court before rumor spins my 'cold' into every imaginable ailment."

He sees the sense in that and takes his leave, swiftly replaced by my ladies, who flutter around me, chattering like so many bright magpies as they dress me.

I go from my chamber armored in queenly raiment. My mother's diadem is on my head and I am ready, so I tell myself, for whatever is to come.

---

"*H*uzzah!"

The crack of a lance snapping in two rebounds off the wooden walls raised between the tilting field and the canopied grandstand where I sit enthroned, surrounded by my ladies and the more favored of my nobles. The tournament in honor of my coronation is finally under way. I smile and offer a queenly wave to Lord Dacre, who has just unseated Baron Chumsley, who should have known better than to position himself quite so high in the saddle when riding full tilt against one of Dacre's experience. Assuming the baron, who at the moment is lying flat and unmoving on the sand, recovers, it is to be hoped that he will learn from the encounter.

The day is a hard, frozen blue. The more agile Londoners have strapped boards on their feet and are slip-sliding along the roads and lanes covered in muddy ice. Thanks be to God, the river still runs. If the Thames freezes, the commerce of the city will cease, and we will have no end of trouble.

My face hurts for smiling. For all my effort, I fear I must look like an animal brought to bay, showing its teeth in fierce defiance. Night cannot come too swiftly. But first I must endure the ritual combat of my nobles, their substitute for the true warfare for which they all supposedly yearn and, not incidentally, a demonstration of their prowess before the foreign ambassadors. Let those worthies write to their masters that the men who would lead my armies are well suited to the task, being both fearless and skilled in the arts of war. Perhaps that will buy us some little time.

The tournament drags on. At least the groundlings are amused. Those good, plain citizens of London smashed up against the far side of the wall, cheering and groaning according to the fortunes of their favorites, spitting, farting, gnawing on goose legs and quaffing ale, both generously provided in my name, seem to be enjoying the effort more than any of their betters.

I watch them as much as I watch the matches for the truth is that I have attended too many tournaments to find any novelty in them whereas my people are still largely unknown to me. They are as good-natured in their contentment as any monarch could hope for, but they have also perfected the art of sullenness, being expert at standing in clusters with their heads tucked into their shoulders, letting their silence shout for them. Only rarely are they bold enough to hurl curses, as they did at my mother. As they will at me if I falter.

My ladies are chilled. They shiver in their silk and damask gowns and sway as close as they can to the tall braziers glowing with coals set to either side of my chair. I, to the contrary, feel heated from within. My new, as yet barely understood, self stirs impatiently. My blood is up and the hunt calls.

At last—at long last—the trumpets sound and Robin rides out into the list on a big black charger that snorts and throws his head in his eagerness. The plated metal armoring man and horse gleams brightly. My darling has vied twice already this day, handily defeating both opponents, and now he will contest for the champion's crown.

I rise, my smile finally genuine, and extend my hand. The crowd cheers well enough but I see the groundlings nudging one another, winking as I draw long silk ribbons from my hair to tie around Robin's lance. He rides as my favorite, as well he should, for no one else so deserves the honor. Let the rabble and nobility alike make of that what they will. His grin is wide and bold in the moment before he drops his visor and turns into the list.

The trumpets sound again and I resume my seat, hoping that no one will see how my hands grip the carved arms. The thudding hooves of the horses throw up clods of dirt as they race toward each other. Robin faces off against Lord Haverston, who, under ordinary circumstances, I hold in some favor. He is brash and ambitious, blindly courageous, and, as far as I know, loyal. In short, much like Robin himself. Were circumstances different, I would have nothing whatsoever against the man. But now I would happily see him gutted in two and spread out as carrion bait rather than have a hair on Robin's head harmed.

Ravens rise into the sky and circle lazily. Sunlight bounces off the steel tips of the lances. The sleek flanks of the horses glow with a fine sheen of sweat. I can smell the wet sand, hear the sizzle of goose fat, see the shards of color that dance in a spray of mist drifting over the river. All my senses are painfully heightened. It is taking too long! My throat constricts and I cannot breathe. Robin's lance is lowered, well aimed, but so is his opponent's. They hurtle toward each other as time suddenly catches up with itself.

The lance strikes directly in the center of Robin's chest. He is lifted half out of the saddle, caught offside as his charger rears, and Robin falls . . . so far . . . falling as though forever. The horse's hooves tear at the air above him. A well of silence swallows me. I move through it without thought or hesitation. My ladies try to restrain me but I throw them off. I am free of the grandstand and at the wall, tearing at it, desperate to get through, when a boy, no more than a child, his grimy face red with winter's chill, sees me and throws open a narrow gate.

I am through and across the sand, hurling myself on the ground beside Robin while the charger still snorts and paws above. Someone behind me is shouting, a great many some-ones.

*To the Queen! To the Queen!*

His blood is on my hands. Sobbing, I wrench off his helmet, see the whites of his eyes rolling, and grasp the hard metal about his shoulders.

"Robin, don't leave me!"

The world is careening out of all control. My heart is set to explode in my chest. I barely see the men-at-arms who seize the reins of the charger and pull him aside in the instant before his hooves would have come down on us both. We are surrounded, caught in a flurry of motion, more shouts, a great bustling to and fro in the midst of which Robin is lifted onto a litter and carried off the field. He manages to raise one hand and wave to the crowd, which roars its approval.

Whatever sense of self-preservation I still have drives me to paste on a smile and wave in my own turn even as I make to follow the litter.

Cecil is standing in my path.

"This way, Majesty," he says, and gestures toward the grand-stand where Robin's distraught opponent awaits, still on his horse. His helmet is tucked under his arm and he looks like a man deciding in which direction to flee.

The crowd is cheering. I walk stiff-legged and climb the stairs I went down so hastily. I take a breath and smooth my gown as my ladies flutter about. Someone thrusts a laurel wreath into my hands. Someone else, I suspect it is Cecil, shoves me forward.

I speak. The words come out by rote. As though from a great distance, I hear myself and marvel at how great a fraud I am.

Haverston, who must be preserved from my vengeance lest my justice be called into doubt, all but sags in relief as I congratulate him on his victory and crown the tip of his lance with laurel for the victor. Grace to God, it bears no trace of Robin's blood or else I swear, I would not have been able to touch it. He has the great good sense not to linger but beats a hasty retreat back toward the competitors' tents. Cecil takes my arm and steers me from the grandstand. Leaning close, he says, "Lord Dudley has been taken to his chambers, my lady. The physicians are with him now."

"I must go—"

Cecil's grip tightens almost but not quite imperceptibly. "His Honor the ambassador from the Duchy of Hesse has asked to speak with you."

"He can wait." For eternity if I have my way, but what are the odds of that? Already I have learned that as queen, I no longer belong to myself.

"With respect, Majesty, if you appear overly attentive—"

He means any more than I have already done, making a spectacle of myself in front of the whole court and the rabble as well. Word of my devotion to Robin will be flying down every lane and byway. Hard upon it will come even more speculation about our relationship. If I am perceived as an immoral or loose woman, the Pope and all the rest of my enemies will claim even greater cause to come against me.

Except for Mordred, of course, who I have to assume has no need of any such advantage.

"I will arrange for word to be brought to you as soon as anything is known," Cecil says quietly.

We move on, back into the palace, through the usual crowd
of hangers-on and petitioners. As always, I nod and smile,
smile and nod. A sudden thought cracks the brittle shell
around me, and for a moment hysterical laughter wells up in
my throat.

"What is it?" Cecil asks, frowning.

"When I am dead, how long do you think it will take the
poor unfortunates charged with laying me out to wipe this
odious grin from my face?"

"Majesty!"

Cecil is dismayed and rightly so. He does not deserve my petulance under any circumstances, not even these. Yet I cannot
help myself. Even as I go through the motions of listening to
the ambassador from Hesse—a dreary, overly earnest man—I
can think only of Robin, his wounds, his pain, his life.

Finally, the meeting is over. I am allowed to withdraw. Cecil
comes to me a short time later in my chambers. At sight of him,
I send my ladies away. Whatever he has to tell me, I do not
want witnesses.

"He is recovering, Majesty. The injury was small, the bleeding quickly stanched. I spoke with him myself. He asked that I
assure you that he is well and will wait upon you very shortly."

The terror that has gripped me since the instant I saw my beloved fall dissolves abruptly. I sag in my chair but only for a
moment. Quickly I stiffen my spine.

"Not tonight." Even as I give fervent thanks to God for Robin's survival, relief of a different kind floods me. The plain truth
is that I do not want him to go with me as I venture out into my
city to do what I must. I do not want him to see, more than he
has already done, what I am becoming.

"Tell him that I bid him rest well and recover fully. He may
call upon me tomorrow."

Cecil does not take his eyes from me as he sketches a bow. "As you say, Majesty. There is other news as well. Walsingham waits to speak with you and Dee is also here."

I take a breath, let it out slowly, gathering myself. "Show them in."

*Night, 17 January 1559*

———

We cross the river again by stealth, taking care to avoid the watch. I am concerned that they may interfere with my plans but Walsingham reassures me, "After the horror the watchmen witnessed last night, they will not be on the streets, Majesty."

I want to believe him but remain concerned. "How can we be certain?" Surely among the watch are at least some men of valor and conscience who will not be deterred from their duty even in the face of such peril?

"They have been told to tend to the safety of their families and let their betters deal with the rest," Cecil says.

"And they are content to do so?" I ask.

"Should they not be?" Dee faces me in the wherry, his cloak drawn close against the chill, his ruddy face alight with excitement. However much the rest of us dread what we are about to encounter, Dee knows no such burden. All things in the universe, be they good or evil, fascinate him.

"Ordinary folk endure much," he continues, "at the behest of their betters. But in return they are supposed to be protected. That is the compact the nobility strikes with them, otherwise surely they would revolt rather than be treated as they are."

I am tempted to ask what is so bad about the lot of ordinary folk, but I suspect the magus of adhering to the radical idea that as all men are equal in the sight of God, they should be equal in each other's as well. Truly, if that addled notion ever becomes common currency, the world will be undone.

We alight at the bottom of the High Street, as before, and quickly make our way up the bank. Barely have we done so than I am struck by the change from the previous night. Whereas before the street and lanes were crowded with drunks, whores, beggars, and the like now they are empty. Scarcely a soul is stirring out of doors. The men of the watch may have held their tongues, but others have been whispering. Sensible folk, well aware of how swiftly disaster can descend, are taking no chances.

For just an instant, I think that a lack of prey may discourage the vampires and make my task all the harder. The thought dismays me. Surely, I have a better care for my people than that?

And yet, I must be realistic. True enough, I have come to stop another wave of killings, but even more important, I have come to do as I must to increase my own power. I make no apologies for that.

"If they hunt tonight," I say, "the vampires will have to go where people think themselves safe."

Every stouthearted Englishman wants to believe that his home is his castle, but I suspect people feel better protected against danger in other places. To our right, I see the dark mass of St. Savior's Church, its square towers looming above the cluster of its outbuildings. The church appears quiet, but even as I watch, a small group scurries through the wisps of fog rising from the river and slips through the gate. A moment later, when the sanctuary door is opened to admit them, I glimpse lamps burning inside and what looks like a considerable mass of people huddled there.

"Perhaps we should make for Southwark Manor," Cecil suggests. "If Mordred really is in residence there—"

"We cannot be certain of that," Walsingham says. He has reported to us earlier about his investigations into the manor, but now he adds, "The absence of property records is suspicious, of course, but hardly unique."

He alludes, without actually saying so, to the confusion regarding property that has plagued the realm since so many church holdings were seized and sold off, whether for profit or to buy the loyalty of the great families. Clear title, so prized and defended in this land down through the centuries, is just one more casualty of my father's reign. Slowly, the records are being reassembled but there are still notable gaps.

"I have confirmed that the property was sold by the late Archbishop of York," Walsingham says, "but as to who purchased it or whether it has been sold again since, I cannot be certain."

I glance again toward the church and decide. "It does not matter. We cannot take the risk that while we look elsewhere, the vampires will come here and wreak havoc."

Cecil looks aghast. "Surely they would not dare to enter a church?"

Would they not? Mordred truly appears to believe that he and his kind are as much a part of God's plan as are we. Or else, he suggests, there is no God. In either case, why would there be any barrier to the vampires entering holy ground?

"I don't know whether they would or not. But I will not leave my people in such peril."

We conceal ourselves as best we can near the approach to St. Savior's. For a time, nothing happens. I am chilled to the bone and at the point of questioning the wisdom of my strategy when a flicker of movement near the treetops catches my eye.

Beside me, Cecil gasps as a pair of vampires come out of the sky and settle lightly on the snow-covered ground. My startled

Spirit and I only just manage to grab hold of Dee in time to stop the magus, in his fascination, from revealing our position. Only Walsingham appears unaffected, standing silently and unmoving as he observes our adversaries.

"Remain here," I say under my breath, and step forward. Hours before, I watched the ritualized combat of the joust with all its rules and conventions. Men argue that the same code must be observed in warfare lest the killing be without honor. Yet from what I have heard, once battle is joined, such niceties are forgotten.

I dispense with any such nonsense from the start. As I draw my next breath, I raise my arm and, without warning, send a spear of light hurtling at the nearest vampire. It hits him full in the chest. He stops stock-still, stares down at himself, and in an instant splinters into nothingness.

The other is turning toward me when I strike again. Give him credit, he manages to leap away from my first blow, gaining the sky before I strike him down with the second. He splinters as he falls toward the ground, showering it with tiny fragments of light that blink out and are gone in a heartbeat.

Power fills me. Glorious, blood-heating power unlike any I have ever known save at the peak of physical pleasure when the world falls away and the spirit soars free. Far from feeling the exertion of my efforts, I am renewed and reborn in a way I could not have imagined possible. Eagerly, I look for more prey.

They come floating out of the sky, hesitating as though they are able to sense the deaths of their kind yet not quite believing what is happening. The light swells within me. Without hesitation, I strike again . . . and again, twice more in quick succession. I am in the lists, on the battlefield, whirling, turning in all directions to confront my enemies, who fall before me, chaff on the wind.

Dimly, I am aware of my counselors, huddled in the shadows under the broad-branched trees where they are illuminated again and again by the bursts of dazzling light that
come from me. Their white, strained faces contorted with
shock put me in mind of the Greek theater masks portraying
tragedy and comedy, the twin aspects of life between which
we reel. Dee, Cecil, Walsingham . . . they are my chorus
urging me on yet at the same time warning of disaster when
pride outstrips reason.

With each death, my strength grows. I feed on those I kill,
gaining in power by the moment. Growing, too, in hunger. My
appetite is ravenous; I am insatiable. I will kill and kill and kill
without ceasing until—

"Stop!"

For an instant, I falter. The vampire I am about to kill shoots
into the sky, escaping me. Suddenly, all is stillness.

Mordred walks out of the night onto the killing ground
where I stand, the greater blackness of his cloak flaring around
him. He is pale as moonlight and as bright. His presence rolls
over me, a wave from the deepest sea of eternity.

"What in the name of all creation are you doing?" he demands.

Face-to-face with him, the yearning I have come to know all
too well rises in me, an elation that fills my spirit and body
alike, banishing all sorrow, all doubt, all mortal weakness. So
powerful is it that I can almost believe that Mordred must be
right, we are fated to be together. Before such a treacherous
notion can take greater hold of me, I must act.

With no thought but to strike him down, I try to raise my
arm, only to find that the weight of it is suddenly too much for
me. I let it sag instead.

"I am defending my people!"

He comes closer still. I see again how beautiful he is. Longing for him threatens to consume me. I resist with all my strength.

"No, you are not!" he exclaims. "If you want to defend them, you will seek peace with me. Instead, you declare war. Are you mad?"

Truth be told, I wonder at times at my own sanity, dark times when the scaffold looms ever present in my thoughts and I cannot rest for the terror it provokes in me. But I am not in the grip of any such dread now. I am reborn as Morgaine's heir; I have her power. I need fear nothing, not even Mordred.

"There can be no peace between us!" The very thought terrifies me, reminding me as it does of my weakness concerning him. "Your kind wantonly butchers mine and you imagine— what? That I will surrender to you?"

A flicker of regret crosses his face, enough to tell me all.

"You did think that!" I crow, unable to contain my glee that he could be so deluded. "You thought to beat me. Let me tell you, that will never happen! From the time of my birth, enemies have sought to destroy me. One by one, they have failed, and so, by God, will you!"

He looks away, long enough for me to wonder what he sees in his mind's eye, what landscape so engages him.

At last he turns back to me. "I thought to give you a lesson. A handful dead, sacrificed so that many more can live and this realm be safe for all time. But you refuse to learn. You go forward blindly, heedless of what damage you do."

He raises his hands and I brace, thinking he means to attack me. But a moment later, he lets them drop as though in resignation.

"Heed me, Elizabeth. Morgaine had to kill hundreds of my kind . . . *hundreds* . . . before she had enough power to come against me, and even then she failed. I survived, she did not.

Have you thought of that? Even more, have you given an instant's thought to what happened to this realm afterward? Or do you imagine that men sit about their fires of a winter night and reminisce about the golden age that followed Arthur?"

"Darkness fell over this kingdom *because* you killed Arthur, not because of what Morgaine did to stop you."

"Arthur was a man, nothing more. Had I not killed him, he might have lived a few more years, but then he would have died, as every mortal man must do. He would have been cut down by an enemy or an injury or by any of the ailments that strike without warning."

Mordred's audacity threatens to rob me of breath. It is all I can do to respond. "You cannot excuse what you did on the grounds that he would have died anyway! He was your father! It is for God to say when that happens, not you."

"Then God has been oddly silent on the matter! Darkness was poised to sweep over England long before I ever made the bargain that I did. And it is poised to do so again. Had Morgaine made the right choice and allied with me, all the centuries of suffering that followed could have been avoided. Will you equal her for wanton foolishness?"

What twisted reason is this? Does he truly think to convince me that he did all for England's sake?

"It is not I who is mad, but you! Your kind *feed* on mine!"

"So do *yours!*"

At my look of shocked disbelief, he flings out an arm. "Look around you, Elizabeth," he commands. "You and your nobility take the lion's share of everything this realm possesses and leave mere bones for the rest. A single failure of crops and there is starvation. A chill winter and the frozen dead stack up like cordwood, while summer fevers sweep away legions too weak to fight them off while you sit in comfort in your palaces."

"That is how God has ordered the world," I insist. "It is not for us to question." I know what I say to be true, yet the words ring hollow all the same.

"How very convenient. But you take far more than my kind ever have. We need only feed in moderation, rarely causing death. Being fed upon is how more of us are made, or did you not know that?"

I did not, nor do I wish to. There is nothing about him that concerns me. *Nothing*. He is the very Devil with his silver tongue. Feed on my own people. What a perverse notion. I serve my people. My life is theirs. There is nothing I would not do for them—

"There would have been no deaths last night," he says, "but for my holding my own kind back too long, denying them all but the smallest opportunity to feed in hope of reaching an accord with you."

"Such restraint." I think to mock him but my effort is a poor, limp thing. What he says strikes me to the core. Worse yet, I am all too aware that I can scarcely control my growing hunger for him. He seeks to undermine my will at every turn, and I, God help me, fear all too greatly that he can succeed.

"And as we are on the subject of moderation," he continues, "you may wish to reconsider before you feed again with such abandon on my kind. Morgaine learned to her regret that such gorging comes at a price."

"I did not—" Horror sweeps over me, driven by the hideous realization that what he says possesses at least a grain of truth. I have fed and ravenously, growing in power each time I killed. But those I slew were vampires, deserving of death. Indeed, all I truly did was release them from their hellish existence. To suggest any parallel between me and Mordred is—

He steps closer, so close that I feel his breath against my skin.

To my heightened senses, he smells of the night wind that blows from distant places under a blaze of starlight. My mind whirls as I struggle not to reach out to him.

He bends closer to me, so close that some fragment of his power seems to leap across the short distance separating us to brush against my neck. Weakness steals over me. The thought of his power . . . his sensuality . . . his possession . . .

"I could kill you now," he says with perfect calm, and yet I see again the flicker of regret in his gaze. "More than a few will say I am mad not to do so."

Abruptly I return to myself. My life is not my own, it belongs to my people and it is of them that I must think. "Then why don't you? What stays your hand?"

He shrugs, and for just an instant I imagine that I see him as the man he was so long ago. A true prince for all that his father could not recognize it.

"Hope," he says, and is gone on the wind and the night.

꒰꒷꒱

"If there is a God, hear me now!"

Not that I thought He would or even that He truly exists, for I had seen scant evidence of Him in all my years on the benighted earth. Even so, from the dark pit of my rage and despair, I called to Him.

"Elizabeth was anointed in Your name! She is Your responsibility. Shine the light of wisdom into her befuddled brain before another millennium of darkness smothers this realm."

No answer came, nor had I expected any. The wind cut slits in the river mist. I slipped through them and flung myself skyward. My only thought was to put the world and all its ills behind me. For a time I drifted toward the sickle moon, hanging in the west. Mars and Jupiter shone brightly in near conjunction at the apex of the heavens. Ordinarily, I would have enjoyed the sight but my mind was in such turmoil that I took scant notice.

Something had to be done, but what? Certainly, I could kill Elizabeth before she became an even greater danger to me and my kind. But without her at my side I would be left to watch England fall to its mortal enemies—the Pope, the Spanish, and the like. Of course, I could wage my own war against them, but when it ended, I would likely find myself ruling over a kingdom of the dead carpeted in bones from Cornwall to Northumberland.

I had told Elizabeth that I still had hope, and I suppose that was true to at least some degree. But hope boils no peas, as the saying goes. I needed a plan.

Given that I have centuries of experience acquiring and holding power, I would say in all modesty that I have a mind given to scheming. Yet just then it was blank. No inspiration of any sort came to me. I was too stunned by Elizabeth's rejection, and by the realization of how powerful she was becoming, to think clearly.

In search of clarity, I alit near the top of the spire that rose above old St. Paul's. From that highest of all vantage points in the city, I looked out over slumbering London. To my left lay the Tower, quiet now that Elizabeth was no longer in residence. Briefly, I thought of Anne in her grave and of Morgaine, both still forces to be reckoned with. But Elizabeth commanded my attention. My gaze traced the path of the moon-silvered river to where it curled past the Palace of Whitehall.

Had she returned there yet? Sated temporarily on the essence of my kind, did she gloat over her victory? Or did she have the stomach to consider that in gorging so wantonly, she had put at risk the very life of her realm? Did she perhaps taste the bile of regret?

Hardly aware that I did so, I lifted off from the spire in the direction of the palace. As once I had called Elizabeth to me, now I felt called to her.

---

*R*eturning upriver, I retreat into my thoughts. The events at
St. Savior's have a dreamlike quality, although perhaps they
would better be likened to a nightmare. I tell myself again that I
have done nothing wrong. To the contrary, it is only good and
right to protect my realm from such beings. And yet—

I cannot confront my doubts any more than I can meet the
eyes of my companions. Cecil, Dee, Walsingham—not a one of
them looks at me directly, but I catch their anxious glances and
see their tight-lipped concern.

Anger stirs in me. Walsingham aside, the other two conspired to make me what I am. Let them dare regret it now and I
will have their heads on pikes adorning London Bridge.

No, I will not. My temper, ever prone to flare hotly, cools as
rapidly. I have need of their wise counsel, but more than ever I
also need their humanity lest I be in danger of losing my own.

More even than all that, I have the most urgent need of
Robin, the touch of his hand, the sound of his voice, the simple
reassurance of his presence.

Straight upon regaining the palace, I make for his chambers.
Coming through the door from the private passage, I startle the
servant who is keeping watch on a pallet beside the bed. At
once, the man stumbles to his feet, bows hastily, and retreats
into the outer room.

Robin and I are alone. My beloved lies pale and unmoving

behind the velvet bed curtains. Only the steady rise and fall of his chest assures me that he breathes.

A deep sigh escapes me as I approach him. A bruise darkens his left cheek, and beneath his eyes are shadows. He murmurs something—can it be my name?—too faintly for me to be sure. I wait, breath held, for him to speak again. When he does not, I give in to irresistible temptation and, having kicked off my pattens, slip under the covers with him.

His flesh is warm even through my clothes, which still bear the night's chill. I lay my head on his shoulder and press my lips to his throat, feeling the pulse of his life. Hunger stirs in me, and as before thoughts of Mordred come hard upon it. I sigh deeply, glad of the exhaustion that draws me away into sleep. When I open my eyes again, I can see through the parted bed curtains the room reflected in the black squares of the window-panes. For just a moment, I catch a glimpse of movement beyond, but the impression is fleeting and I am too distracted to take note of it.

If hope has caused Mordred to spare my life, assuming that he could have taken it, what does he hope for? Mere power and the triumph of his kind, as I have assumed? Or something more?

He warns of the darkness that will sweep over England again as though he himself is not its harbinger. He claims to want to prevent it but how is that possible, for surely evil cannot negate evil?

That seems a worthy problem as much for an alchemist as for a queen. Perhaps I should ask Dee. He can explain to me how evil is transmuted into good, if any such thing is possible.

If Mordred could have killed me, surely he would have done so after I slew so many of his own. What king would suffer such a threat to endure?

One with higher aspirations than his own survival?

What is wrong with me! I am here with Robin, comforted by his nearness and content to remain where I am until the break of day expels me. What claim has Mordred on my mind?

And why can I not chase him from it?

Lying beside my beloved, giving thanks to God for the continuance of his dear life, I refuse to think any further of my undead foe. There will be time enough and more for that later. After all, what was it that Mordred said? That he had held his own kind back from feeding while he tried to reach an agreement with me? If he wants my surrender that desperately, I can be assured that he will do nothing to jeopardize it, at least not yet.

I slide my fingers down Robin's chest, feeling the thick bandage just below his heart. Dear Lord, how close I came to losing him, this cherished friend of my childhood grown to be the man I love. He deserves far better than for me to go mooning after a demon! Yet Mordred . . .

No! I will not think of him. In a rage at my wayward self, I sit up in the bed and press my fists against my brow, fighting to drive him out. Yet for all my effort, the sense of him grows within me. I can almost . . . smell him?

Smell the night and the wind as though the air all around me is charged with his power.

As though he is near.

I leap from the bed, cross the room at a run, and throw wide the windows.

A whirl of snow dislodged from the roof immediately above falls over my outstretched arms. I see only that . . . and a ripple of blackness moving away across the sky.

## 18 January 1559

---

*I* remain with Robin as long as I dare, lying sleepless beside
him as late night yields to the creeping stealth of day. Only
then do I slip off down the passage to my own chambers. Once
there, I suffer myself to be bathed and dressed by my ladies. Kat
eyes me with concern; I know she wants private speech with me
but I contrive to avoid it. She disapproves of Robin and will tell
me so . . . again. I have no patience for that at the moment.

Cecil, who finds some pretext to have a private word with
me each morning, is not in evidence. His absence further jan-
gles my already strained nerves.

The usual breakfast of cold meats, breads, and ale is laid out
in my withdrawing room. I glance at it in passing but can find
no appetite. I am not looking forward to the coming hours,
crowded as they are with yet more celebrations of my coronation. Scarcely are morning prayers concluded despite the constant whispers and murmurs of my attending courtiers crammed
into my ill-named "private" chapel than I progress to my audience chamber, where I am subjected to a performance of son-
nets written in my honor, all flattering to be sure, if somewhat
insipid. Yet I do my best to appear pleased. My intent is to encourage the arts in my realm both for my own glory and for the
glory of Britannia, which are, after all, one and the same.

Directly afterward, I am feted in front of a tableau depicting
me as Athena, the goddess of wisdom, defending England from

the twin forces of ignorance and sloth. Were that all I have to worry about I would have slept better the previous night. As it is, I am grateful for the stiffness of the whalebone corset beneath my buckram-lined bodice. Both help to keep my spine ramrod straight until the performance finally ends.

I am rising to leave when I spy Robin standing toward the back of the audience chamber. My first thought is relief at seeing him up and about. Hard on it comes surprise when he does not hurry forward to greet me. It is not like him to hang back.

Nor is it like him to stand with his arms crossed over his chest, glaring at me.

With a quick swish of my skirts, I turn and leave the chamber. My ladies trail after me but not too closely. They have the sense to steer clear of my temper, as apparently Robin does not. And to think that I practically wept over that man scant hours ago.

My mood, already soured, does not improve when Cecil sidles up. Without meeting my eyes he murmurs, "A word, Majesty?"

I am resigned to speaking with him when suddenly a wave of nausea sweeps over me. I press a hand to my lips. The feeling ebbs quickly enough, but in its place comes a gnawing hollowness that makes me gasp. I have never felt any such sensation before—a combination of the most acute hunger and desperate urgency that drives me to do something, anything, to sate it.

Yet the mere thought of food brings another wave of sickness worse even than the first. I stagger against the wall. Cecil tries to take my arm but I shake him off.

"Away!"

The craving that has seized me is overwhelming. I struggle to breathe but there is no space in my lungs, no room in my body.

Even my heart is being crushed. Suddenly, Robin is there, his anger stripped away and replaced by concern.

I bare my teeth at him, snarling, "Do not touch me!"

The pressure of my own skin is intolerable. Frantically, I look around in search of escape only to reel back the moment the light streaming through the windows touches my eyes. I am burning! Without thought, heedless of who sees me, I run, my heavy skirts clutched in both hands.

Startled servants and courtiers alike flatten themselves along the walls of the corridor as I fly past. My hair slips from its carefully tended coif and streams behind me, a banner of fire. Faster, faster! The hunger is devouring me. I must get free!

The floor tilts suddenly. I land hard, scratching and clawing in a desperate effort to escape the iron-hard arms that have brought me down. Robin looms in my vision, his eyes dark pools of horror, his cheeks torn and bleeding. Yet he does not release me. I am lifted, carried swiftly into a place made blissfully dark by the quick action of my ladies, who dash past to yank shut the curtains.

Even then, there is no ease. The hunger remains a monster inside me. I am trapped and crying out. "Help me!"

"She is burning up!"

Robin's voice, a silver thread in the dark, pierces my terror. If I can catch hold of it—

My clothes are stripped away. I am lowered into a bath so chill that at once my teeth begin to chatter. Every muscle in my body clenches in agony.

"Bring more snow!"

The voices fade. I hear only the pounding of my heart, which must soon burst and then it will be over. Thank God for that! I will be dead and will gladly face whatever fate is mine rather than endure such suffering a moment longer.

Perhaps I am dead already for surely I am floating, my body seemingly weightless, the terrible constriction of my skin eased. Weak with the ebbing of the voracious hunger, I try to lift my head but can only just manage to turn it slightly.

My chamber is gone; I float in a world I have never before seen. The landscape around me stretches to distant horizons. I can make out shapes—rocks, perhaps, and stunted trees. The wind blows as though from eternity. Light glints off what appear to be mountains of darkly gleaming ice. Somewhere far off a wolf howls.

"Did you know," Mordred asks, "that the Norsemen believe Hell is a frozen wasteland rather than a fiery inferno?"

I try again to raise my head and this time only just manage it. He is standing a little distance away, leaning up against a large rock. Despite the wind, his cloak hangs unmoving. He appears at his ease.

"Are we in Hell?" I ask.

He frowns. "You have to be dead to go there, don't you?"

"Then I am still alive?" The prospect does not fill me with quite the pleasure that it should.

"For the moment. I did warn you."

I try to remember but nothing comes to me. "About what?"

He straightens away from the rock and comes nearer, staring down. I squirm a little under his regard.

"The wages of gorging yourself as you did. The same thing would happen to Morgaine. I met her here more than once."

Questions crowd my mind: Where is here? How have I come to such a place? But one rises above all the rest. More than anything else, I want to know about Mordred and Morgaine.

"Why would you do that? The two of you were enemies."

He sighs and looks away. "We were lovers first."

I cannot conceal my shock. It drives me to seize on what he must surely mean. "When you were still mortal?"

"And afterward." Perhaps I gasp for he adds quickly, "I'm sorry if that dismays you. Our relationship was . . . complicated."

"I don't believe you."

"As you wish. I will leave you now." He moves to go but glances back. "You will feel better soon, but know that every time you feed upon my kind, you will experience to some degree what you have just suffered. The more you feed, the worse it will be."

"You only say that to weaken my resolve."

"Believe what you will, it makes no difference."

"Wait! Don't leave." As the truth of his going sinks in, I experience a moment of panic. I cannot bear to be alone, fearing as I do that he really is telling me the truth and, worse, what he has not said but what I feel, that in taking such power into myself, I am becoming something other than human.

To my relief, he turns back. His hand brushes my brow as he smiles gently.

"Shall I tell you of Morgaine?"

Helplessly, unable to take my eyes from him, I nod.

She could fire an arrow from the back of a horse at full gallop and strike her target. Then wheel, race back across the training field, and do it again.

The men of Arthur's army grumbled that a woman should not be allowed such liberties. The High King laughed at their umbrage and urged her on, understanding as he did that her skill challenged every man to prove himself her better.

Few could, at least not consistently. I got off a lucky shot every once and again, but I was never Morgaine's equal with a bow. That might have bothered me more had I not been so infatuated with her.

Her hair was as dark as the sky on a moonless night. Gaze up along the arch of the heavens on a warm day and you will see the same shade of blue as were her eyes. Her skin, where the sun did not touch it, was very white, but winter or summer, she always had a bloom of color in her cheeks. As for her mouth, the swains who bumbled about her likened it to a lush, ripe rose, which I suppose was fair enough.

Days on horseback, hard training, and her love of the hunt made her lithe and strong. Had she been a man, she would have been a warrior. Instead, she settled for being a priestess.

Arthur was a Christian, but many of those sworn to him were not. The Druids remained a force at his court. Morgaine was chief among them for he loved her. Lies have been told about what bound them to one another; the truth is simpler by far. Her father had been one of the closest and dearest friends of his youth. That Arthur had caused that lord's death by sending him into a battle that could not be won explains the care he showed to Morgaine. Guilt is a powerful motivator.

I loved her, too, in an entirely different way. For me, she was the light in the darkness of my life. I could remember a time when my father and I had not always been in conflict, but only just. Rarely have two men seen the world so differently.

The vampires came into England when I was a child. Their leader was Damien, not a bad sort, kingly in his own way. The Christian priests spewed spittle at sight of them, so frightened were those men of God by what they called devil spawn. You would think they would have had sufficient faith in their own deity to be unworried, but no. The Druids took the vampires much more in stride, understanding as they did that the real danger came from the Saxons.

With the fading of Roman order, the way lay open for rapacious tribes to fall upon our fair isle. The old Anglo-Roman families—my father's being first among them—banded together and held off the invaders for a while, but the flood tide that washed up against Britain could not long be repulsed. We were overrun and in danger of extinction when Arthur raised his banner. My father swore that he would do all that was needed to protect our families, our fields, and our hearths. He vowed to leave no measure untaken, no effort unfulfilled.

He lied.

When Damien proposed an alliance with his kind, Arthur—under the influence of the Christian priests—refused it. In his arrogance, he said that he preferred to die and have all his kingdom die with him rather than make common cause with demons.

I was with Morgaine in the great hall of Camlan when the High King announced his decision. In a fury, I challenged him, demanding to know by what right he could choose death for all of us. We quar-

reled bitterly. Arthur called me a faithless son and sent me from him.
I went gladly, vowing that if he would not save us, it fell to me to do
so.

Morgaine went after me. We stood just beyond the timber hall,
the night filled with the scents of winter pine and smoke, the swollen
moon so bright that I could see her as well as if by day. Better perhaps, for moonlight always became her well.

"I will go to Damien myself," I declared.

"No!" she cried, and made to grasp my arm. "You must not! We
will find another way."

Later, I came to believe that her effort to stop me stemmed, at
least in part, from her sense of what she was becoming. If the arrival
of the vampires in England had not fully awakened her as a Slayer,
the process had certainly begun. But by the time I discovered that, it
was too late.

She followed me and we argued further, then made up on a bed of
sweet moss beneath a sacred oak. I stole away before dawn and
sought out Damien. My plan was to reach an accord with him, then
gather a combined army of vampires and mortals to stand against the
Saxons.

It almost worked. Morgaine, having followed me by some Druid
means known only to her, burst in upon us. While she yet lacked the
power to kill Damien, she wounded him grievously. Well aware of
what the coming of a Slayer meant to his kind and desperate to protect them, he passed his power to me before giving up his light.

What shall I say of the years that followed? Morgaine loved me
still even as the hunger to kill me grew within her. I do not underestimate the battle she waged inwardly. Arthur continued to insist on
fighting the Saxons alone, with little success. More and more, he
turned to the Christian priests, who grew in power.

So, too, did the Saxons, who benefited from the conflict between
the vampires and the Britons. Ultimately, Morgaine succumbed to

the force within her. She attacked my kind with wanton abandon, finally becoming strong enough, she thought, to challenge me.

Against all evidence, driven by my love for her, I let myself believe that if I could only put a stop to Arthur's bloody folly, I could keep both my kingdom and my beloved safe for all time. I truly did not want to kill my father, but urged on by his priests, he had no such reluctance regarding me. In the end, I had no choice.

Arthur fell and Morgaine came against me. The rest is too dark and tragic to dwell upon. I will say only that she and I both left the field of battle sorely wounded. I survived; my beloved did not.

I thought her gone and wept for her, but now I wonder if she did not have another plan. Has the essence of her lain in wait all these years, abiding until another Slayer could be born and the terrible destruction she unleashed be at last completed?

And if she has, what chance have I this time to persuade her otherwise?

Love proved to be my greatest weakness so long ago. Now I must turn it on the lathe of fate and contrive from it a weapon to save all.

*Evening, 18 January, 1559*

-----

My heart beats steady and strong, a herald proclaiming my return to the world of men. Yet still I resist, clinging to Mordred's voice and the tale he told: Morgaine, devoured by the terrible power within her. Arthur, valuing his immortal soul above the life of his people. And Mordred himself, the valiant champion of Britain, still intent on saving her.

How much is truth? How much a fantasy contrived for my seduction? For he does mean to seduce me. Of that, I no longer have any doubt.

Worse yet, the notion has a certain appeal.

I am so cold!

I burrow deep, seeking warmth, but find only icy water and come up sputtering.

"She lives!"

Hauled from the tub, I am wrapped in blankets. My ladies chaff my legs and rub dry my hair as Kat spoons broth down my throat. I stare into the fire fed to roaring and try to understand what has come upon me.

Madness or something even worse? I cannot ignore the sense that I have seen past the thin veneer we call this world into a corner of the vast reality beyond. Not Heaven, not Hell, not anything we are capable of imagining. By comparison, mere madness seems the better bargain.

"We should put a stop to this right now." Robin is speaking. I rouse just enough to see that Cecil is near as well, as are Dee and Walsingham. I should be dismayed at any of them witnessing me in such a state, but I cannot manage it.

"Her Majesty cannot be put at such risk," Robin continues. "I will not allow it."

*He* will not allow it? My gratitude for his concern vanishes in an instant. Never—*never*—will I give any man governance over me.

"Perhaps we should not have"—Cecil is sputtering, something he does only when he is nervous—"we should not have ventured down this road to begin with."

What a fine time for him to think of that! When he and Dee all but dragged me into that accursed chapel and set me on this course!

I am gathering my breath to say so when the magus does it for me. "Now is not the time for doubts," Dee insists. "To the contrary, Her Majesty is becoming exactly what she is destined to be. We should rejoice in the evidence of her growing strength."

"You may do so," Robin says in a tone that makes it clear that he does not. "But dozens of courtiers saw her run down a corridor screaming that she was burning. Hundreds will be speaking of it already. How long before the common rabble believe she is possessed? And what do you think will happen then?"

What indeed? The raw instinct for survival imbued in tenderest childhood stirs. It is a cunning beast, sharp of fang and claw, and it tramples over every other concern.

"Help me up."

At the sound of my voice, all turn—my ladies, my counselors, my ambitious beloved. I am, as I should always be, the focus of their attention.

"You cannot," Robin begins.

Truly, the man is caught in a hole of his own making and his solution is to dig it deeper?

I ignore him. To Kat, I say, "I must dress at once and return to my people before such foolish rumors gain common currency."

"That may not be wise," Cecil begins. Clearly he doubts my capacity to appear as the strong and trustworthy monarch I must be seen to be.

Standing, only just managing to hold myself steady, I glare at him. "It is not seemly for any man to be here. All of you, go."

They go, but reluctantly, with backward glances and deep frowns. Barely has the door closed behind them than their anxious chatter starts. Truly, they are worse than a gaggle of old women.

My ladies have the sense to keep silent as they cluster around me. In their presence, Kat, too, holds her tongue, even though I can see that she is bursting to know what Dee and the others were speaking of.

Rather than put on what I wore before, I don an even grander ensemble of black and white silk brocade embroidered over every inch with thread of gold. With it I wear a high ruff of intricately pleated pure white lace sewn with tiny pearls. I choose the colors deliberately, symbolizing as they do eternal virginity. It is time that my counselors begin to accept my aversion to matrimony. So, too, I make a point to wear my mother's diadem. Let anyone dare to think me other than their anointed sovereign, set by Almighty God to rule over them.

I will return to the court where I will appear delighted by every festivity, give solemn ear to every courtier and ambassador, and, I have just decided, dance with every gentleman who can turn an ankle, each and every one of them save Robin. He can stand on the sidelines all night and glare at me if he likes, but he cannot now—or ever—order me about. For the sake of the love I bear him, let him recognize that without delay.

I brush past the quartet of anxious men on my way from my chambers, pausing only long enough to whisper to Kat, "When I return, we must talk."

She will assume that I mean to confide in her as I always have in the past, for truly there is no one I trust more. Who else knew my mother so well and has kept Anne's secrets locked in her heart all these years?

But first there is the court to reassure. I must be seen to be well and whole in mind as well as body. I must smile and laugh, offer a sally here and a riposte there. I must move among my lords and ladies in all my glory—a gilded idol in velvet and silk, adorned with gems and pearls—and convince them to both love and fear me.

I was born for nothing less, and with no desire to give myself undue credit, I carry it off with aplomb. Only once during the evening do I falter. When Robin approaches me to dance our special dance—lavolta, the only dance that allows us to embrace publicly—I keep to my resolve and turn away from him. At once the courtiers begin to whisper. What has cast him into such disfavor? Or was he ever truly so favored as they thought?

The moment pains me but at the same time I savor it. Let him never again take anything to do with me for granted.

Cecil is not so easy to ignore. He hovers nearby, not approaching me but also never releasing me from his scrutiny. He saw what happened at St. Savior's—he, Dee, and Walsingham. Not a one has said what he makes of it, but I can imagine. As unattractive as the thought is, they witnessed their Queen transformed into a creature of death, driven to feed voraciously. Cecil, at the least, is frightened by that.

My Spirit wavers in his resolve because he is no longer certain that I am up to the task and perhaps because he fears that he is not. But what of Dee? The magus is at court this night. I give him my particular regard, trying to divine what hides behind his smooth countenance and cordial manner. He claims to rejoice in my growing power, but does he really? Dee harbors sentiments I do not pretend to understand except to know that I do not agree with him. What did he make of Mordred's claim that I and my nobility feed upon our people? Is he still trustworthy?

And what of Walsingham, the new man in my service? He stands apart from all the rest, a black-garbed, solemn presence observing the proceedings with a faint smile. The schoolmaster is amused by us, but when my eyes meet his across the room, he bows most graciously.

Mordred has sown doubts in my mind about those upon whom I must rely. Whether he means to or not—and I suspect that he does—he is setting me apart, isolating me in ways that make me ever more susceptible to him.

Mindful that I must guard against that, I raise my hand and summon the schoolmaster to my side. As he is new to court, my favoring of him draws immediate attention. Walsingham shows no awareness of it. His expression never changes as he comes near, bows again, and waits for me to speak.

"I would take the sounding of your mind, good sir," I say quietly so that we cannot be overheard. "What do you think I should do?"

He appears neither pleased nor displeased to be challenged by me. I see no sign in him that he is afraid anything he says will be held against him later, as so many of my courtiers are when asked for an honest opinion. Indeed, he seems to have no concern whatsoever for himself.

Cecil has done me a favor bringing him to me.

"Mordred will use any trick he can to stop you," Walsingham says, pitching his voice low for discretion's sake. "He will seek to confuse your mind and make you question yourself. But if you hold true to your course, you will prevail. Of that, I have no doubt."

"Do you not? We have seen now the cost to me of gaining power as a Slayer, and yet I am nowhere near as strong as I must be if I am to defeat Mordred. Have you considered that in order to become what I must be, I may have to make myself into something my people cannot accept?"

Truth be told, until that moment I had not fully posed the question to myself. Yet it was there, lurking in the swirling mists of my mind since my return to the world. Can I be Queen and Slayer both?

"You will be what you were born to be," Walsingham continues. "Nothing more and, God willing, nothing less."

Cecil is watching us and Robin as well. I take a breath and let it out slowly. The gaudy court recedes from my vision yet remains uppermost in my mind, as it always must if I am to survive.

"There are more than a few who believe that no daughter of a witch can be rightful Queen of England."

I have never voiced my deepest fear to anyone, yet the schoolmaster draws it from me as though his unbending reason can wipe away my sin of doubt.

"If you have concerns about your mother," he says, "resolve them with all speed, else you can be certain that Mordred will use them against you."

I nod, my throat too tight for speech. It is a truism of kings—and of queens regnant—that the most valued counselor is the one who will dredge from our own minds the truth we already know but hesitate to speak.

God bless the schoolmaster for doing so.

Although I suspect that Kat would not be so gracious in her thanks.

I tarry a little longer after Walsingham withdraws. Robin continues to stare at me as though by doing so he can compel my love. At length, he tries another tack and partners a lady in a dance. Her name is of no consequence and better for her that I do not dwell upon it. He makes a great show of favoring her, and she seems simpleton enough to think he means it. That at least affords me some little amusement, although I will also admit to a twinge of jealousy. But only a twinge whereas scant days ago before all this began my reaction would have been far stronger.

My distraction grows as the hour wears on and night's embrace deepens. Briefly, I indulge the thought of taking to the hunt again to feed upon the light. The price for doing so gives me pause, but I tell myself that this time I would be moderate, pace myself as it were, and escape such dire penalty.

Still, I put the thought aside. For the moment, more urgent matters summon me. As soon as I can, I make a show of yawning and bid all good rest. Through torchlit passages lined by bowing courtiers, I make my way to bed.

*Night, 18 January 1559*

———

*K*at is asleep in a chair in my chamber. The fire has burned low. I can only just make out her dear face, slack with dreams. I dismiss my ladies, shut the door behind them, and touch her arm gently.

"Wake, old friend, with my apologies. It is urgent that we speak."

She is alert at once in the way of the elderly—she would curse me for describing her as such—who only skim the surface of sleep. I suppose they hesitate to sink too deeply out of fear that they will not wake again, although it is hard to think of Kat's fearing anything. Her eyes blink once, twice, and see me.

"My lady." She starts to rise but I press her back into the chair and take the footstool at her feet.

When she makes to protest, I insist, "No formalities tonight, for pity's sake. I have had a stomachful of them."

Kat laughs, perhaps remembering how she and I used to sneak away to hidden places within the gardens at Hatfield where I could be only a child and she the woman who loved me. No concern for rank and none at all for the world where my life hung so precariously. Memories of those times and of her love have kept me knit together through the darkest days.

She is of an age to be my grandmother but has been mother to me, the one constant in my life of turmoil. Twice she has been ripped from me, imprisoned by my enemies seeking a path to my destruction. Each time she proved valiant and true. If I had to trust someone with my deepest secrets, I could not choose better than Kat Ashley.

On sudden impulse, I lay my head on her lap. She sighs and gently strokes my hair. Her fingers brush against the diadem I still wear. It pains me but I do not remove it. Tonight above all I must be Anne's daughter.

I look up and catch her gazing at me with such tender devotion that my throat tightens. She has ever been a woman of character, has Kat Ashley, the Devonshire girl of middling good birth who contrived to acquire an education any man would envy, avoided marriage until she was nigh on to forty years, when she took the husband of her own choosing, and drew the eye of a queen who entrusted her with that which she held most precious.

"What troubles you, dearest?" Kat continues stroking my hair, soothing me as she did when I was a fretful child, unable to calm myself without her touch.

"My mother—"

Kat goes still. She has always discouraged questions about Anne, knowing as she surely did that my only chance of survival lay in unswerving loyalty to Henry. My father wavered dangerously enough as it was, alternately declaring me a bastard and restoring my birthright. If he had ever had reason to suspect that I nurtured love for my mother, he might well have thrown me to the wolves, for I was ever the living, breathing reminder of what he had done to her.

"Was she guilty?" I ask. So few words, yet they contain all the wretched terror that threatens, like acid dropped upon a copper plate, to etch their design into my very soul.

A moment passes, long enough for me to fear that Kat will not answer. Finally, she touches my shoulders gently.

"Sit up, sweetling." When I obey as I child would, she instructs, "Tell me what you think you know."

Kat's discretion not withstanding, I have heard the whispers. I know something of the crimes for which Anne was called to account and for which she died. Even so, I can barely give them voice.

"She was accused of unlawful . . . even unnatural relations with many men." Including her brother, my uncle, but I will not speak of that.

"Lies," Kat says implacably. "Mad, wild lies that everyone knew could not possibly be true. Your mother was a woman of honor and pride. She would never have debased herself in any such way. Moreover, she understood full well the precariousness of her position as queen. She did all she could to avoid giving her enemies anything to use against her."

"Those who still loved the old queen, Catherine of Aragon, and blamed my mother for my father setting her aside?"

Kat nods. "Those and others. Your mother believed in the true reform of the church. Many at court, including many close to your father, did not. They sought to undermine her."

"But the charges went beyond adultery. The King . . . my father thought her guilty of witchcraft." This, too, I have heard. Henry did not bring that charge into court where it would, of necessity, become public; he settled for accusing her of treason instead. But he made no secret that he thought her guilty of consorting with the Devil, even to the extent of toying with the notion of burning her.

Kat leans forward, looking directly into my eyes. Without hesitation she says, "Your mother was no more guilty of that than of anything else."

Relief floods me, of course, but hard on it comes fresh pain. As grateful as I am to know of my mother's innocence, it raises the question that has haunted me since I first began to glimpse the outlines of her terrible downfall. She had failed to bear a son, so be it. But why had Henry felt driven to destroy her so utterly? Why had he not simply divorced her, as he later did Anne of Cleves when he found her unpleasing as a wife?

True, my father had executed a second queen, poor Catherine Howard. But she was a foolish girl who really had crowned him with cuckold horns. Humiliation more than anything else had driven him to slay her. What compulsion swung the sword that severed my mother's neck?

"You are convinced," I ask, "that nothing ever happened that could have even remotely given my father cause to believe that my mother had dealings with the supernatural?"

And there it is, the flick of an eye, a quick tilt of the head. Kat has never lied to me, of that I am sure. But I am equally certain that just then she is tempted to.

"I had hoped," she says softly, "that it would not come to this."

To what? What does she know? What does this woman who has loved me dearest and best all my life, who has never hesitated to do what was right for me, now hesitate to say?

She slips a hand beneath the bodice of her gown and draws out a packet of yellowed parchment folded over and sealed by wax cracked with age. "I have carried this next to my heart since Mary died and you were proclaimed Queen. Before that, I kept it locked away, never touching it from the day your mother put it into my hands."

Something of my mother after all this time. I can scarcely credit it. I have nothing of Anne's except the diadem made for her and curiously kept by my father when he might have had it melted down and recast instead. No other item that she ever touched has been preserved, at least not to my knowledge. Perhaps something is hidden away here and there, but if so, no one speaks of it.

Now suddenly there is this—what?

"Your mother told me to give this to you only if you ever asked the question you have just posed. Otherwise, she wanted you left in peace, untroubled by its contents."

"Do you know what they are?"

Kat shakes her head. "I do not. They are for you—and only you—to know. Your mother made that clear."

My impulse as I take the packet is to break the seal right then and there and devour whatever lies within. But the circumstances under which I have received this message from my mother fill me with caution. Whatever I am about to learn of her, there will be no turning back from it.

"Do you want me to stay?" Kat asks.

Of course, I do. I want her to gather me into her arms, rock me back and forth, and tell me that everything will be all right. I want to roll back time and be a child again with no awareness of the sword that hangs over my life. I want to sleep without dreams of a woman swinging me round and round in a garden full of roses, and of the love she had for me shining in her eyes.

It does not matter what I want. I am Queen and I must do what is needed whatever the cost.

"Go to your rest." When she hesitates, I add, "You have fulfilled your duty. Now I must do the same."

She obeys, reluctantly and not before embracing me most lovingly. I cling to her for a moment before finally forcing myself to let her go. Even then I have to resist the impulse to call her back.

When I am alone, I sit in the chair before the fire and stare at the packet. My hands are steady as calm seeps over me. This is my mother, who will speak to me from across the grave. The woman who bore me, who died for doing so, and who still managed to endow me with power I can barely comprehend.

I heard her voice once in the moment of my awakening.

Now I will hear it again. Please, God, let me be guided by it.

I split the seal and unfold the parchment, bending closer to the candle to make out the fine hand written there. A quick glance at the first words and my breath catches. The letter is dated two days before my mother's execution.

*At the Tower, London*

*17 May, Anno Domini 1536*

    *My beloved daughter, light of my heart and comfort of my soul, I rejoice at your continuance on this earth for my only wish has ever been to keep you safe. Pray God that Kat remains with you. If it has pleased the Almighty to take her to Him, I abide in faith that she will have entrusted this letter to the best of hands.*

    *Know that it is my hope that you will never read this. I yearn for you to live in peace, perhaps as a comfortable country woman far from the treachery that is the court. Should it please you, I hope that you are wed to a kind and loving lord, and that many children play at your feet.*

    *But if the secret horoscope that I had cast at the time of your birth proves true, none of that has come to pass. Instead, you are Queen. No doubt you are surrounded by those who believe that a woman is not suited to rule. Do not be swayed by their petty minds. Only you can protect our realm in the great struggle that will determine England's fate for a thousand years and more. It is for this that you were born a woman and my daughter.*

    *In those days when I basked in the constancy of your father's love, all swore that I carried the longed-for*

*prince. So, too, did I swear to your father. Only one*
*dared say otherwise. On a bitterly cold night in February*
*in the year of your birth, I received a most unexpected*
*visitor . . .*

A tear slips down my cheek and falls on the parchment, followed swiftly by another. I break off reading to brush them away
before they can smear the ink. In the stillness of the room,
where every pop and hiss of the fire seems magnified ten times
over, I can manage only a single thought: my mother loved me.
I have always wanted to believe that but now I know for certain. She did not blame me for her fate or regret my existence.
She went to her death wanting only the best for me.

To be the recipient of such love is humbling in the extreme,
yet I am also exalted by it. She has reached across the grave to
soothe my greatest fears and strengthen me in this time of trial.

Regaining control of myself, I quickly read the next few para-
graphs, my astonishment growing with each word. My mother
describes her first encounter with Mordred, how he appeared in
her apartment in Whitehall on that winter night, entering un-
hindered despite all the protection surrounding the newly wed
Queen carrying the King's child. He came, she believed, through
a window that, though high above the ground, presented no barrier to him.

At that time, she wrote, she knew only a little about the existence of vampires in England, stories passed down through her
mother's family, which had deep ties in Cornwall where Arthur
had dwelt. She was afraid, naturally enough, at Mordred's
sudden appearance, but he made haste to assure her that he
meant no harm. That was the first of his many lies.

And then he warned her . . .

*        *        *

. . . Mordred told me that the child I carried beneath my heart was not the fervently desired prince. I would bear a girl, and unless I took steps to prevent it, her birth would mean my death. I did not believe him. Such was your father's power and will that I could not imagine the Almighty denying him the son he desired above all else.

In the spring, with you in my belly, I went to my coronation. The night before, I was in residence here at the Tower. I cannot explain the impulse that took me into the Chapel of St. Peter ad Vincula, but once there, I remained to pray. As I knelt before the altar, the world as I knew it fell away. I found myself standing on a hilltop within sight of the river Thames. A lovely woman beckoned to me. In the way of dreams, I recognized her as Morgaine, who is whispered to be the ancestress of my mother's line.

She, too, said that I would bear a girl, but she added that you would be the means by which either great evil or great good came to reign over Britain. She cautioned that if I was to protect you and this realm both, I would have to make a terrible choice.

And so the war for my soul began.

You were born, my beautiful daughter. Even as I rejoiced at your life, the shadows deepened around me. Mordred's visits grew more frequent. Despite Morgaine's warning, I came to look forward to them. Alone of everyone I knew, he expressed no disappointment that you were a girl. But he did caution that the King, curdled by his disappointment, would in time strike out against me.

Even so, the blow came sooner than I expected. I had not considered that Henry would set spies on me, searching for any grounds to free him from the wife he had come to despise. Nor that my association with Mordred would give them what they sought.

By the time I realized the extent of the danger, it was too late. Henry was determined to be rid of me, and nothing I nor anyone else could do would stay his hand. Except Mordred. He pointed out that if Henry died before he could dispose of me, you would be Queen. Until you came of age, under the laws your father himself had set in place, I would be Regent.

As such, I would be able to reform the country in ways that Henry balked at doing. There would be true freedom of religion and a rebirth of learning. So Mordred promised when he laid out his plan for me. All that he said would come to pass provided I agreed to one small concession: when you were of an age to wed, he would become your consort and rule as king over this realm.

I love life as much as anyone and I long to be at your side as you grow. The thought that I must climb the scaffold that I can hear them building even now on the green and lay my head upon the block fills me with terror. But the alternative . . .

I have arranged for your protection. Darkness will hover over you, but, God willing, by signs and symbols, prayers and portents, you will pass safely through into the light of your true destiny—Queen Regnant, protector of this realm, victorious over the demonic forces that, should you falter, will rule to the end of time.

Beloved daughter, joy of my heart, know that with my last breath I think of you.

Your loving mother, forever,
Anne B.

## 19 January 1559

Someone has come into the room and is opening the shutters. I blink in the sudden light, not waking for I have not slept, but roused nonetheless from the dark pool of my thoughts.

Kat is there. She stands by the chair where I have remained all through the night. Gently, she takes the packet still lying open on my lap, folds it, and slips it beneath her bodice.

"Come now, my lady, you must dress."

She speaks with cheerful firmness but I can hear the quaver in her voice. She does not know what I have learned but she can see the effect it has had on me.

I stand stiffly. The room, the day, even dear Kat herself, scarcely seem real. In my mind, I am back in the Tower, listening to the steady pounding of hammers as the scaffold rises.

"My lady—"

Her concern touches me at last. With an effort, I drag myself into the here and now.

"By heavens, Kat, what hour is it? I will be thought the worse layabout in the world if I am not about my queenly business soon."

She snorts but pretends to be persuaded that nothing is wrong. All the same, she keeps a close eye on me as I dress. We are not alone; there is no chance for private speech. To please her, I manage to eat a little but her frown remains. As I take a sip of ale, I notice Robin lurking on the other side of the door left just far enough ajar for me to see him.

At my raised eyebrows, Kat shrugs. We both know that she does not approve of him, convinced as she is that he is somehow a danger to me. Yet on this day, under these circumstances, she has taken pity on him.

I can see why. He looks dreadful—pale with deep shadows beneath his eyes, unshaven, his dark hair barely brushed, and, unless I am very much mistaken, still wearing the same clothes I saw him in yesterday, only now badly wrinkled.

I crook a finger at him. He comes quickly, stopping just in front of me, and, despite his haggard state, executes a lovely bow. When he straightens, he is grimacing.

Perhaps I really should forgive him . . . but not quite yet.

"Do you have any more instructions for me, Lord Dudley? Anything more that you will not allow?"

He flushes and ducks his head. Not for a moment do I believe that he is penitent. Men by nature believe that women should not have the ordering of our own lives. But he has been caught out and now he must retreat, cover his flanks, and maneuver for a defensible position.

Truly, if I am ever called upon to lead men in battle, I will acquit myself well enough for I understand the way of it in my very bone and sinew.

"If I were in a position to do so," Robin says, "I would order the world in such a fashion that I might bask continually in your favor as in the radiance of the sun. As it is, I can only beseech you to forgive your poor servant who loves you and thinks solely of your well-being."

A pretty speech nicely delivered. The last of my anger at him slips away. I hold out my hand.

"Lawd, Robin! We have a tiny tiff and you magnify it into high drama. You know that you are my dearest friend as, indeed, all the world should never forget."

I raise my voice just enough to assure that the courtiers hovering on the other side of the door can hear me. With those few words, the strain slips from his face and he smiles. As well he should for I have restored him to my favor and, perforce, the court's. The uncomfortable night he no doubt spent worrying about exactly how far he had fallen is over and the new day has broken.

Truly, power is an amazing thing. I find I have even more of a taste for it than I would have anticipated.

When he is done kissing my hand, I draw him a little away so that we may speak privately. Now that we are friends again, I have a use for him.

"There is somewhere I must go tonight. I want you to arrange it for me very quietly, and accompany me."

"Of course but Cecil—"

"I don't want him to know anything about this. It is strictly between the two of us. You understand?"

Whether he does or not, Robin is pleased. Not only is he back in my graces, but I am trusting him above my Spirit, who, like Kat, is no friend of his.

"Absolutely, have no doubt, I will arrange everything just as you wish. Where do you want to go?"

In all likelihood, he expects me to say that I want to return to Southwark and I do, but not yet. When I tell him what I intend, he looks surprised but he is wise enough after my recent coldness to ask for no explanation and raise no objection. I am content that the matter will be well managed.

That leaves me to get through yet another round of celebrations. I have been Queen for scarce three days and have had precious little opportunity to see to the ordinary business of the realm. Somewhere laws are being proposed, cases are being adjudicated, foreign affairs are being hashed over or made a hash of, but I am not there. I am here, the amazing, performing royal puppet. See her smile! See her wave! See her pretend to be interested in an endless parade of preening blowhards.

And to think that I once believed that all my worse problems would be solved by becoming Queen. I would laugh at my own idiocy if I weren't so tempted to weep.

Of course, I will do neither. I will, instead, do my best to assure all concerned that the hand that holds the scepter is steady and sure. Admittedly, my task would be easier if the ambassador from the Hanseatic League would conclude his peroration on the vital necessity of expanding the tax and customs concessions granted to his trading guild, including listing each of them in excruciating detail. By the time he has finally done, I am nearly limp from the tedium.

Still, I manage one diversion, that of avoiding Cecil, who spends the entire day attempting to gain my ear. Each time he approaches, I wave him off while pretending rapt interest in whoever is speaking to me. My attentiveness wins frowns from him but startled smiles from the recipients of my unexpected interest. I must assume that Walsingham told Cecil of my fears concerning my mother. But perhaps he did not. Perhaps the schoolmaster trusts no one fully, not even the man who brought him to my notice.

If so, he is wiser by far than most.

Of all the questions that have bumped and tumbled through my mind in the hours since reading my mother's letter, one stands above the rest: why did Anne raise no alarm when Mordred visited her, not once but repeatedly? It was a curious omission on the part of a queen who must have understood the precariousness of her position. But upon reflection, I think I understand why she did it. *He expressed no disappointment that you were a girl.* What a balm that must have been to a frightened woman confronted by her royal husband's fury. How easily Mordred played on her loneliness and dread to insinuate himself into her graces and win, if only for a time, her trust.

How shocked he must have been when she chose death over all he offered.

If it comes to it, will I have the courage to do the same?

No matter if I do, for plainly and simply I must not die or England will be caught between civil war and foreign invasion. No realm, no people, can survive such dual threats.

I must live and I must prevail. If only I can determine how. To do that, I must seek counsel of a very particular kind.

So, when night descends at last, the candles in the great hall are gutted, and the court wends its way to bed—though few will remain in their own—I join Robin in the passage beyond my chamber. He is at pains to assure me that all is in readiness.

"The river is running too high just now to risk it, but I have horses at the ready and a handful of good men who can be trusted to keep their silence."

I fasten my cloak over the simple woolen gown I have got myself into without any assistance. Kat and my other ladies think me so exhausted that I have retired early. I would not have them know otherwise.

"They had better or they will not keep their tongues."

We go swiftly out through the walled garden to the road beyond where his men wait. They keep their eyes forward, not a one so much as glancing at me. I am reassured that he has chosen well.

Robin cups his hands and bends to give me a leg up into the saddle. We are away, our mounts' hoofbeats muffled by the fresh fall of snow. I smell the banked fires of my city mingling with the icy wildness that blows from the north where it is said that all manner of marvelous creatures dwell. I am inclined to be-

lieve it for truly creation holds wonders we can barely comprehend. It is that I seek in dark depths of night when all the world
lies wreathed in stillness and decent men and women do not
stir.

The guard on watch at the Tower bars our way until Robin is
recognized. Then they stand aside swiftly. We pass over the
moat and through the gate before Lion Tower. I dismount on
the green—for all I know on the very spot where my mother
died or near enough—and look toward the Chapel of St. Peter
ad Vincula. The high windows are silvered by moonlight. Nothing moves within.

On sudden impulse, I reach for Robin's hand. I should go
alone, but the mere thought makes me falter. The wooden door
leading to the chapel, much battered and stained, creaks as it
swings open. Just inside, I stop and look toward the altar. Is it
my imagination or does a faint mist rise near it?

"Stay here," I say. "Do not come any farther."

"Elizabeth—" Robin uses my given name only in our most
private moments, but I cannot blame him for doing so now.
Standing alone in a place that has encompassed so much pain
and fear has a certain intimacy.

Even so, I release his hand and turn to face him. "Whatever
you see—or think you see—do not attempt to interfere. Stay
here if you can, leave if you must, but do not approach the altar
or anywhere near it."

His eyes darken with dread but such is his devotion to me
that he says, "You cannot expect me to—"

"I order you to. Damn you, Robin, listen to me! There are
forces at play here that you do not understand."

"But you do? This involves Mordred, obviously. Is he here?"

"No, at least I don't think so. It isn't about him, not directly.
I need to—"

What can I say? That I need to reach out across the chasm of time to try to find the one person who might be able to tell me how to defeat Mordred without destroying myself in the bargain?

Robin would think me mad, and who is to say that he would be wrong?

I take his hand again and raise it to my lips. He stiffens in surprise. I look up, meeting his gaze.

"As you love me, do as I ask. If I think you are in peril, my resolve will weaken and we may both be lost."

He takes a breath, lets it out slowly, and nods. With difficulty, I release him. Even more reluctantly, I turn to gaze down the aisle toward my mother's grave. The mist really is there and it is deepening.

I step away from Robin, and in all honesty, with that step he is forgotten. I can think only of what I have come to do.

*Night, 19 January 1559*

---

The mist dissolves and I am standing on a hilltop within sight of the river Thames. Tumbled walls covered in moss give way to fields running down to the water. A lovely woman is nearby. Her hair is black as a raven's wing, her skin like cream kissed by the sun. She wears a crimson robe caught at her shoulder with a golden broach. The fabric presses against her as she moves, revealing a figure at once slim and strong. A bow and quill are hooked over her shoulder.

A moment ago, I knelt beside my mother's grave in the chapel, praying that I would find a way to bridge the chasm across time. So swiftly my prayers have been answered! I am without breath, left gaping as the woman strides toward me.

"Elizabeth." Her voice washes over me like fast-running water, exhilarating and daunting all at once. "At last we meet."

"Morgaine?" I know who she is—as my mother said, in the way of dreams—yet the circumstances are so strange that I can scarcely believe it.

"I am she. The Slayer before you and the one who has awaited your coming all these years."

A thousand years spent waiting . . . where? "What is this place?"

"My home." With a graceful movement of her arm, she indicates the hill, the river, and the shore beyond. "Like everywhere else, it exists first and foremost in eternity. When I needed it, I found it there."

"I was in the chapel a moment ago—"

"You are in a different moment now, a much longer one that beats to a time vastly greater than the flicker of a human life. But you have come here for a reason. Tell me what it is."

So much draws me to her—my awakening beside my mother's grave, Anne's letter, the desperate struggle to save my realm. But even in that vast moment, urgency grips me.

"Mordred—"

At once, she nods. "Yes, of course, Mordred. He is at the center, after all, which I suppose you realize is where he was always determined to be."

"I'm not sure that I do." I am struggling to understand anything at all. What has happened to me in the past few days is beyond comprehension. By comparison, the rest of my life seems plain and ordinary.

"You, whose father exiled you into the darkness where you were left to wonder if every breath you took would be your last? You fought your way back to nothing less than the throne itself. What drives you drives him."

The notion that Mordred and I are alike in some way offends me deeply. Far more important, the suspicion that it is true terrifies me.

"I was born to be Queen," I say stiffly, "anointed before God for that purpose. How can you compare me to such a creature as—"

"But he wasn't always," Morgaine says. Sadness flits behind her eyes, so intense that it pierces my offended dignity. "He was a man and, before that, a child as innocent as any. Mordred chose the path of darkness for what he truly believes is the greater good. If you do not understand that, you will have no chance of defeating him."

"But I must." The notion that I may not fills me with despair. "What he wants for England cannot come to pass!"

"Because it would offend your god?"

*Your god,* not simply God. I remember then what Mordred told me, that Morgaine is a priestess of the old faith. A pagan, and as such, perhaps not so deserving of my trust as I would wish her to be.

Even so, she remains my only hope.

"Mordred is not human," I say. That is the crux of it, but I wonder if she—who has waited a thousand years for me to come—can understand what is missing when humanity is gone. I am not sure that I fully grasp it myself.

"Because he does not die?" Morgaine asks. "He can do so but only under extraordinary circumstances. In the normal course of events, he is immortal."

"As you are?"

The idea seems to amuse her. "Not in the least. My spirit lingers here because I will it so, but my body—of which I was quite fond, by the way—is long gone. No, Mordred and his kind are entirely different from any who know death. They don't live in the shadow of the scaffold, the sword always descending toward their necks."

My stomach tightens. I know far too well what she means and yet I perceive that she is speaking of much more than my private fears.

"You are saying that to be human is to know the inevitably of death?"

"Oh, more than that. It is to know life as a flash of lightning against a darkening sky. We exist and are gone—*poof.* However much we suffer in the world or whatever joy may come to us, we know at the core of our being that we are tiny and insignificant. Yet we are driven to become so much more."

"Surely," I venture, "God determines what we are?"

Morgaine shrugs, as though what I believe is of no great import compared to what truly is.

"God—in any form—gives you the gift of creation but it is up to you how well you use it. Mordred has convinced himself that he can rule England and eventually the world without any real harm to humans. Of course, you will have to be fed upon by the ever-growing legions of vampires that he intends to create. But in return for that, he will free you from all pain, all suffering, all need to strive or dream. You will be so drained of spirit, so lulled into lethargy, as to be as lowing cattle content to chew your cuds even as the blade slices through your necks."

My mind reels, not because I cannot grasp what she is saying, but precisely because I can. Too clearly, I remember the empty gazes and vacuous smiles of the laudanum users. A handful of such fools is regrettable but no real danger. A few hundred, even thousands, are a different matter. And a world of them . . . all of humankind drenched in apathy, daring nothing, achieving nothing . . .

"How can I stop him?"

Morgaine hesitates long enough for me to realize that I am asking her how to accomplish what she herself could not. Granted, she did Mordred such damage as has required a thousand years to heal. But she did not destroy him. If I cannot do better, his victory will merely have been postponed, not denied.

"You will prevail," Morgaine says, "if you avoid the mistake that I made."

"The mistake?"

She looks away for a moment, out over the rolling hills illuminated by light that seems to come from everywhere and nowhere. The mournful caw of a raven drifts across the sky.

"I loved him . . . from the beginning when we were both children and right to the very end, when I struck the blow that should have killed him. I have had a thousand years to come to terms with the fact that when I unleashed that blow, I held back just enough to assure that I would fail. That is why he won."

"You were defeated by love?" It seems a frivolous notion considering how great the matter that hangs upon it. Yet do not people say that love makes fools of all men—and women, too? Pride, dignity, honor, even the most basic sense of survival, seem to fly out the door when the heart lets love come in.

"You doubt it?" Morgaine asks. "You think I should have been stronger, and I would not disagree. But think of this, Elizabeth. Unless you guard yourself with the utmost vigilance, the same can happen to you."

"But I do not love Mordred." Never mind how drawn I have felt to him. That is lust, troubling in its own way but not remotely what Morgaine is describing. "I never knew him as you did, before he became what he is. From the moment of our first meeting, he has been my enemy."

I could add, but do not, that I have even more reason now to think of him as my foe. By his doing, my mother came to be suspected of adultery and, worse, of witchcraft. I cannot be certain that he led her into such a thicket of danger deliberately, believing that she would have no choice but to turn to him. Yet neither can I discount that possibility. In the end, it does not matter. He made her vulnerable and for that I can never forgive him.

"He will try to convince you that he is your ally," Morgaine warns. "Even your best, if not your only, hope. He will tempt you with what no one else can offer—protection for England and yourself, and more. If you give him everything he wants, he will make you immortal."

"Did he offer all that to you?"

"Oh, yes, and I was very tempted. But in the end, I chose to stand against him, or at least so I believed. Because I did not recognize the weakness within myself, I failed and have kept this lonely vigil ever since, waiting for the one who will not falter as I did."

"Believe me, I will not." I make this vow with all my heart. Whatever lay between Mordred and Morgaine, it has nothing to do with me. I will steel myself against him, make fast all my defenses, and from behind the strong walls of my queenly state, I will strike him such a blow as to be certain that he will never rise again.

He will shatter, light on the wind, and be gone forever.

So I am resolved, but as with any great enterprise, practical matters must be considered. I turn to the most important of them first.

"Is there a way to increase my power more quickly and without suffering such ill effects as I have experienced?"

Slowly, never taking her eyes from me, Morgaine nods. When she speaks, I listen with the greatest possible attentiveness.

What did they talk about, there on the hilltop above the ruins of old
Londinium? Morgaine and I used to scamper among those tumbled
walls, trying to imagine the giants who had built them. Did she tell
Elizabeth about that or did they speak of other things?

I have my suspicions, of course, but I cannot claim to know for
certain. From my perch on the far side of the altar window outside
St. Peter ad Vincula, I could see the two of them but faintly through
the veil of time. Frankly, I was astonished that Elizabeth had managed to pierce it so readily, but Morgaine may have helped her. They
were two of a kind in some ways, although I had yet to fully realize
that.

The insufferable Robert Dudley was lurking toward the back of
the chapel where Elizabeth had bade him stay, a good dog heeding his
mistress's command. What could she possibly have seen in him that
made her trust him so? A queen of such intelligence and strength
should have known better, but truly, who can fathom the mind of a
woman, much less her heart? He paced back and forth, looking anxiously toward the grave beside which Elizabeth stood, her lips moving
as though she were at prayer.

Except that she was not. On the other side of the veil—Morgaine's
side—she was talking all right, but above all, she was listening.

What did Morgaine tell her?

Whatever it was, it took long enough. Dudley became impatient.
After several false starts, he strode halfway down the aisle only to

think better of it and retreat back toward the door, where he resumed his incessant pacing. I was almost reconciled to wasting the entire night trying to determine what she was up to when the mist surrounding Elizabeth suddenly vanished and she was back on this side of the veil.

She looked exhilarated, which could not possibly bode well. Worse yet, she had an air of implacable resolution about her that reminded me all too much of Morgaine. Once my beloved conceived of an idea, it was impossible to dissuade her of it.

Dudley, who had been looking more whipped and worried by the moment, snapped to as she approached. She gave him a smile that could only be called incandescent—which he most certainly did not deserve—and strode right past him out into the night. He followed at her heels, yapping about something.

To her credit, she ignored him and made straight for her horse. Or at least she did until he dug his heels in, grasped her arm, and turned her to him.

Bad dog!

In her newly awakened state, Elizabeth's senses were too keen for me to risk venturing closer. I could contrive for her not to see me, but I suspected she would feel my presence all the same. Hovering as near as I dared, I strained to hear what they were saying.

"What happened?" Dudley demanded. "Why did you come here?"

For a moment, I thought she would reprimand his impertinence. But instead she touched a gloved hand gently to his cheek.

"My poor Robin. Are you feeling ill-used? I would not have that for the world."

Staring at her, he shook his head. I swear that I heard its scant contents rattle.

"Of course not, beloved. I care only for your welfare, which is always uppermost in my mind."

If by uppermost he meant right beside his constant scheming to re-store his treacherous family to the wealth and power they had squan-dered in disloyalty, then I suppose he spoke truly enough. She could not possibly be so deluded as to believe him.

She kissed him. Right there in front of the guards, who affected blindness even as their eyes bulged. She raised herself on her toes, brushed her fingers through his hair, drew him to her, and kissed him long and deeply.

A thousand years, beyond even the measure of Methuselah, and still I could not comprehend what passes for reason in a female. Was she merely amusing herself or was it possible that her feelings for Dudley truly ran that deep? Could she truly be so shallow as to be drawn to a weak-minded, contemptible villein better suited to walk behind an ox plowing fields than dare to lift his eyes to a queen?

So distracted was I in contemplating that mystery that I lost track altogether of whatever it was that she and Morgaine had found to talk about.

Ultimately, I would remember that to my regret, but by then it would be too late.

*20 January 1559*

---

*I* kissed Robin because Morgaine's tale of what her love for Mordred had cost her reminded me of how glad I should be to have so loyal and willing a man who never, ever would burden me with the slightest fear or loss.

And because I am Queen and may do as I wish . . . if only occasionally.

And because returning to the world from the netherworld where Morgaine and I met reminded me of the pleasures to be found here, sprinkled though they may be amid the trials and tribulations of life.

But as I take the heat of his mouth, savoring his taste and scent, I remember what Morgaine told me. The only way to gain sufficient power to stand against Mordred is to do what she had realized through the most painful experience—kill not merely any vampire that came my way but the most powerful vampires I could find and defeat.

Until she told me that, it had not occurred to me that one kill would be different from any other, but with hindsight, it makes perfect sense. The only problem that remains is how to find those most worth killing.

Even as dawn comes and I am trapped once again in the pantomime of queenship, I ponder how to accomplish what I must. Kat hovers near, watching me with concern. I know she wants me to tell her what I discovered in my mother's letter, but I cannot bring myself to do so. She is too good a woman to be burdened with knowledge of the danger that afflicts us.

Robin is another matter. Either he knows me less well than Kat, despite all we have shared, or he is undeterred by what he must surely recognize is my reluctance to talk of what happened in the chapel. All day he remains close, watching me with intentness surely designed to draw the notice of the court as well as my own. Having only just restored him to my favor, I cannot dismiss him nor would I wish to do so. His presence soothes me even as I weigh how much I am willing to reveal my thoughts to him or anyone else. I am only just recognizing that to be queen is to be alone in a sense that ordinary mortals, even those of exalted state, will never know.

Ever since my encounter with Morgaine, a strange energy has filled me. It carries me through the day's interminable round of appearances and celebrations, into the inevitable banquet, and on to the only part of the day I can truly say that I enjoy, the dancing.

I am at once elated and on edge, certain as I am that I stand on a precipice from which there is no retreating. I will fall or I will soar. The coming days, or more probably the nights, will determine which it shall be.

In flight from the image of myself lying crumbled and broken on the sharp rocks of failure, I lift a hand to summon Robin to my side. At the same moment I call out, "Play lavolta!"

The court applauds but no one else takes the floor as the music begins. This is my and Robin's dance, the only chance we have to truly be ourselves before others. Let heads bend together in eager speculation; let foreign ambassadors whose masters would presume to wed and rule me grimace in dismay; let Cecil scowl fiercely. Fie on them and all the world. Robin's hands are strong at my waist; he lifts me with ease. I float above him and the world on the music and my own laughter.

Looking up at me, he smiles boldly and whispers for my ears alone, "How I adore you, Elizabeth! Truly, you are the sun in my sky and the stars in my heaven."

When he lowers me, our bodies brush against one another in silent promise of the intimacy to come when all the world is held at bay and only the two of us are adrift on the island that is my bed.

But not this night, for there, sidling up beside Cecil, comes Walsingham, the black-garbed schoolmaster. They exchange a word. Cecil responds with what appears to be a sharp question. Walsingham smiles with the benign patience of a man who knows his worth, or at least the worth of the information he commands.

Robin lifts me again. Over his head, I meet my Spirit's gaze and see in his eyes that the pleasures of the evening are at an end. I have had my tiny taste of what it is to be a young woman with no thought but for love. It is time once again to be Queen.

We meet in my withdrawing room—Robin, Cecil, Walsingham, and Dee, the magus appearing as though from the ether, though I suspect he has more likely been making use of the library my father assembled from the pillaged manuscripts of the churches he destroyed, which are said to contain many secrets. Whatever Dee has found there still seems to have a grip on him; he appears distant and preoccupied.

I have no interest in his esoteric meanderings. Far more practical concerns beckon.

"What have you learned?" I demand of the schoolmaster, for truly I am in no mood for pleasantries.

Nor, it seems, is he.

"The rumors regarding Southwark Manor appear to have some substance, Majesty. In addition, I believe that the record of ownership there has been obscured deliberately."

Cecil does not hide his surprise. "You have not been able to discover who owns a manor of significance so close to the seat of government? A former possession of no less than the Archbishop of York? How is that possible?"

Walsingham sketches a small bow suggestive of apology without actually offering any. "Given the"—he pauses delicately— "the recent disorder, it is easier than it has been in centuries to transfer property without due attention to legalities. This is far from the first such case that I have seen, although, I must admit, it appears to be the most elaborate and effective."

"Surely," Robin says, "that is indicative of a sinister force at work, is it not?"

Before Walsingham can reply, Dee appears to awaken from whatever has so preoccupied him. He blinks owlishly and strokes the beard that I suspect he cultivates to make him appear wise beyond his years. But then perhaps he truly is so.

"You may be right, my lord. I have been making my own inquiries in my own way. It seems that there is more to Southwark Manor than may appear. The estate is extremely old. Although there are gaps in the record, large gaps as Mister Walsingham has said, I believe the lands were part of an Anglo-Roman property dating back as far as the age of Arthur."

"What does that matter?" Cecil asks, but I scarcely hear him. I already know the answer. The manor has some significance to Mordred. Perhaps he lived there, on the opposite side of the river from the place that Morgaine called home. As in eternity she sought what was dear and familiar to her, Mordred might seek the same in this world he aspires to rule.

I reach for the cloak thrown over my chair. Instincts I have long since learned to trust urge me to action. Morgaine has shown me how I can prevail, but that knowledge will do me no good unless I am strong enough for the task. Swiftly, before

Mordred realizes what I am doing, I must find and kill the most powerful vampire possible. Where better to find my prey than among his court?

"We are going there," I say.

Cecil looks alarmed. "Now? Is that wise?"

"It is if Her Majesty says that it is," Robin declares. Clearly, he is determined not to be found guilty of presumption again. However, that does not stop him from having an opinion.

"On the other hand, if Her Majesty prefers, I will go alone and through cunning and subterfuge discover what is afoot there."

Cecil snorts, but before he can comment, Dee intervenes. "With all respect, Lord Dudley, that would not be wise."

Anger flashes across Robin's face. His temper is formidable but the dangers and difficulties that afflicted his life from a tender age have schooled him to mask his feelings from all save me. I, alone, know his heart. Indeed, I possess it.

"Why do you say that, magus?" he asks with false calm.

"Because if the manor is indeed a nesting place for vampires, you will make a tasty snack for them."

For a moment, I fear that Robin will erupt with rage at so great an offense to his honor. No lord of such prowess in the lists and on the field of battle could tolerate such a slight. So certain am I that he will strike at Dee that I move to insert myself between them.

I needn't have bothered. With a visible effort of will, Robin keeps control of himself, if only just.

Through gritted teeth, he asks, "Then what do you propose, magus?"

"That we accompany Her Majesty but do not hinder her."

I would prefer to go alone but I cannot yet contrive how to cross the Thames and make my way through Southwark without assistance. Queen of the realm, slayer of vampires, I have never ventured of my own volition anywhere without retainers and guards. For that matter, not only have I never handled the coin needed to hire a wherryman, I have no idea where to lay my hands on it.

I could ask Walsingham, of course, but I suspect that the schoolmaster would find some way to deny me. He is ambitious, as are they all, and the best route to realized ambition is to stay as close as possible to the source of power.

"Well enough, but once we attain the manor, I will proceed alone." Robin opens his mouth to object but I forestall him. "It is my intent to draw Mordred into a ruse of my making that will give me the strength I need to defeat him. If you interfere, my plan will fail and we will lose our best chance to drive this scourge from our realm."

"How do you intend to accomplish this miracle?" Robin demands. His relief at being returned to my favor seems to be wearing off swiftly.

"That is my affair. If you prefer, you may remain here."

"Don't be ridiculous."

My breath catches. As a woman, I am struck by his sudden disparagement. But far more critically, as Queen I cannot possibly tolerate such presumption without risking the disrespect of all those around me. Worse yet, Robin knows this.

I step away from him, drawing myself to my full height, and bestow on him what I hope is a sufficiently regal glare. "Lord Dudley, your injury in the list is affecting you more than I realized. You have my permission to withdraw."

He takes a step toward me, his gaze commanding mine. A pulse beats in the shadow of his jaw. Deliberately, he challenges me. "I am entirely fit, I assure you."

I grasp my skirts tightly in both hands, the better that I may not pummel him. His strength and will that I so enjoy in the bedchamber have no place here and now. Is this the price he wishes to exact for the pleasure he gives me? Have I been a fool to trust him?

Ice etches my response. "You are mistaken, my lord. In fact, I would say that your condition is worsening by the moment. Withdraw while you still may."

Cecil, realizing the extent of my anger as Robin apparently is incapable of doing, grasps his arm and attempts to draw him toward the door. Under his breath, he murmurs, "Do as Her Majesty says, Lord Dudley, or it will go the worst for you."

When a man speaks to him, Robin seems to awaken suddenly to what is happening. He pales and stammers an apology, but I ignore him. If there is to be a reckoning between us, better that it wait. In my present mood, I may do something irreparable.

Cecil urges Robin from the room and, to my satisfaction, shuts the door in his face. I imagine him standing on the other side, wondering—I hope—if this time he has truly cast himself into the outer darkness permanently. In my heart, I know that he is growing impatient to take what he believes to be his rightful place at my side. I can never permit that, but how long can I keep him suspended in a state of unfulfilled hope before I risk losing him altogether?

It is a problem for another time. Just then, I am almost glad to have Mordred to divert me. The vampire who threatens my realm seems less challenging to deal with than does the lover who demands more than I can ever give.

And so we four—Cecil, Walsingham, Dee, and I—cross the Thames bundled tightly against the chill night. I keep my head tucked down not only to avoid the wherryman's curious glances but also because an icy rain descends on us, bringing more

misery than the deepest snow ever can. Mercifully, halfway
across it stops, but the cold continues to bite bone deep as we
scurry up the bankside.

This time we do not tarry near St. Savior's but continue directly up the High Street toward Southwark Manor. As before,
the area is strangely quiet. Nary a whore nor beggar is in evidence. Several of the inns and taverns we pass have their shutters drawn, although from behind them I catch glimpses of
light. As we pass, a door opens and someone peers out, only to
quickly retreat back inside.

The High Street climbs following the contours of the hill
that rises above the river. Near the top, the bear- and bull-
baiting rings lie shrouded in darkness. I hear the sleepy snuf-
fling of the animals kept penned below them and smell the
copper stink of old blood on the air.

The manor lies behind stone walls so high that only the
chimneys can be seen from the road. A tall iron gate bars entrance to a wide drive lined by ancient oaks. Mullioned windows are aglow with light. Whoever dwells within keeps late
hours.

I expect that the gate will be secured and that I will have to
contrive some way to get through it, but when I press my hand
tentatively against one side of the iron scrollwork, hinges creak.
The gate swings open just wide enough to admit me.

For a moment, I hesitate but the matter is of too great import
to let any personal consideration, including concern for my
own safety, dictate my actions. Having come so far, I must go
the whole way.

"Follow the course of the walls," I instruct the others, "and
discover whatever you can about this place, but on penalty of
my greatest displeasure, do not attempt to venture within. I will
meet you all back here."

"How long do you think you will be, Majesty?" Cecil is pale with fear, but whether for himself or me, I cannot say.

"I have no way of knowing, but if I have not emerged by day-light, return to Whitehall. Do all you can to cast obscurity over my absence and deflect all rumor. I will rejoin you as swiftly as I can."

Unspoken among us is the realization that I may not return at all, in which case it will fall to Cecil to deal as best he can with the chaos that will follow. I regret afflicting my Spirit with such a fraught task, but I can think of no man better able to carry it out should the need arise.

As though he knows the content of my mind, Dee says, "Have no fear, Majesty. The stars show clearly that your path continues on far beyond this night."

I believe him, of course, but I also believe that nothing in what the stars reveal to us is inevitable. The destinies they blaze across the heavens come to pass through the agency of our own will. I can only pray that mine proves equal to the challenge I am about to face as I slip through the iron gate and enter the ancient grounds of Southwark Manor.

———

*M*oonlight slips through skeletal branches that arch above the drive leading to a large stone house with three wings, all built in the style popular during my father's reign and still much in fashion. The exterior walls sweep up three stories to a gabled roof. Above the center wing, a tower rises dark against the night sky. At the very top, behind round oriel windows, I can just make out the flicker of lamps.

Clutching my cloak tightly, I proceed with as much confidence as I can muster. My steps crunch over the hard-packed snow that covers the drive, unmarred by a single footstep. An icy fog drifts in tendrils across the ground. With hindsight, my plan of going on alone appears less than well conceived. However much I do not want to be distracted by concern for Cecil, Dee, or Walsingham, I would welcome their company as I pass through shadows into silvered light, all my senses painfully alive. For that matter, I would even welcome Robin's pretended deference as he busies himself attempting to order my life.

But I am alone, with only my mother's and Morgaine's courage to guide me. When an owl hoots nearby, I startle and for a moment forget to breathe. My heart hammers against my ribs. I should be cold for the night bears the sting of the north in a thousand pinpricks that assail the skin, but I am heedless of any such discomfort. Indeed, my blood runs hot as I begin to feel the power growing nearer with each step I take.

A wide stone terrace leads to double doors of oak bound by iron. I pause, listening intently. I can make out voices, laughter, and music. Someone is playing the virginal and doing it quite well. Others are singing, their voices melding in perfect harmony.

I would be hard-pressed to say what I expected to find, but this is not it. I stand in darkness, all but pressing my nose against a window, and peer into a world of light and warmth. A fire roars in a vast hearth on the far side of the large room. Golden candelabra hanging from the ceiling glow with the light of a hundred pure white tapers. The music is clearer now; it sounds like a chorus of angels, but that is far from the greatest surprise. The beings—what else can I call them?—at home within that sumptuous chamber are the most beautiful I have ever seen. Dressed more exquisitely than the most elegant of my courtiers, they appear uniformly young and physically perfect. Male and female alike, they are quite simply stunning. Their jewels and cloth of gold, the deeply rich velvets and finely sheened silks that adorn them, are all eclipsed by their own insurmountable beauty.

I am still contemplating how this can possibly be—for surely God would not gift creatures of the dark with such unearthly loveliness without some purpose—when a faint sound alerts me that I am no longer alone. I turn swiftly, intent on defending myself, only to freeze when I behold Mordred, lounging against the wall that runs around the terrace. He wears black—velvet, I think, and a fine wool—with a splash of silk shot through with thread of silver at his throat. Despite the cold, he is without a cloak, but then I suppose he has no need, the chill becomes him so.

He looks at me with amusement and pleasure and something more I do not care to recognize, for it appears perilously close to the hunger I know too well myself.

"Elizabeth, what an unexpected delight. But there is no reason for you to be hovering out here alone. Come inside and join the festivities."

*Alone.* Does he use that word deliberately to underscore my vulnerability. Or because he senses the burden of solitude I have known since becoming Queen? He is, after all, a king in his own right. How has he managed in so long a time not to be crushed by the weight of rulership? For a moment, I am tempted to ask him. Only refusal to acknowledge any common ground between us stops me.

He extends his hand in invitation. "Allow me to introduce you to the others. I think you will find them . . . interesting."

At that instant, I want nothing in the world more. To be a part of such youth and beauty, such gaiety and careless ease . . . the thought is irresistible. But I stand with my feet firmly planted on the snowy ground and I will not allow myself to forget the purpose for which I have come.

"By all means. If I am to weigh what you offer, I must learn all I can of you and your kind."

He stares at me and I am suddenly afraid that he sees beyond the mask of queenship to the woman within. If his vision is as penetrating as it appears, he must surely know that I remain sorely tempted to accept his proposal even as I am determined not to do so. The battle raging within me seems almost to eclipse that which I must win against him. Yet he gives no sign that he is aware of either my weakness or my treachery.

Instead, he merely says, "You surprise me."

I allow myself a small exhalation of relief. If he truly is taken unawares, so much the better. Perhaps my mad plan can succeed after all.

I reach out, taking the hand he offers. His touch is warm, almost comforting, and entirely pleasant. I sense neither evil nor danger. Indeed, I feel as safe as I did when I soared in his arms on the night we first met. But beneath the void where fear should be lurks a faint awareness that I see him as I do because he wills it, and that, should his desires change, so shall my experience of him. This genial manner is only one more mask among the uncountable others that he, I, and all of us wear.

"Come then," he says, his smile deepening. He tucks my hand into the crook of his arm and covers it with his, moving close. I feel my body drawn to his for safety. Together, we walk through the wide doors that have suddenly swung open as though at his silent command.

An odd figure waits just within, wearing what looks like a monk's hooded robe that completely conceals its form, including its face. It stands, hands tucked into its sleeves, head bent in obeisance. Mordred ignores it and continues on, drawing me ever closer to him.

We pass through the antechamber hung with ancient banners and shields that appear to have survived many battles. Beyond lies the great hall I have seen through the window. But before we go there, Mordred draws me aside.

"What do you know of this place?" he asks.

I let his arm drop and move a little way off, trying to take in as much of my surroundings as possible. Everything I see— paintings, furnishings, wall hangings, carpets—bespeaks both wealth and taste. Much of it strikes me as far older than the building in which we stand.

"I know that you bought Southwark Manor from the Archbishop of York, who I have to assume had no idea whom he was selling to. I know also that the manor has existed for far longer than is commonly recognized. Did you live here as a boy?"

He shows no surprise at my knowledge but answers forth-rightly, "I was born on this land. My mother was of an old Anglo-Roman family who had held the estate for centuries. It was a good alliance for Arthur, good enough for him to overlook that she was pagan. They were wed according to the old rites. Later, when he found it convenient to do so, that allowed him to deny my legitimacy."

"I am sorry." The words are out before I can stop them, but I should not be surprised by my own candor. I, above all, under-stand what it is like to be rejected by a parent.

"When his union with the Christian Guinevere proved barren," Mordred says, "Arthur found it necessary to acknowl-edge me as his son. Had he any better alternative, I am certain that he would have taken it."

As my father would have if he had been able to contrive any other way to secure the Tudor succession beyond my brother, Edward, who reigned so briefly, and my sister. I was his last, most desperate gamble for the continuance of his line. Did he ever consider that by his own actions he had assured that I would choose barrenness over subjugation to any hus-band?

"It seems neither of us was what our fathers wanted."

Quietly, so that I have to strain a little to hear him, Mordred says, "At least your mother loved you."

I freeze momentarily. "Do you truly wish to discuss her?"

"Why not? I am sure that by now you have questions."

Does he know then of Anne's letter? Could he possibly be

aware that I have found Morgaine? Whatever prompts his willingness to bring up so delicate a matter, I decide to take full advantage of it. To begin with, I will test his truthfulness.

"How would you characterize your dealings with Anne?"

"Plainly and simply, I tried to keep her alive. To my great sorrow, despite her undeniable intelligence and courage, she could not see beyond the superstitions of her faith. She chose death and in so doing almost condemned you to the same."

That is a slur I cannot leave unanswered. "She left me well protected."

He lifts a brow. "Who told you that? Your so-called magus, Dee, or perhaps it was the one you call your Spirit, both pretending knowledge of matters far beyond their ken?"

"Yet here I am." My continued existence on this earth is all the proof I need that the mother who I now know truly loved me did everything she could to keep me alive.

"You are here," Mordred says, "because each time your life has been in peril, I have taken steps to preserve it."

So audacious is this claim that I cannot help but gasp. "Surely, you do not expect me to believe you?"

"Believe what you will, but know this: After your mother's death, certain high lords sought to convince your father that your continued existence was a threat to the children he was certain to have with his new queen. They hoped to gain his approval to end your life quietly. He did not give it, not right then, but neither did he reprimand them for suggesting so vile an act. I did away with them before they could persuade him."

"What lords?" I demand even as my stomach tightens. Kat

has never spoken to me of such matters, but I knew in the way that children do that some terrible fear weighed down on her when I was very young.

Mordred names them—great lords all, all long dead. All men that I know were my mother's implacable enemies and apparently mine.

"I still do not believe you." I cannot bear to. It is hard enough to accept that my father killed my mother, but that he would also have sanctioned the death of his own helpless child . . .

"The threat to you did not end with him. Three times during your sister Mary's reign, emissaries were sent from Spain and the Pope to convince her to execute you. They were all highly persuasive men who understood her mind very well. Any one of them could have succeeded, but none ever reached these shores alive."

Again, I know that Mary was tempted to do away with me but I have assumed that it was sisterly love that stayed her hand. Am I to believe now that I live only because those who would have persuaded her to kill me never reached her side?

"Why would you go to such lengths on my behalf when I am a danger to you and all your kind?"

Mordred shrugs. "I saw the strength in you from tenderest childhood. I sensed the woman you could become. Admittedly, I had no idea at the time that another with Morgaine's power would ever walk this earth again, much less that it would be you. However, had I known, be assured that I would not have acted differently. On the contrary, the forces that have awakened in you make it all the clearer that you and I are meant to be allies and more."

I choose my words with care, determined as I am to lull him into a false sense of confidence.

"Surely some would say that we are destined to be enemies?"

"They would be fools to do so. The power you possess makes you a formidable slayer, that is true, but it also can make you the greatest of us all. Greater even than me."

He is lying, he must be, trying to seduce me with visions of my own invincibility. I cannot succumb to them for all that they present a formidable temptation. I must remember who I am and why I am there.

In battle, the greatest advantage is to be gained from surprise.

"Has it occurred to you that I have an entirely personal reason for wanting to kill you, one that has nothing to do with the protection of this realm?"

He starts slightly and stares at me. "I cannot conceive of what that would be."

A shiver ripples through me. I can feel his closeness almost as though we were actually touching. A current of energy flows between us, heating the air through which it passes and threatening at any moment to burst into flame.

How is it possible for a creature of his kind to look so entirely, so genuinely beautiful and innocent? I must struggle to remember what he truly is and what harm he has done.

"You tempted my mother into trusting you in order to make her all the more vulnerable and force her to accede to your demands to save her own life. How disappointed you must have been when she chose death rather than promise me to you."

He tilts his head slightly and looks at me. I fancy that I can see the reflected glow of candles burning behind the dark shadows of his eyes. "Is that really what you think? That I conspired at her death? Believe me, there was no need for me to do so. Your father was determined that she should die. Nothing on earth could have saved her, short of his own demise."

"He had no reason to want her dead. A divorce would have sufficed."

Mordred's sigh hovers between frustration and regret. "You truly don't understand, do you? Your mother led your father a pretty chase for *eight* long years, denying him her bed when almost any other woman would have welcomed him gladly. Indeed, more than a few did, including her own sister. But he would have none other than her in his heart. She was his holy grail, the chalice that would produce the longed-for son who would carry the Tudor name into the future. For her, he remade the world, and what did he get in return?"

My throat is tight, I can scarcely speak. "Me."

"Precisely. God denied your father what he wanted most and used your mother to do it. In Henry's mind, the fault had to lie with Anne. The only other possible explanation was that Henry himself had incurred the Almighty's disfavor."

"Even if he believed it was her fault, he did not have to kill her. He could have spared her, let her live in honorable retirement as he had Anne of Cleves. He could have allowed us to be together."

"For pity's sake, Elizabeth, your mother's death was the blood sacrifice your father made to regain his god's favor. When your brother, Edward, was born a year later, Henry took it as a sign that the Almighty was pleased with what he had done. He basked in the glow of that pleasure the rest of his life."

Too vividly, I see my mother mount the scaffold, lay her head on the block, see the swordsman draw his blade, see it cleave the air, and then the blood . . . so much blood flowing into the earth. Blood of my blood, life of my life, my beginning and, unless I am fortunate indeed, my end. The image makes me tremble.

"What you are suggesting is a perversion of our faith, a rejection of the God who loves and forgives us our sins. It is monstrous."

"Men become monsters when the fear of their own mortality overtakes everything else. Only those of us who are free of the shadow of death can cultivate all that is good and pure in ourselves."

How easily he casts himself in the light of the angels! I could say that men also become monsters when they put their own needs above those of all others. But that would not serve my purpose.

"You tried to convince my mother of that?"

He nods. "As I said, her faith prevented her from seeing it. She went to her death in the name of the selfsame god your royal father sought to placate with her blood."

My heart twists with pain so great that it is all I can do not to weep. I am the anointed representative of that same God, Queen of this realm in accordance with His will. How can I serve that which doubly slew my mother?

How can I not?

The music coming from the great hall grows in power. For a moment, my wounded spirit is in danger of being swept away. Perhaps Mordred senses my susceptibility for he offers me a dazzling smile and once again extends his hand.

"In simple fairness, Elizabeth, at least see for yourself who and what we are."

I could not ask for a better opportunity to persuade him that what he has sought for so long is within his grasp. My power wedded to his, England his to rule, its enemies crushed by his will, and beyond all that an entire world waiting to be fed upon by his kind as the light of humanity flickers out and is extinguished.

Only let him believe that and I will have what I need to destroy this trickster king who drenches all my senses in desire and tempts me so dangerously.

But before all that I must survive the heady surge of excitement that sweeps over me as Mordred leads me into the hall and I see for the first time the full otherworldly beauty of the vampire court.

Of course, I was not entirely blind to Elizabeth's intent. At the least, I knew that she had mixed reasons for coming to me. Curiosity no doubt played its part, but more important so did the desire that I felt coursing in her each time we touched, desire I fully reciprocated. Still, it took rare courage to do as she had done, which suggested that she had a higher purpose. Hope swelled in me that she truly was on the verge of accepting my proposal.

As I stepped into the great hall with her on my arm, I indulged the pleasant fantasy that she was already my queen, ruling at my side. England was safe and at peace, her enemies crushed. The kindred were strong, growing in number, poised to move into the larger world.

Still wearing her cloak sodden with melting snow and ice, her face so pale as to make her hair appear as a nimbus of flame, she trembled slightly. I could not blame her. The lords and ladies of my court fell silent at our entrance. As one, they turned to stare at her. A dozen were missing of our number, those she had killed. The remainder knew her for a Slayer, a being who had not been seen in a thousand years, beyond the measure of any of their lives. She was the stuff of legend . . . and terror.

No doubt she feared how she would be received but there was no reason for her to do so. My presence beside her, the manner in which I presented her, lifting her hand high, and the firmness of my tone when I spoke told my subjects what I expected of them.

"*Behold, Elizabeth Regina, Queen of these isles and my honored guest. She is welcome among us.*"

I released her hand, moved behind her, and removed her cloak. She wore a gown of golden brocade embroidered with pearls over an overskirt of deep blue velvet that complemented her eyes, simple by the ornate standards of her official appearances but effective all the same.

Polite applause rang out, hardly unfettered in enthusiasm but sufficient to my purpose. Elizabeth inclined her head regally. I took her hand again and escorted her farther into the hall. A passage opened before us, framed on either side by bowing courtiers. At the far end, on a dais raised beside the hearth, I had caused a second chair to be placed next to my own in signal of my intent to take a queen. Blanche had made it clear that she wanted to claim that position as her own, but she knew better than to test my authority. Even so, she hovered close and glared at Elizabeth, who took no notice of her. She was far too occupied looking in all directions, trying to take in everything at once.

"*I will value your opinion of our music,*" I said as I seated her. "*Several of my subjects are quite skilled in that regard.*"

Elizabeth sat without allowing her back to touch the chair. I followed her gaze out over my court, trying to see it as she did. In all modesty, my kind cannot be surpassed for beauty and elegance, and with centuries to devote to the cultivation of skills, a certain proficiency is expected whether in the arts, gambling, or whatever the chosen field.

After a flurry of cautious glances in her direction, my courtiers resumed their pursuits. Dice flew, the music soared, and the usual flirtations were pursued. I was glad to see that the latter were restrained by a certain decorum not usually in evidence. We are sensual beings inclined to indulge our carnal natures and indulgent of those around us who are doing the same, but that night care was taken not to shock Elizabeth too much. A degree of preening and posturing did go on, no doubt to draw her attention, but there was no overt hostility.

A thrall approached bearing a pair of Venetian glass goblets that contained a rich burgundy that I favored. I took both and gracefully handed one to Elizabeth.

As our fingers touched, I said, "I believe you will find the vintage worthy of your palate."

She took a sip and followed the thrall with her eyes as it resumed its position against the wall.

"What is that?" she asked.

"What is what?"

"The . . . servant who brought the wine."

I shrugged dismissively. "Oh, that. We call them thralls. Do not trouble yourself with them. What do you think of the wine?"

"It is . . . pleasing. Do they all conceal their faces?"

"They are of no account, Elizabeth. Forget them."

But it was clear that she could not. After a moment, she said, "I would find it disturbing to be served by people whose faces I could not see."

"Whereas I prefer menial servants to be as unobtrusive as possible."

That should have settled the matter but she continued to stare at the thrall a little longer before finally looking away. Her interest in the creature irked me. I wanted her to think only of me . . . and of my kind as well, of course, of all she could find among us.

Blanche must have sensed my darkening humor. Garbed in shimmering white, her ebony hair cascading down her back, she approached the dais but waited for a nod from me before making her curtsy to Elizabeth.

"May I present the Lady Blanche," I said. "She is among the most trusted and beloved of my subjects."

Blanche straightened and smiled. She looked very well that night, I will admit, but then she always did.

"*Dear Queen,*" she said, "*how honored we are to have you among us.*"

Elizabeth studied her cautiously. I watched as the perception of a monarch changed to that of a young woman a little uncertain about her own looks, confronted by an experienced beauty of sensuality and sophistication.

"*Lady Blanche . . . forgive my curiosity, but have you been long in service to your king?*"

"*I have, Majesty. It has been three centuries since I was freed from the shadow of death. My gratitude for my liberation is boundless. I am devoted to my lord's service in every way.*"

Elizabeth raised a brow, but whatever else she thought of this declaration, she was distracted by her discovery of Blanche's age.

Gazing at skin so smooth, hair so luxuriant, a figure so perfect as to belong to a woman no older than herself, Elizabeth passed her tongue over her lips.

"*Three hundred years?*"

"*Indeed, Majesty. In that time, I have gained beyond measure in experience and wisdom.*"

"*How fortunate for you . . . and for Lord Mordred, whom you serve so well.*"

Blanche bristled at the hint of sarcasm. I felt the power rising in her and sought to quell it with a glance. She ignored me, her gaze fastened on Elizabeth.

"*I am of a noble lineage, Majesty. My family served this realm with valor and distinction, even at great cost to themselves. Though they are long gone from this world, I honor them still.*"

Elizabeth nodded slowly. "*Surely your power is greater than theirs could ever be?*"

Blanche smile, mollified. "*You are correct, Majesty. Indeed, as a Slayer, I suspect that you can sense my strength.*"

"*I certainly sense something,*" Elizabeth replied, a little tartly I thought, but then Blanche's mention of my guest's proclivity for slaying our kind was hardly tactful.

I stood and, with my hand outstretched, silently bid Elizabeth do the same. "Allow me to introduce you to more of my kind, and perhaps you would enjoy joining in some of their activities."

Blanche stood aside to let us pass but not without a mocking smile. I drew Elizabeth away as hastily as decorum allowed while reminding myself to have a word with Blanche. She would have to rein in whatever jealousy she felt once Elizabeth became my queen.

By all appearances, Elizabeth was fascinated by my court. She inclined her head graciously to everyone she met and only gasped a little when several lofted into the air for a better view of her. I watched her watching them and was well pleased. Her eyes gleamed with fascination and the delectable pulse beating in her throat quickened. After a second goblet of the excellent burgundy, she even agreed to play a tune on the lute, for which I will say she had a pretty hand. Applause rang out again but this time accompanied by cheers.

When she was finished, she turned to me. "How enthralling this all is. I had no idea that you lived in any such way."

"What did you imagine," I asked with a smile, "that we lie about in crypts or hang from the ceiling like bats?"

She laughed and I joined her, so good was my humor. Seduction finds so many paths—the pleasures of the flesh, of course, most especially when combined with the promise of eternal youth. But for some individuals—and I believed that Elizabeth was one of them— safety and security are the greatest treasures to be desired. I told myself that she would find both and more within my court. She would find a home.

It was on the tip of my tongue to ask her there and then if she had come to a decision. Perhaps she sensed that for she moved to forestall me.

"Most regrettably," she said, "the hour is such that I must return to Whitehall. If I am gone longer, my absence will be noted and it will raise suspicion."

I was disappointed, of course, but I saw the sense of what she said. Having already waited for so long, surely I could wait a little longer?

"Allow me to escort you."

I could see that she was tempted; who would not be to soar over the ground free of all earthly restraint? But after a moment, she shook her head.

"I did not come alone. My attendants will be alarmed if I do not return with them."

"Lord Dudley in particular, I presume?"

To my surprise, she flushed and looked away.

"Lord Dudley is indisposed following an incident in the lists," she said.

This passed all belief for surely his entrails would have had to be dragging on the ground for him to willingly remain behind.

"How regrettable. I do hope he will recover soon."

"So do I," she replied with an edge that suggested Dudley had damn well better or risk her permanent disfavor.

I could not have been more pleased. Cecil I could tolerate; he had his uses. Walsingham, too, perhaps, if what I had seen of him so far held up. Even Dee might find a purpose serving me. But Dudley had to go. The combination of ambition and obsessive love that he had for her would make him a danger to me so long as he breathed.

Perhaps when the time was right, she would join me in feeding on him.

I saw her through the main doors and partway down the drive toward the gates. There she left me, going on alone. As I watched her move through the darkness with swift grace, I told myself that everything I had yearned for through the centuries was at last within my grasp.

In my own defense, I will say that I did wonder at her coming to me right after her encounter with Morgaine, but I did not allow myself to dwell on the implications of that. Instead, I lofted back to the manor lighter in my spirit than I had been in a long time. So excellent was my humor that not even Blanche's angry glare aroused more than amusement in me.

The rest of my subjects were eagerly chattering among themselves, clearly well pleased with their soon-to-be queen. Inclined to be indulgent now that everything had gone so well, I summoned Blanche to my side. We slipped together onto one of the low couches scattered about the hall for such purposes. I lifted her white gown, caressing her thighs as I tasted her lightly. With that came a general loosening of restraint. My kin diverted themselves as they are like to do—in twos and threes, sometimes more. Velvet and silk littered the floor; candlelight glowed on revealed flesh; the night flowed on, filled with the promise of the glory that I was certain nothing could prevent.

———

*C*ecil, Dee, and Walsingham are huddled, shivering, near the gate when I emerge. They spring at me with mingled relief and curiosity that leads me to believe they have spent the past few hours imagining me dead . . . or worse.

"Majesty," my Spirit gasps, "praise God that you are safe!"

"Indeed, madam," Dee joins in. "We had come near to despair for your well-being."

"As you can see, you need not have," I reply with some asperity for I am in no mood to listen to their complaints. Indeed, haste nips at my heels. I believe that I have the means now to achieve my ends. Only the precise time and circumstances remain to be determined.

As we hasten toward the High Street and from there to the wherryman who will return us to the Whitehall steps, I question my companions.

"Did you discover anything in your surveillance of the manor?"

Walsingham replies, "As Your Majesty instructed, we did not attempt to venture inside but we made a complete circumnavigation of the outer wall, which is, by the way, in good repair. There are four additional gates, one on each side of what amounts to a square. We saw no evidence of guards, however we were puzzled by the presence of what appear to be monks on the grounds."

"They are thralls, not monks, and they are servants, although I suppose it is also possible that they stand watch."

"Are they vampires?" Cecil asks.

"I do not believe so. At least, they appear nothing like Mordred's court, who are all young, beautiful, and gloriously garbed. I think the thralls must be something else entirely."

"And Mordred himself," Dee asks, "he saw nothing suspicious in your coming to him as you did?"

"He saw what he wants to see, and that suits me for now. I have led him to believe that I am inclined to accept his proposition."

"Majesty!" Cecil protests. "Is that wise?"

I step in a clump of snow and grimace. "It is essential if I am to prevail. But enough, I am weary and I must think. Give me the gift of your silence until we have regained the palace."

They obey, of course, but clearly with difficulty. Cecil scowls as we take our seats in the wherry; Dee fidgets; only Walsingham appears unconcerned, but I see him looking back toward the High Street and catch the calculation in his gaze. He is trying to determine what I have in mind.

He is not alone. Barely do I regain my chambers than Kat is upon me. I find her sitting in the chair by the hearth when I come through the passage door.

"There you are," she says. "It's worried sick I've been."

This is blunt talk for Kat, who has treated me with deference ever since I was old enough to understand what that is. Nor is she finished.

Having risen from the chair and smoothed her skirts, she approaches me with a look that I have not seen since I ripped up a rosebush at Hatfield when I was eight years old.

"What are you thinking of, going off in the middle of the night yet again? Do you truly believe that no one notices what you are

about? You disappear with Dudley, whisper has it, to no less than
the Tower. Next we know he has his tail between his legs again
and you're off to who knows where? My dear child, how long do
you think you can keep this up before it crashes down around you?"

"I am not your child."

How cruel I am to speak such words to the woman who
raised me, protected me, and loved me all my life. What darkness dwells in me that I can do such a horrible thing?

She flinches, and for a moment I see the sheen of tears in her
eyes. But Kat Ashley is made of sterner stuffer than even I can
dent. She squares her shoulders and stares me down.

"No, you are not, but that changes nothing of what I have
said. As you seem ill-disposed to have a care for your own well-
being, I have no choice but to do so. Where have you been?"

In the realm of the vampires, sipping wine, playing the lute,
and doing my utmost to ignore the temptations that Mordred
presents.

"About the business of being queen. What else would you
have me do?"

She reaches out to me, catching both my hands in hers as
though she would draw me back from the brink of terrible
danger.

"I beseech you, Elizabeth, share at least a little of the burden
you carry. Tell me what message your mother sent to you from
beyond the grave and what it drives you to do."

"She—" I fumble for words and find none. The strength goes
from my legs. I am suddenly almost unbearably weary.

Kat helps me to a chair, fussing over me as she sets my feet
on a stool, lays a blanket over me, and pokes up the fire. She
leaves the poker in it to heat while she lights more lamps, then
returns to plunge the hot metal into a cup of cider. When it is
warm, she places it in my hands and urges me to drink.

"When did you eat last?"

I swallow and wipe my hand across my mouth, heedless of decorum. "Whenever the last banquet was."

"You never eat enough at those things. I will send for food."

She turns to go but I seize her hand. "Don't leave me. I have so much to tell you."

Kat hesitates, but after a moment she nods and pulls up a stool beside me. Still holding my hand, she says, "Begin where you will, my dear, but leave nothing out. I would know it all."

———

I speak for I do not know how long. I tell her of my awakening as a vampire slayer beside my mother's grave, of the contents of Anne's letter, of the visit to the Tower chapel and my encounter with Morgaine, of what I saw at Southwark Manor. I mention Mordred's claim to have tried to save my mother and to have protected me, but do not dwell on either. Lastly, I tell her what he wants of me.

She is pale long before I finish, her mouth taut. Silence settles over us when I am done. Slowly she speaks, "Truly, the world is stranger than we can know."

A faint laugh escapes me. Her plain good sense and honesty are exactly what I need. "Wiser words were never spoken. But now you understand what I am facing. I have a plan that I believe will enable me to stop Mordred. But I fear that my will may not be equal to the temptation he presents."

I would make that admission to no one in the world save Kat and the moment I do make it, a great weight seems to lift from me. I slip from my chair, kneel before her, and lay my head in her lap.

"My mother had the courage to die rather than yield to him. How can I do less?"

Kat strokes my hair gently. "What makes you think that you will? Of course he tempts you, how could he not? From what you have said, he offers you eternal youth and more, safety for yourself and this realm. How many do you suppose would have the strength to refuse that?"

Glancing up, I meet her eyes. "Do you think that I should?"

I half expect Kat to express shock that I would ask such a question for I know her to be a godly woman. But she is also a woman of keen intelligence who, despite her musings on the strangeness of the world just now, has rarely if ever been surprised by it.

"You stand to gain a great deal," she says. "But from what this Morgaine person has said, the price could be very high."

"Humanity will be extinguished. That is what she believes."

Kat nods. "Of course, she could be wrong."

If only she were, but I cannot believe that. "I have seen the laudanum users; they are drained of all spirit and will, mere shells of men. Mordred intends to create more vampires, who, of course, will need to feed in order to sustain their lives. He claims this will be a small price for the benefits he will bring to humanity, but I do not believe him. Far better souls than mine have resisted him. And why would they if what he says is true? His own experience of being human is so far in the past that he likely can scarcely recall it. He has forgotten how fragile and precious humankind really is."

"And you cannot convince him to see the matter differently?"

"After a thousand years spent seeking the same goal, what chance have I to change his mind? I can accede to his demands or I can destroy him. Those are my only choices."

"I am glad to hear you say it, but I wasn't actually thinking of all of humanity. It is your own soul that concerns me."

I straighten up, forcing myself to rise and walk a little distance away. Standing before the window, gazing out at the winter night, I struggle to express what lies heaviest in my heart. "My mother's faith was firm. I am not certain that the same can be said of my own."

There, I have admitted it. I rule in the name of the one, true God—who I believe to the depth and breadth of my soul does exist—but about whom I have so many questions that some might well judge me a heretic.

Kat comes to stand beside me. She puts an arm around my shoulders and hugs me with strength that belies her age.

"You will find your own source of courage and you will do what is right. Of that, I have no doubt."

I turn away, hoping that she does not see my tears but suspecting otherwise. Treacherous yearnings rise up in me. At this moment when I need my greatest strength to resist what Mordred offers, I am dangerously weak.

"But there are times," Kat says, "when we all need to be reminded of why life—human life—is worth fighting for." She looks at me directly. "There is no shame in wanting that."

I do not understand her at first. Only when she continues to stare at me as though she can will my poor, sluggish brain to work do I grasp her meaning.

"Oh . . ."

"Go to your Robin, love. Take from him whatever it is you need in order to accomplish what you must."

How tempted I am! And not only because of carnal urges. The moment I allow myself to contemplate finally and completely being with Robin, I realize how desperately I need the comfort of human love to protect me from the lure of Mordred's darkness. Yet still I hesitate.

"You have always made your disapproval clear—"

"Because he is a danger to you, my chick, you know that. But right now you face a greater danger. How fortunate for him."

The sharp edge of her tongue makes me smile. I hug her tightly. She goes with a tender backward glance over her shoulder and a warning.

"Be certain that you are back here before dawn. Your ladies rise early. I cannot hold them off very long."

I promise her most fervently that I will be just where I am supposed to be before the first faint finger of dawn edges above the horizon.

The door closes behind her but the warmth of her smile lingers.

I hurry about the task of removing my clothes, which I almost never do for myself. Finally, I accept that tearing at the silk laces down my back will accomplish nothing and look around frantically for a pair of scissors, finally finding one in a sewing box one of my ladies has left in a corner of the room. Straining with both arms, I snip the laces and breathe a great sigh of relief when they fall away. Moments later, my corset and petticoats follow. I strip off my shift, bathe in water that I scarcely notice is cold, and put my night shift on. Wrapped in my robe, I slip through the door to the passage and hurry toward Robin's rooms.

---

Robin is lying in bed, his arms folded behind his head, when I come through the passage door. He is not asleep. His eyes flick to me but otherwise he does not react. I am left to approach the bed where I stand, gazing down at him.

"Are you very angry at me, Robin, love?"

He is silent long enough for me to wonder if he truly means not to answer, and how I will deal with such defiance. Finally he says, "I can never be angry at you, Elizabeth. You are my love."

The thought flits through my mind that he knows why I am here. Or at least he senses the possibility on some primal level that spurs his response. I do not care. Robin loves me. I have always known it and am a fool to ever think otherwise. The truth is that I take advantage of his love in a thousand shameless ways.

"I wonder sometimes how you can love me. We both know that I can be horrid."

He laughs and sits up farther in the bed, lifting the covers beside him in silent invitation. "It is true, you can be."

I feign of look of shock at his agreement and he laughs again. "But at your worst, you are always Elizabeth and I would not have you catch a chill. Get in."

I comply with as much grace as I can muster. Inwardly, I am trembling but I try my best not to let my beloved see that. Not until he takes me in his arms, his hands stroking all along the length of me as he eases my night shift up and over my head do I lean close to him and whisper against his neck.

"Do you still have those French gloves?"

At once he stiffens. Propping himself up on an elbow, he stares down at me. "Do you mean . . . ?"

I am struck by embarrassment, ridiculous under the circumstances. "Yes, those. If you still have them—"

"I may . . . Yes, I do." He scrambles from the bed. I lean back against the pillows and watch him. Robin has a fear of the dark, but no one knows of it save for myself and his most trusted servants. Candles are always lit in his chambers. By their light, his back and flanks appear sleek and burnished. I give myself up to the simple pleasure of admiring his body as he throws open one chest and then another, searching until he finally raises a hand triumphant.

"Here they are!"

He returns to the bed and we spend a few moments examining what he has brought. I am almost overcome by self-consciousness, but my curiosity gets the better of me. Truly, the lengths of sheep intestines folded over and stitched meticulously tight at one end while threaded through with a silk tie at the other appear ingenious.

"Are you sure that they work?" I ask finally.

"Absolutely . . . at least, so I have been told and I see no reason to doubt it. But Elizabeth, tell me truly, are you sure . . . ?"

He looks at me with such longing that I would be hard-pressed to deny him even if I had not already made up my mind.

"Yes, my love. But how do you . . . ?" I am trying to envision how the contraption is put in place when Robin demonstrates.

"The male member must be erect before the glove can be donned," he explains, "but as you can see, that is no impediment."

Indeed, Robin always seems to find my presence most arousing. I stare in fascination as he attempts the task and am obscurely pleased when he has difficulty with it. I would not like to think that he has experience in such matters for then I would have to question with whom.

After several awkward moments, I offer my assistance, which he accepts most gratefully. When I am done, I sit back on my haunches to observe my handiwork. "Remarkable, truly. However did the French think of them?"

"I suppose we should be grateful that they did." Robin's voice sounds unusually thick. His face is flushed and he appears to be having difficulty breathing. Even so, he asks me, "Elizabeth, are you certain?"

That is the question, is it not? What I contemplate is irrevocable. Once gone, my virginity cannot be regained. Perhaps I will regret its loss, but with all that lies before me, I am determined to know this most essential part of human life no matter what the risk.

Truly, it is vital that I do so for even as I consider what I am about to do, my gaze strays to his throat. A need that is other than human rises in me.

Repressing it, I bend over him, brushing my breasts lightly across his chest. He groans and takes hold of my hips.

What shall I say of what follows? I assumed, without even knowing that I did so, that the passion we had already shared had prepared me for what was to come, and to some extent that was true. Yet the sheer intimacy of allowing him into my body was unlike anything I could anticipate. Men make such a great deal of that act of penetration that they do not seem to recognize how utterly and completely they are taken by a woman. Perhaps that is for the best.

But I, riding him vigorously after the briefest flash of discomfort, feel supremely in control. By the rhythm of my body, I control his release and my own. When we both scale the heights of physical joy, I know that my instinct to come to him was right. I give my virginity gladly, a sacrifice for the boon of courage, of which I have vastly greater need.

Afterward, lying in Robin's arms, I listen to his heartbeat slowing as my own does the same. Contentment washes over me and with it a kind of peace I cannot recall ever feeling before. I have known pleasure well enough, to be sure, but the change I have allowed to take place within me seems strangely liberating. Queen that I am, anointed in the name of Almighty God, I am also completely and utterly human.

And determined to remain so.

"I have a plan to defeat Mordred."

Robin takes a breath and hugs me closer. "I was certain that you would. Tell me of it."

"I have seen him in his lair. He is . . . formidable but arrogant. I think that he truly does not believe that he can be bested."

"How do you mean to do it?"

When I tell him, he is silent for several moments. Finally he asks, "How did you come to this?"

"The Druid priestess Morgaine told me what to do. I went to St. Peter ad Vincula in hope of finding her and I was not disappointed. She was there, as she has been for a thousand years, waiting for the one to come who would relieve her of the burden of defeat that she has carried all that time."

He shakes his head slowly, struggling to comprehend. "I do not understand. How could you—"

"I don't know and I will not pretend to. But scarcely did I begin to think of her than she was there, across the veil of time. She and Mordred are knit together far back to when they were both children. She knows him better than anyone."

"And she has told you how to defeat him?"

"How I may possibly defeat him, nothing is guaranteed."

He turns slightly, easing me onto my side. His eyes are liquid pools of dark passion in which I . . .

Truly, I am ridiculous. Romance is all well and good, but I have had my tryst with it and I must now return my mind to business.

"Did you find what you needed at the manor to accomplish this victory?" he asked.

I think for a moment and slowly nod. Indeed, I believe that I know precisely what is needed. It only remains to be seen if I am right.

———————

True to my word to Kat, I am back in my own bed before dawn, although not before Robin and I make use of two more of the French gloves. If only our Gallic neighbors across the Channel concentrated their attention on what they are so good at, namely pleasure, rather than dabbling in government, we would all be better off.

The day is, once again, taken up with queenly duties of little import compared to what else I face. Yet amid the usual demands lightly cloaked as requests from various parliamentarians, churchmen, diplomats, bureaucrats, social climbers, and the like, I am free to send my mind ranging over what must be done to save my realm from evil threat. By the time night falls, thankfully so early in the chill of winter, I have settled on how I will proceed.

To begin, I write a letter:

> *Honored Lord Mordred, if I may address you as such, kindly receive my thanks for the hospitality you have so generously shown me. Truly, the fascinating hours I spent in your most gracious home were at once enlightening and thought provoking.*
>
> *As I believe you know, since you so eloquently made your proposal to me, I have struggled to understand what*

is best for my realm and myself. I would be less than
honest if I did not admit to you that my efforts to that end
continue. I am as yet unresolved in my mind although I
wish most sincerely to put an end to the turmoil of my
doubts and confusion.

   To assist me in better determining the proper course for
me in this matter, I beseech you to send me the Lady
Blanche, whom I confess to wishing to know far better
than is possible on such scant acquaintance as she and I
have already shared.

   The counsel of a woman who has already joined with
you may prove invaluable to me. I wish to draw upon her
wisdom and experience in this matter.

   With thanks for your understanding and patience, I
am—

                                   Elizabeth Regina


I read the letter over several times, wondering if it is too
much. Mordred possesses undeniable intelligence that I would
be a fool to abuse. If I rouse his suspicion by too fulsome prose, I
will have cause to sorely regret it. Will he think me serious or
will he smell betrayal?

   Yet the more I consider the letter, the more convinced I
am that it will lull my adversary into a false sense of confidence. Let him believe that I yearn for the eternal youth and
beauty of the Lady Blanche, as though I were a poor, shallow
female called to no higher purpose. Let him send her to me,
this once mortal daughter of warriors who boasts of her own
power.

   I seal the letter with hot wax into which I press my personal signet. By the time I do so, the new day has arrived. Banishing the last of my doubts, I summon a servant.

"Find Doctor Dee and tell him to wait upon me here."

Who better to send with a message for the king of the vampires than the magus who played so key a role in bringing about my confrontation with them?

The illustrious Doctor Dee did everything but grasp his balls with both hands and bend over moaning in fear while he waited for me to read Elizabeth's letter. Beads of sweat shone at his temples. His mouth twitched as his eyes darted here, there, and everywhere. I could smell the fear rolling off him like the stench of a fetid swamp.

He was an interesting fellow, was Dee, at once as frail a human as any who has walked this earth, but at the same time possessed of insatiable curiosity and a need to make sense of the world that bordered on obsession. I could almost have sympathized with him had I not fully appreciated the futility of trying to understand this strange, contradictory place in which we find ourselves, washed up like amnesiac survivors on an alien shore.

"Tell your mistress that I will grant her wish," I instructed finally as I rolled the parchment up again and placed it on a nearby table.

He appeared relieved that he would not have to face Elizabeth's wrath, yet even so he could not contain his restless mind.

"If I might ask," he ventured, "what it is that she wants?" In his anxiousness, he tugged on his beard so hard that he winced.

His willingness to admit his own ignorance if only to assuage it amused me and won him a measure of tolerance I would not otherwise have extended.

I raised a hand and at once Blanche was at my side. With a private smile for her, I replied, "The Queen requests the counsel of a lady who may advise her as to the best course to follow in this matter."

Dee's eyes darted between us, widening yet farther as Blanche's beauty had its usual effect. Not even a man who aspired to the wisdom of ages was immune from it.

"This lady?"

"The selfsame."

I took Blanche's hand, brushing my lips over her fragrant skin as her gaze met mine. "Will you undertake this commission for me? I can trust no one else with it."

I was asking her to persuade Elizabeth to agree to my proposal, join with me, and become my queen, thereby denying Blanche what she had so long sought for herself. I took it as a measure of her true devotion and submission to me that, after the briefest hesitation, she nodded.

A doleful assent to be sure but good enough under the circumstances.

"I will inform Her Majesty then," Dee said, looking anxiously toward the door, through which he scampered scant moments later with speed suggesting that all the imps of hell were nipping at his heels. Even so, he could not resist a last glance over his shoulder and what I took to be a sigh of regret that he could not bring himself to tarry longer.

Having draped herself over the arm of the chair where I once again reclined, my dutiful inamorata blinked back tears—leading me to wonder if she could actually still cry—and pouted.

"How can you send me to that mindless ninny? It is too cruel."

I accepted the wine offered by a thrall but handed it to Blanche in a small service intended to soothe her temper. I took another for myself.

"You have nothing to fear. She is merely the means to an end."

I was lying, of course. Already Elizabeth fascinated me, partly because of her connection to Morgaine but increasingly in her own right as well. Her fiery will and courage, the sensuality glowing behind the façade of virginity, and, most particularly, the raw power she possessed, the equal or greater of my own . . . all that and more convinced me that I could love her as I had not loved since Morgaine. Indeed, perhaps I was destined to do no less.

That being so, I did not hesitate to use Blanche but kept her in good humor with a gift of a strand of pearls, each bigger than a man's thumb, that I twined around her neck amid assurances that no touch, no presence, no companion, could ever please me so well as she did.

Yet I also cautioned her, "I know your temperament better than you do yourself. Once with the Queen, do not forget your duty to me. Fulfill your mission and you will have reward beyond any you can imagine. But fail and—"

"I shall not. You will have your foolish mortal for whatever good she may do you." Blanche bent closer, inhaling my scent even as I breathed in hers. "But afterward, when you have used her to the fullest possible extent and there is nothing left of her save an empty husk, then I will still be here and we will be as one, shall we not, my most dear and precious lord?"

I kissed her long and deeply. "Be assured that it will be so for I would never have it otherwise."

She went smug in her certainty that she had me well in hand. I watched the stars drift by beyond the high windows and told myself that my long wait was almost over. The coming hours would see the fulfillment of all my desires.

*Evening, 21 January 1559*

———

I count the hours until Dee's return as I try to estimate when I may legitimately begin to worry. Half an hour perhaps to secure a wherry and make his way to Southwark. The same again to reach the manor and enter it. An unknown length of time while Mordred considers my request. Assuming, of course, that he does consider it and allows Dee to return with his answer. If he does not, if he harms the magus—

My mind cannot encompass that possibility. Queen a pair of months, crowned mere days, I have not yet sent men to their deaths. That inevitably awaits me as it does any sovereign with ambitions to remain enthroned, much less one such as myself beset by enemies from all directions. But please, God, do not let Dee be the first to fall in my service.

Robin senses my distress and strives to ease it so much as he can in full view of the court. Memories of all we shared lighten my burden somewhat, but I fear that I may reveal too much whenever I look at him and so must ration my glances. He seems to understand, or at least he takes no umbrage. To the contrary, he exudes a newfound cheerful confidence, for which I can scarcely blame him. No doubt he believes that with the deed now done, it is only a matter of time—and little enough of that—before our betrothal is announced.

How disappointed he will be to discover that intercourse, pleasing though it is, has changed my view of marriage not one whit. It has, however, made me think more deeply of what it means to be human, which is to say frail and vulnerable yet capable of such soaring exaltation of body and spirit as to dazzle the mind. What counts it that our pleasures and our pains alike are so brief? Only the world beyond this truly matters, or so I have been taught from tenderest childhood with no chance ever to consider otherwise.

I watch the water clock from the corner of my eye even as the thought creeps over me that as gloriously arrayed as are my lords and ladies—not so much the foreign ambassadors, although the French make a good enough display—they cannot compete with the magnificence of the vampire court. It is unfair, of course, for humans to be compared to immortal beings, or as close to it as it is possible to come in this world. Better Mordred and his kind be held to the measure of angels, in which case they would surely be found wanting.

Or would they?

How wayward is my mind! My course is set and I will not waiver, yet still temptation stirs within me. To be as they are, forever young and beautiful, forever free of the shadow of death. What is the measure of my soul that makes it worth so great a price as death?

I raise a hand, summoning a servant, who steps forward quickly with a goblet of my favorite Rhenish wine. Sipping it, I take distant note of the velvet-clad lad, his back erect, his eyes bright, his step secure. How different from the . . . what was it Mordred called them? . . . the thralls I saw in his court. Who are they exactly, that one dull note among so much vibrant beauty?

Perhaps Dee will know. I will ask him when he returns, if he does. And if he does not?

A sudden pause in the conversation and I realize that a representative from the Low Countries' merchants has asked me something. Lacking any notion of the topic, I flounder until Cecil steps in.

"Her Majesty and I were discussing that very matter only yesterday," my Spirit says. "Truly, the sober industry of the people is a country's chief adornment. Every caution must be taken to prevent distraction from that."

By which I suspect that the fellow has in mind the discontent spreading among his people as they chaff under Spanish rule. Perhaps he wishes to raise the topic with me more directly. Perhaps he hopes for some sign that were the good folk of the Low Countries to decide to throw off their Spanish yoke, I would look favorably upon their cause.

Perhaps I would, but it's all far too premature and I have far more urgent matters to concern me.

"Have I thanked you for that excellent cheese?" I inquire. In fact, I have no memory of it, but with Netherlanders cheese is always somehow involved.

He manages a weak smile and a moment later is eased aside by one of the majordomos charged with managing the crush around me. So many wish to be seen in conversation with the Queen, even if they have nothing in particular to say, that a constant ebbing and flowing occurs in my presence. Were it not properly handled, I swear they would press so close as to leave me without breath.

As it is, I can feel the tightness building in my chest. Despite the chill of the winter night, the room is overly heated with roaring fires along both long walls, added to the flames of several hundred candles and the warmth of so many bodies packed too closely together. I have the sense of being in a hothouse on a sultry summer day when the air within is torpid and heavy, almost too thick to breathe.

Dear Robin, who, all things considered, has been a model of

discretion this evening, murmurs an order to the majordomo, and suddenly the space around me clears.

"Her Majesty is too good," he declares loudly. "She thinks only of us, her most fortunate subjects, and nothing of herself. Therefore, let each and every one of us resolve to protect her well-being and let no harm ever come to her."

A cheer goes up that threatens to crack the ornately plastered ceiling, for who would fail to second such noble sentiments? Robin ushers me through the crowd and into my retiring room, where, I will admit, I gasp with relief to find cooler air and blessed quiet.

"Your cheeks are flushed." He pours water for me from a beaded carafe. I sip it gratefully but try to dismiss his concern.

"The presence chamber is overly warm, nothing more."

Servants hover nearby. He dismisses them with a flick of his hand. For once, I do not resent his ordering of my life. There is some relief in allowing another to make decisions, however small. Glancing around, I notice that Cecil is absent. Generally, my Spirit stays closely attached to my side. Robin, it appears, has outmaneuvered him, if only temporarily.

"Elizabeth—" He breathes my name as though from the very center of his being and, having taken the goblet from me, clasps both my hands in his and draws me near. "Every moment we have been apart is torture, and yet nothing gives me greater happiness than to watch you in all your loveliness and majesty. Truly, you outshine the sun."

Even I, susceptible to flattery as I am and well know it, think this a bit much. All the same, adoration is not to be despised in a lover—or in a subject, for that matter.

I smile, brush my lips against his, and succumb to the far deeper kiss he insists upon. When at last we break apart, he is more flushed than I.

"We could bar the door," he suggests, glancing at it as though already reckoning how the task can be accomplished.

Laughter wells up in me, spurred by shock and amusement in shared measure. "And do what, couple on that table there? Fie on you, good sir. Have a better care for my posterior."

He leans closer, his lips trailing down my throat to the edge of the lace ruff. "There are any number of ways to spare your sweet rump, lady. Positions you will find most—"

"Enough!" My skin is heating once again, though for far different cause. My heart beats too quickly and I am at risk of letting reason slip just when I most need it.

"There is no time." I push him away and walk a few paces across the small room, struggling to collect myself. "Dee will return shortly and then—"

"Return? Where has he gone?"

"I told you that I have a plan to defeat Mordred."

"But not the particulars. You did not share those with me but you entrusted them to the magus?"

I see the instant jealousy that springs forth in his gaze and shake my head. "He is my messenger, nothing more. If Mordred takes the bait I have laid out, I must be prepared. I count on you to help me."

He hesitates a moment before, with a small bow, assenting. "Of course, my Queen, I will do anything that you require. Only tell me what is needed."

"A private place, somewhere none will think to look for me, and just as importantly, I need for no one to be searching lest they see more than they should. Kat, my ladies, Cecil, all of them must think me safely occupied."

"We speak of now, this night?"

"We do . . . I hope. If all goes as planned, Mordred will send an emissary to me whose power I must contrive to take."

A flash of concern speeds across his face and is quickly masked. "As Morgaine instructed you to do?"

"Just so. I will acquire great power but without the terrible cost that comes with killing many times over."

"What if this vampire is stronger even than you think, what then?"

Stronger than me, he means. I have wondered the same myself. Exactly how powerful is the Lady Blanche? How formidable a foe will she prove to be?

"I will take her by surprise."

"Her? Mordred sends a woman?"

"Of noble lineage, so she boasts, more than three hundred years on this earth." I cannot cease to marvel at how long Blanche has lived, though I know well that I must put aside such thoughts or risk being betrayed by them.

Robin is silent for a moment. At length he says, "Three centuries ago this land was torn by war and rebellion. The barons rose up against their king, taking his power as their own. You are certain the lady is of that time?"

"So she says." I had not thought about the circumstances in which Blanche passed from mortal woman to vampire, but now I wonder. "You think her family could have been involved in the rebellion against the crown?"

"If they were of noble lineage, it is very likely that they were. The plain truth is that very few of the nobility stood with their king. I wonder what befell them when fortune's wheel turned and victory became defeat."

*My family served this realm with valor and distinction, even at great cost to themselves.*

"Nothing good, I suspect. If I recall my schoolroom days, the rebels who did not die in battle were executed, but the blood-letting did not stop there. Whole families were wiped out."

"A dark time," Robin says quietly.

Such darkness as I pray will never come upon me. Even my father at his worst spared the wives and children of his enemies, if not his own.

"It was a different world," I say as though the words alone make it so.

Robin agrees. "Barbarous, lacking the refinement and rationality of our own."

If such virtues can encompass the burning of those deemed heretics, the heads displayed on Tower Bridge, the crows' feast of bodies left hanging from the gibbets, and all manner of other actions my immediate predecessors thought necessary for the maintenance of civil order and the well-being of the realm.

"Whatever the lady's origins, I must prepare to meet her."

"Your fierce Kat will never be held off by me, but the rest I can manage well enough."

I hide a smile, wondering what he would say if he knew that the pleasures of the previous night came at Kat's urging.

"I will let her tuck me into bed, then send her to her own."

"Good enough, now as to the place . . ." He frowns as Robin is always wont to do when considering a knotty problem. I remember him as a boy toiling with me over Latin declensions while wearing the same expression.

Abruptly his manner lightens. "I have it. Somewhere no one goes at night that will afford you ample room to maneuver. But how to lure her there?"

"Is it in the open at all?"

"It is."

"Then she will find me for, as I have experienced myself, these creatures have the power of flight."

Robin's smile fades as quickly as it came. Fear for me falls as a shadow across his eyes. "Such dark devices they possess beyond the ken of mortal man. Have you thought well on this, Eliza-beth? If you are wrong about your ability to defeat her—"

"I am not." My answer speaks of confidence that I do not en-tirely feel, and yet I have taken the measure of the Lady Blanche. As my own powers have grown, so, too, have I become better able to sense that which lies within my prey. The lady is . . . distracted. Yes, that is the word. She thinks too much of Mordred to think enough of herself.

Another fool then, like Morgaine. Praise God that as tempted as I am by thoughts of eternal youth and the death of all my enemies, no hint of treacherous love stirs within my well-fortified heart.

Robin tells me of the place he has in mind. We are discussing it when a knock comes at the door. Dee has returned and seeks most urgently to speak with me.

---

The magus, who appears no worse than shaken by his so-journ in the vampire court, assures me that my request is granted, the Lady Blanche will call upon me. He has gleaned nothing more of use. I thank him for his diligence all the same and send him on his way. He goes most willingly, I hope to con-template the wages of involving his Queen in such dire matters without winning her permission first.

The evening wears on and eventually winds down. I scarcely notice what fills the intervening hours apart from more of the tedium that seems my royal lot. Although to be fair, were I not engaged in such strange and otherworldly matters, I would no doubt enjoy the amusements that surround me.

At long last, I am snug abed, watching as the door closes behind Kat, who, her smile tells me, assumes that I am about to hie off down the passage to Robin's rooms. Would that I were. Instead, I am on my feet again instantly, throwing on such clothes as I can manage while striving despite my awkward fum-blings to look my best when I meet the beauteous Lady Blanche.

Wrapped in my warmest cloak, I take the passage but go right by Robin's rooms. He is not there in any case, being busy divert-ing Cecil and the ever-lurking Walsingham. Hurrying, I make my way through the winter garden and from there to the long, low wing of the palace that my father had constructed to accommodate the sporting activities he pursued before failing health robbed him of their enjoyment.

Since my awakening, and most especially as my power has grown, all my senses have sharpened. I can see as readily by night as I can by day. Whereas I would once have stumbled or risked becoming lost, I proceed without hindrance. Twice, I hear the far-off approach of patrolling guards and conceal myself until they have passed. The air smells of frost and the river, of wood smoke and the distinctive odor of London, which some describe as sour or fetid but which I find has a curious appeal, carrying as it does the evidence of a human presence ever striving to make more of itself.

The tennis courts, open to the sky to allow for sufficient light and air, are filled with shadows and the mournful whistle of the wind. I skirt past them quickly and, going around the bowling alleys, hurry across the archery yard. All are deserted at this hour, but by day my nobles congregate here to vie against one another in every manner of contest. I encourage their competitiveness, preferring that they exert it against each other lest they be tempted to turn it on me.

Near the far end of the wing, close by the river, is the cockfighting pit. I have been here only a handful of times for the sport, such as it is, holds no appeal for me. If I wish to see an animal bloodied, I will hunt it down myself, galloping over miles of fields and streams, vaulting fences and walls, until in a rush of victory it is brought to bay. No venison tastes sweeter than that seasoned with one's own sweat.

Yet there is no denying the popularity of cockfighting for my lords and more than a few of my ladies. They flock to it, betting on their favorite birds with even more enthusiasm than they bring to the gaming tables. Several hundred of them can fit into the circular arena open to the sky and surrounded by tiers of wooden seats. At the center is a flat, sandy floor where the birds have at each other, pecking and slashing with razor-sharp beaks and claws until one or both are too wounded to continue. The sand is clean and well raked, yet I fancy I catch a whiff of the blood spilled here and imagine the dead birds carried away by their disappointed owners.

I walk out upon the sand, directly beneath the open roof, and stare up at the wisps of clouds floating across the glory that is the stars. The wind dies down; a hush settles over the night. I wait, pacing, looking up from time to time, all the while wondering if Dee misunderstood or if I have. Is Blanche coming? Can she find me?

At length, when my feet have begun to ache from the cold despite my fur-lined boots and my patience has worn thin, I curse under my breath. What game is Mordred playing that he thinks to toy with me?

"Damn the miserable bastard."

That faint sound from above and behind me . . . is it a laugh? I turn so swiftly that my cloak flows out as a black wing behind me and stare up into the highest reaches of the bleachers.

Blanche is not there; instead, she is higher still, perched on the very edge where the curving wall meets the open space above the arena, between the poles from which banners fly by day. She is wearing the same white silk gown that caresses her body with the addition of a strand of pearls so opulent as to take my breath away, and she looks well amused. The cold does not appear to touch her.

"Don't let Mordred hear you call him that," she says. "Even after so long, he remains sensitive about his birthright."

I start to sag with relief that she has come but catch myself and straighten my shoulders resolutely.

"Descend, that we may talk face-to-face."

She looks at me mockingly but comes away from the wall and floats down, alighting a few feet in front of me. Her black hair flutters down the full length of her back. I have never seen more perfect skin, as white as the moon, or eyes more filled with secrets.

"As Your Majesty wills. I am instructed to answer all your questions fully and honestly. Will that satisfy you?"

Did Mordred truly send her with such orders? If so, his confidence gives me pause. Rather than reveal my unease, I reply, "I can ask for nothing more."

"Then begin. What is it you wish to know?"

I have lured Blanche here for the sole purpose of slaying her. Yet I hesitate to do so too precipitously. She may be the best chance I have to learn about Mordred and his kind.

"Why did you become what you are? Was it forced upon you?"

She raises a perfectly arched brow. "Forced? I pleaded with my dear lord to grant me so great a boon. I swore to him that he would not be disappointed and I have kept my vow. That is why I am here now and only for that reason."

"Had you no care for your soul? No desire to stand in the light of the Almighty and know His grace?"

Blanche sighs and the world seems to sigh with her. I tell myself that it is only the wind picking up again.

"The same Almighty who, despite my most anguished prayers, declined to spare any of my family even to the tiniest child? Is that the God of whom you speak?"

"Death comes for all mortals." It is a feeble answer even to my own ears.

Blanche does not spare me her scorn. "My family, of proud and noble lineage as I told you, rose in rebellion against a mad king intent on bringing ruin to this land. For that crime we paid the highest price. Only I escaped."

I have known my own days of terror and imprisonment when the sword of death swung so close as to leave my skin feeling scraped. All the same, I can think of only one reason why she would have made so dire a choice.

"You wanted Mordred's help to claim your revenge."

She twines a length of the pearls around her fingers and smiles. "Oh, yes, bright Queen, I did! The mere thought of it sustained me through the darkest hours when my very sanity hung in the balance. It gave me the strength to call out, not to the god who had forsaken all those I loved but to the power I sensed in the darkness itself. Power that redeemed me and made all things possible."

"But not the vengeance you sought. I know the history of this kingdom. Henry's son, Edward, redeemed his father's throne. He and his dynasty ruled this realm until my own supplanted them."

"And you think that means I lost? How foolish you are! I watched them one by one grow old and wither and die. I was witness to their disappointments, their fears, their tragedies. I saw them weep and curse and try to bargain with their god who listened no more to them than he had to me. And all the while I remained as I am now—young, strong, beautiful, awaiting the day when my own kind will rule in the place of you weak mortals."

"Don't you mean when you will rule at Mordred's side?" I saw how she looked at him in the hall at Southwark Manor. She had the proprietary air of a woman who has staked her claim, whether a man, vampire or otherwise, has the sense to recognize it.

"After three hundred years," I continue, "surely you deserve nothing less. Haven't you served him all that time, helping him step by step toward the power he has craved for so long? Yet now he wants to toss you aside and put me in your place."

I am trying to provoke her, perhaps to justify what I must do. In that instant, it appears that I have succeeded. A dark flush of color spreads over her skin as her eyes glitter dangerously.

But I underestimate Blanche at my peril. The centuries have taught her patience. A moment later, she is once again in control of herself.

"Whatever my lord Mordred commands, I obey."

Would that I had servants so steadfast in their loyalty.

"Convince me then," I challenge. "Tell me why I should give up all I hold dear and join with him."

She looks at me with scornful pity. "Give up what? The constant danger that surrounds you? The certain knowledge that like every mortal you will grow old, your body betraying you more and more with each passing year until you wither and die? That is, of course, if you manage to avoid assassination or execution. You are what—twenty-five years old now? I give you no more than two chances in ten of seeing thirty."

Her calculation of the odds against me is chilling, all the more so because I cannot refute them.

"If it pleases God to take me, I will find my reward in the life to come."

That is, of course, the appropriately pious response, never mind whether I really believe it.

Blanche shakes her head as though I am so great a fool as scarcely to be endured. "You have a chance to live far beyond the scant span of days allotted by your jealous god. You can bring peace and security to your people while pursuing all that interests you—art, music, natural philosophy, the pleasures of the flesh, all are yours for the taking. And you can do it in perfect health and beauty, never growing old, never dying. How could any person with a claim to sanity reject that?"

"You paint such an idyllic picture, yet surely it is incomplete."

A frown creases her alabaster brow. She leaves off her play with the pearls as both her hands drop to her sides. "What do you mean?"

"What of your need to feed upon humans? You drug them into a stupor to facilitate your use of them. Some few become like you, but I presume that is only possible for those chosen by Lord Mordred?"

When she nods, I continue, "The rest, whether they die or not, are robbed of the spark of life that is most essential to their humanity. Does that not trouble you at all?"

Apparently not as it seems the question has never occurred to the Lady Blanche. She looks puzzled by it.

"They live," she says. "What else matters?"

"The quality of their lives is so greatly diminished as to scarcely be life at all, but I perceive that is not a concern for you. Perhaps like Mordred you have forgotten what it means to be human. Let us go on then. What are the thralls?"

Since first becoming aware of the existence of those beings, I have been troubled by them. Not vampires, yet seemingly not human either, they hint at something amiss in Blanche's paradise.

"They are servants, nothing more. I marvel that you notice them."

"Servants whose faces are never seen and who never speak. Where do they come from?"

She shakes her head in disgust. "That does not concern you! How weak is your mind to be drawn in so meaningless a direction when Lord Mordred offers you so much. Do you truly still not understand all that can be yours?"

The moon casts long shadows over the tiers of seats surrounding us. I turn away and close my eyes, imagining the crowd, feverish with excitement, roaring for blood. Blanche has nothing more to tell me. It is time.

"I had another purpose in asking that you come here," I say, and turn back to her. In the instant that I do so, her mouth pulls in a taut smile as her eyes go flat and hard.

"Did you, Slayer? What could that possibly be?"

She knows. I cannot be certain how or why, but whereas my ruse duped Mordred, it has not fooled Blanche. Yet she does nothing.

Not so myself. In the quickening of a breath, I seize my chance and hurl a bolt of light directly at her. The air between us ripples. Before my horrified gaze, the light slows, leaving Blanche ample time to step away from it.

Yet she does not, or at least not fully. She allows it to just slightly graze her, severing the strand of pearls, which shower down onto the ground, and rending her garment to expose pure white skin gashed by scintillating fragments of light.

Pain contorts her face but fades too swiftly. Before I can overcome my surprise and gather myself for a second blow, Blanche strikes.

The blackness that comes from her is as deep and suffocating as that I experienced from Mordred. I must call on all my will to hold it back and even then only just manage to do so. She, on the other hand, seems to have strength in reserve.

"I know your kind," Blanche says, "far better than my lord Mordred ever can. I know how treacherous and scheming you are, the lengths to which you go to hold on to the only power you are capable of understanding. Did you truly think that I would come into the presence of a Slayer without being pre-pared to defend myself?

Defend and more, for even as she speaks, the darkness thick-ens. I gasp for breath, my heart pounding and will from deep within myself a strike of such power as I have never unleashed before. The light flows from me as a spear cleaving the night, aimed directly at its target.

Blanche avoids it easily and rises into the sky, hovering above me.

"Fool," she taunts. "In striking at me, you have done exactly as I hoped you would. Now that I bear your mark, I may return to my lord with proof of my loyalty and your treachery. He will understand that I had no choice but to end your pitiful life. I will reign at his side while you rot in the ground, unlamented and forgotten."

Clearly, the thought gives her great pleasure for she is smiling as she prepares to unleash what I do not doubt will be my death blow.

---

*I* run, heedless of dignity, with no thought but survival. My skirts catch around my legs. I grab them in both hands and leap, hurling myself into the maze of columns that hold up the tiers of seats around the pit.

"There is nowhere to hide, bright Queen!" Blanche calls out. "I see in darkness as well as you, even better. I hear your every movement. I smell the scent of you. Come out and die swiftly. Otherwise, I promise, you will curse your last moments on this earth."

I am cursing already, regretting my arrogance and stupidity. How did I imagine that the sole survivor of a line that dared to topple a king would give up what she believes to be her rightful place simply because Mordred bid her do so? And, moreover, that she would cede it to me, heiress to the throne from which her family's ruin was decreed?

She will kill me to gain the place at Mordred's side that will come to her when I am dead but also for the vengeance so long awaited.

But not if I can kill her first. Please, God, let me truly be as treacherous and scheming as she claims I am.

"Wait," I call out. "There is no need for this. I have no quarrel with you. Mordred is my enemy."

"And you imagine that I am not?" Again, she laughs.

With my back pressed against a pillar, I dare a swift look into the pit. Blanche has settled on the ground again. Her wound still glitters, but she seems unaffected by it. Her arms flung wide, she paces like a beautiful, agitated beast anxious to be done with its confinement.

"Come out, come out, bright Queen!"

"Why should we two be foes? Mordred contrived at my mother's death and he conspires to take my throne. I sought your power so that I could kill him, but now I see that was a mistake. Far better that we should be allies. Tell me, what is it that you wish?"

Silence for a moment, broken by the murmur of the wind, before she says, "To rule in my own realm, Queen regnant of all vampires."

Poor Mordred, so convinced of Blanche's devotion! Yet she seems more than able to embrace existence without him. Indeed, he stands between her and the power she seeks.

"What of vengeance for your family?"

Again she hesitates, but at length I hear, "You did not kill them."

"I sit in the place of those who did."

"True . . . do you think that I should kill you for that?"

I manage a faint laugh. "I would prefer that you not, but consider that if I die, there will be chaos in this land. Out of it, the remnants of the same lineage that destroyed yours will have a chance to rise again and take the throne once more. Is that what you want?"

The wind is growing stronger, whistling down the river from the direction of the distant sea. I would draw my cloak more closely but that I must keep my arms unencumbered.

"You know that it is not."

"Then let us make common cause. With Mordred dead at last, we will both achieve our ends."

I dare to peer once more around the column. Blanche appears to be considering what I have said. I could try to strike her now but the distance between us is great enough that I could miss, and for certain there will no other opportunity.

"Let me come out," I call, "that we may discuss this face-to-face."

She tosses her head, the dark mane of her hair fluttering out around her. I marvel that she does not feel the cold, but in truth my own sense of it is fading. The power is rising in me, eclipsing all else.

"As you will," she says.

I step out slowly from behind the pillar, knowing even as I do so that I may be taking my last steps in this life. If Blanche only means to lure me out . . .

"Come closer," she says. "You fuss so about the faceless thralls, I would see you clearly."

Crossing the sandy floor, I affect such confidence as I can muster while seeking to divert her. "You will admit that they are passing strange."

"I suppose, although it's been longer than I can remember since I thought of them at all. Still, you could say that they are Mordred's little joke."

Despite the circumstances, my curiosity stirs. "How so?"

"They are his former foes, men and women who have dared to go against him. He has taken that essence of humanity you make so much of from them and left them able to do naught but his bidding."

A shiver runs down my neck as I consider what such a living death must mean. Does sufficient spark of consciousness still exist for any of the thralls to know what is happening to them?

I almost hope that it does not for surely the knowledge of their torment would be torment in itself.

"Why doesn't he simply kill them?"

"Because death would be a release. This way their punishment goes on and on."

"And you call that a joke?"

"It is for him, for he certainly enjoys it." Something in my expression must alert Blanche to my disgust for she adds, "Did you think him too refined for such cruelty?"

"I hadn't really thought of it at all." This much is true. I have considered, and been tempted by, what Mordred could provide to me—eternal youth and beauty, safety of a sort for my realm, and so on. I have given scant attention to his essential nature, yet I am not surprised.

"In my experience," I say, "power does not bring out the best in people. To the contrary, it tends to be corrupting."

I will be the exception to that, of course. Alert as I am to the sins committed by my father and my sister, Mary—both of whom only just refrained from adding my own death to their litany of offenses—I will never allow such cruelty to take root within my soul.

Bless God, let that be so.

"How perceptive of you." Blanche beckons me nearer. "So we are to be friends, you and I? You to rule over England while I rule over the vampires? Is that what you propose?"

"It is, but none of that can come to pass while Mordred lives."

"How then do you suggest that we destroy him? I can tell you that your power is not sufficient to the task. Go against him as you are now and you will find yourself in the ranks of the thralls."

The very thought fills me with cringing horror. It is all I

can do to refrain from crying out against so loathsome a
fate.

"Your power added to mine and mine to yours will surely accomplish what we both desire," I say as I come closer still.

"Indeed it will," Blanche says, "but for that, one of us has to
die." She raises her arm.

"Wait! We can attack him together."

She hesitates, but I sense that she is only playing with me.
Mordred's cruelty has its equal in her. "We could," she says, "if I
were willing to trust you, but I learned long ago that trust is for
fools."

I do not need to hear more nor am I likely to, for just then
she releases a dark, suffocating blow. Rather than attempt to
flee again, I leap forward and dive toward the floor of the pit.
She is just sufficiently surprised for me to have a chance at the
desperate plan I have conceived.

Rolling over and over across the sand, I unleash a spear of
light that misses her entirely and strikes instead a tier of seats
rising over the pit. They collapse with a shriek of rending
wood into a cloud of dust. Blanche's face contorts, her beauty
replaced by stark hatred as she prepares to deliver another
blow.

Scrambling to my knees, skittering backward like a crab, I
strike at her again. This time, against all odds, my aim proves
true. Blanche cries out and lurches back, but not before releasing another blow at me.

I throw myself desperately to the left, rolling again, and do
not get to my feet until I am once more within the shelter of
the columns, where I leap upright and run, darting in between
them. She howls with rage and comes after me.

As she steps across the sand, I raise my arm and, calling
upon all my strength, take aim at her again. Once more, I

miss her. Snarling, she continues forward. So dark and thick a cloud of life-draining energy as I have not seen before hurtles across the sand. It passes by so close as to threaten to suck me in. I cling with all my strength to the column, knowing that the contest between us is almost done. I have little left.

Indeed, I can muster only one more blow and I have scant hope of that succeeding. Blanche has withstood everything I could throw at her, and now she comes at me remorselessly. I take a final breath, gather myself, and—

She slips. Her feet roll on the pearls scattered across the floor of the pit when I struck her first. Her balance lost, she flails.

In that moment, I gather myself and whisper the only prayer I can think of.

"Morgaine, help me."

Does the priestess hear? I have no idea, but I do know that in the instant when Blanche struggles to right herself, everything I am, all the power I possess, combines within me into one fierce, final blow that holds nothing back and leaves nothing in reserve.

I live or die on this, my final chance.

The spear of light strikes her midchest. For a moment, she teeters, forward and backward, staring down at herself in dumb amazement. With aching slowness, the glittering wound expands, spreading in all directions until she is engulfed in its pulsating glow.

The other vampires I slew died quickly, but not so Blanche. She fights against the light, twisting this way and that, her face contorted in rage and agony.

"Damn you!" she cries, even as the thin web of cracks begins to swallow her. Her form disappears, only her face remains to the very end, her eyes filled with consuming hatred.

"Damn you and all your kind!"

Then she is gone, only the light remaining to fall like frozen stars onto the sandy ground, where, long after it has flickered out, the pearls continue to shine.

I double over, struck down by mingled relief and weakness greater than any I have ever known. My knees strike the sand as I hover on the edge of unconsciousness. Darkness threatens to engulf me until, first as a faint glimmer but growing rapidly into an incandescent core, I feel the new power within me. Blanche's power, all the strength and will of a three-hundred-year-old vampire, second only to Mordred himself in supremacy.

My power now, added to that which I already possessed, and gained without the terrible price I paid before. As I get to my feet, all weakness falls away. Every part of my body feels reborn and remade. I hold out my hand, staring with wonder at the glow of strength that emanates from it. As it does from all of me, I am certain.

Abruptly, I throw back my head and laugh. I have won! Or very nearly so, for what chance has Mordred to stand against me now? I am stronger than any Slayer has ever been, certainly stronger than Morgaine, weakened as she was by love. No one is my equal for power! I will defeat all my enemies and rule forever, eternally beautiful, everlastingly—

A gasp of horror catches in my throat. What am I becoming? I sought Blanche's power to preserve my humanity, not to sacrifice it. Morgaine never warned that this might happen. Is it possible that she did not know?

Too late, I realize that my experience has gone beyond where she can guide me. I am in a realm entirely separate and apart. I am alone.

Or I am not. For even as the crushing sense of inhuman solitude threatens to descend upon me, a familiar voice calls my
name.

"Elizabeth!"

He is there, stepping out of the shadows around the pillars,
striding toward me. Impetuous in his desires, vainglorious in his
aspirations, sometimes infuriating and frustrating. But always
and unceasingly my love.

"Robin!"

He throws his arms around me, fierce in his embrace. I am
lifted free of the pearl-strewn ground, hugged so that my ribs
threaten to crack and all the breath is expelled from me.

And I glory in it. I love and am loved. I am human.

"I feared the worst when you did not return." He sets me
back on my feet but keeps me close, cupping my face in his
hands. "What happened?"

Never will I tell him the truth of what I so nearly felt myself
become. Instead, I say only, "Blanche is gone. Her power is
mine."

"Praise be to God!"

Indeed, but I will withhold my thanks until the greater battle
is done.

"Come." Taking him by the hand, I lead him away. In the
morning, the court will see the collapsed tier of seats and
wonder at what brought them down. I will have it put about
that they were shoddily constructed and must be dismantled entirely before any come to harm. The pit, the sand, the whole of
it, will be erased. I want no reminder of the place where I did
battle with Blanche only to discover that the greater threat remains within myself.

But for now there is the sweet seclusion of Robin's bed, his body strong and eager against mine, and the reminder of all that makes human life so precious.

I sleep at last, wrapped in his arms, and dream of pearls falling one by one through the narrow neck of an hourglass, winding around its bottom like an opalescent ribbon that will shortly reach its end.

When Blanche departed, I retired to my library. I did not wish to dwell on what I would do if, even after such persuasion, Elizabeth remained uncertain as to her course. Rather than consider what I hoped most fervently would never come to pass, I sought diversion.

My eye happened to fall on Malory's Le Morte d'Arthur. I had acquired the volume shortly after its publication almost seventy-five years ago but had barely glanced at it before tossing it aside in disgust. The fevered romance about my father and his court, intended to pander to the most maudlin sentiments, infuriated me. Or at least it had. With my objective at long last in sight, I was prepared to take a more benign view of the work.

I even thought that I might glean some insights into how to present myself to my human subjects when the time came to do so. It amused me to think that I would claim the mantle of Arthur's fictional honor and nobility. Perhaps I would rename the court Camelot and install a round table.

In such manner, I passed a pleasant interlude. I was deep into the fanciful account of Arthur's birth—which, if it had held a shred of truth, would have made him a bastard, too—when the first awareness struck that something was not right.

I felt from a distance what seemed like a glancing blow, inflicting pain but bringing hard upon it a surge of strength and resolution. My first reaction was bewilderment. Who among my kind was I sensing?

*I considered any who might be absent from the manor, but no name occurred to me; none, that is, save Blanche's.*

*My instinct was to pursue her at once and put an end to whatever was occurring. I leapt up, but the quick exchange of blows that followed disoriented me and robbed me of the ability to react immediately. My mind screamed out against the battle even as I was held captive by it.*

*That Elizabeth had attacked first was beyond doubt. Such foolhardy treachery! But so, too, was I aware that Blanche did not fight merely to defend herself; her clear intent was to kill. She would deny that afterward, of course, stressing that she had only meant to preserve her own life, but I knew the truth and even felt a stirring admiration of her for it. Not so submissive after all, dear Blanche. Indeed, the thought came to me that if she survived, she might prove a worthy consort after all.*

*Not that I wanted to see Elizabeth perish, of course I did not. But one does not live a thousand years without learning how to make the best of an unsought bargain.*

*Blanche summoned all her power to launch a final blow. I braced myself, expecting that the next moment would bring Elizabeth's death. Caught between shock and dismay, I paced in extreme agitation. Had anyone entered, I would no doubt have been found with hair in disarray and eyes aglow.*

*Fortunately, no one did come in, for truly I would not have wished to be seen in such a state. Worse yet, an instant later I felt the death blow that struck not Elizabeth, as I expected, but Blanche. The stunning impossibility of that rendered me all but insensible. When next I fully recall, I was on my knees beside the hearth and the sound of my own howling was ringing in my ears.*

*Someone was pounding at the door, calling my name, but I paid no need. I could think of nothing but what had just occurred. Blanche destroyed and Elizabeth . . .*

*Rage filled me at the certain knowledge that this was what she had intended from the beginning. Her pleading letter, hinting that she was on the verge of submitting to me. Her request for Blanche to be sent to her. Even the meeting beyond time's veil. All now became clear. Morgaine had learned through trial and tribulation the most effective way to grow in power as a Slayer. She had passed that knowledge on to Elizabeth, who had acted on it with ruthless speed and will.*

*Again I howled, but this time I also acted. At a flick of my hand, the high windows in the library flew open and I passed through them. Southwark flashed beneath me, followed swiftly by the river. In moments, I reached the palace and swiftly found the place where Blanche had fallen. It was deserted.*

*I settled upon the sand, turning in all directions, and bent space and time to my will as I saw the battle played out again before me. So, too, did I see the instant when Elizabeth teetered on the brink, almost but not quite falling victim to her own newfound power. Had she done so, I might still have been able to bring her to my side or, failing that, used her vaunted confidence as a weapon against her.*

*But there came her good dog Dudley, moaning of love, drawing her back from the precipice of darkness. Damn him and all he was to her!*

*Of Blanche, there was no trace. Or so I thought at first. My gaze fell on the pearls strewn all about. I held out my hand and several rose into my grasp. I touched them lightly, expecting nothing, but was surprised to feel some indefinable quickening stir deep within.*

*With a sweep of my arm, I gathered up all the pearls and slipped them into a pouch inside my cloak. What had changed in them, if anything truly had, was a question for another time.*

*Nothing mattered just then save for Elizabeth. I could no longer deny that she would go to the greatest lengths to slay me. That being the case, I set out to prepare myself for the climactic battle that I was certain was almost upon us.*

*Morning, 22 January 1559*

---

"I cannot stay here." It is morning and I am still in Robin's bed. Kat will bar my ladies from my chamber for as long as she can, but even so there will be talk.

He turns onto his side to look at me and smiles. "Pray God the day comes swiftly when we can be together without any hindrance."

If ever a man has dangled an invitation for me to declare my intentions, Robin has just done so. As my silence draws out, a frown moves behind his eyes.

"That isn't what I meant." I rise quickly, heedless of my nakedness, and begin casting about for my clothes. "I can't stay here in the palace." I turn, holding my shift, but making no effort to cover myself. "Meet me at the stables in a hour."

I am gone before he can reply.

"What are you thinking?" Kat demands when she finally has me in her clutches. "Do you imagine that your ladies are blind? Every one of them has been trying to get in here since shortly after dawn, not to mention that Cecil. By God, he is the most persistent of the bunch. An old woman could not natter more."

I refrain from suggesting that she should know and thrust my arms into the jacket of the riding habit she has fetched for me, a pretty thing of ruby brocade and silk.

"I had matters to attend to."

Kat snorts. "One matter certainly. All things in moderation, my chick. *All* things."

Partly to divert her but also because I am curious, I ask, "What is the gossip of the day?"

"You are lucky there," she admits, however grudgingly. "Instead of wondering what you are up to, something else has caught the court's notice. Part of the cockfighting pit collapsed last night. Not only that but there are strange marks on the sand, traces of scorching as though there was a fire, though there's no sign of what might have burned."

"How odd." I speak by rote, my mind turning over the scene in the pit. Abruptly I remember the pearls. "Was anything else found?"

Kat thinks for a moment, then shakes her head. "Not that I've heard mention of." She looks at me shrewdly. "Should there have been?"

It is possible, of course, that someone passing by the pit, drawn by the sight of the collapsed bleachers, found the pearls and appropriated them. But they are far too large and sumptuous to be peddled safely within the city. Perhaps some bold lord or lady will present them to me as a gift and then I will know who took them. They matter little, in any case.

"Tell Cecil I will return in better humor and that he should be glad not to have to deal with me in my present state."

"He had that fellow Walsingham with him," she calls out, but I am through my private door and do not answer.

Robin is at the stables. Coming round a corner, I pause for a moment to look at him. He wears only an open shirt, a loosely laced doublet, hose, and boots, with a short sword at his side. His skin is tanned by the sun, his coutenance open and cheerful. Never has a man looked finer.

"There you are." Gesturing to the chestnut mare whose velvety nose he is stroking, he adds, "Newly arrived from Ireland. Do you like her?"

I wait while a groom leads the mare out, then look her over carefully. Robin is a superb Master of the Horse, the first of many important appointments that I intend to give him. He shares my love of the hunt, but nothing pleases either of us so well as a full-out gallop across open ground. Never mind that Cecil and all my counselors live in dread certainty that any day I will fall from the saddle to my death. At times I can scarcely bear being cooped up within my own skin. Nothing will do but to fly free and fast, heedless of all but the power of the horse beneath me.

We are away to the north. Robin has arranged for a small escort, but we leave them behind once we reach the manor of Hyde, purchased by my father and enclosed as a deer park for his pleasure. The deer are safe from me this fair morning; I want only to feel the sun on my face and the wind against my skin.

The ground is hard-packed, covered in places by drifts of snow and frost. The bare branches of the trees stretch against a sky almost painful in its brightness. I set spurs to the mare and send her flying. Her legs stretch out, gobbling ground, as the world flows by in all its spare winter beauty. Robin follows, but the mare is swifter and carries less weight. Though his mount makes a valiant try, when I draw rein several miles hence it is to tease him for his laggardness.

"You are a slugabed this day," I tell him.

He laughs and sends me a kiss off his gloved fingertips. "Would that I were, fair lady, provided you were with me. Be assured, I would give you a good ride."

His boldness makes me laugh in turn. We continue on, walking the horses until we are deep within the park. A doe, feeding near a copse, lifts her head and looks at us. In an instant, she is gone. I hear the crash of her movements as she leaps through the underbrush. My heightened senses, so surprising at first, are becoming second nature to me. That easily do we change, if we do not take care to preserve ourselves.

"My father loved this place."

Robin stares away toward the far horizon as though it holds something of great fascination. He knows our history well enough to sense where this is going.

"He acquired it from the canons at Westminster Abbey," I continue. "They had held it since the Norman Conquest."

"A wonder then that they wished to part with it."

The words fall from his lips as though each weighs a stone and more. Clearly, this is not a topic that he wishes to pursue.

I am of a different mind. This day above all I will speak of Henry. "I suppose he offered them a decent enough price. And, of course, they would not have wished to incur his disfavor."

"Let us speak of other things."

"He bought it not long after my mother's death."

The manor was one of the gifts the king gave himself after disposing of his queen in order, it was said, to lighten his mood, much lowered by all that he had suffered in ridding himself of her.

"He swore his undying love for her before man and God." The mare, feeling my tension, shies beneath me. I soothe her firmly. "He wrote her poems, composed ballads in her honor, draped her in jewels, and remade the world all so that he could marry her."

"Elizabeth—"

I hold up a hand, silencing Robin. "Let me finish. The nearer one stands to the throne, the easier it becomes to see people as no more than a means to an end. That is how my father saw my mother, for all that he claimed otherwise. When she failed to give him the son he thought his due, he allowed her name to be dragged through the filth and attached to every infamy. And then he butchered her."

"He sent for a swordsman from Calais. Only a single blow was needed—"

"That changes nothing! All my life I have heard him called merciful because he did not burn her as was his right! *Burn her!* She trusted him with her life, her honor, her body, even her soul, and look what he did to her!"

The mare shies again. I pull hard on the reins, compelling her to settle.

"He was ill served by ambitious people who conspired to bring her down," Robin says.

"He was cleverer than all of them put together. Do not tell me that he failed to see through their machinations."

"So be it then. Do not look to me to excuse him, but what purpose does this have? The world has gone on and you with it. Surely it does you no good to dwell on such sad matters now?"

"You do not understand."

He reaches across the small distance separating us and clasps my hand. "Then for pity's sake, help me to do so. What is your meaning here?"

Words, once spoken, can never be recalled. Our greater safety lies in silence. I, who have kept my own counsel since tenderest childhood, know that far better than most.

Yet, there comes a time when silence is itself a lie and there is no way forward but the truth.

"I can never marry you."

He stares at me in shock, then pales. His hand falls away. I watch the muscles work in his throat and dread the moment when he speaks.

"You would put a foreign prince over us?"

"No! You mistake my intent. I will never give any man such power over me as my father held over my mother's head until the day he had it hewn from her body!"

Dear Robin, sweet Robin, he truly looks appalled. "I would never—!" The very thought appears to sicken him. He sways slightly in the saddle.

In desperation, I try to make him understand. "Power corrupts, and none worse than the power that comes from the throne. It can take the purest soul on earth and twist it into something you could not recognize. Look what happened to my father. In his youth, he was a kind and cheerful man, a scholar and a poet. He ended his days steeped in madness, seeing conspiracies everywhere, willing to wade in the blood of his friends."

"I am no Henry! For pity's sake, Elizabeth, you know me better than this!"

"I know who you are now and whom I wish you to remain. Be my friend, my lover, my confidant, the one and only man with whom I can truly be myself. But do not ask to be my husband, for that can never be."

He turns away, and for a moment I fear that he means to ride off, leaving me alone in the vast park where my father sent stag after stag to its death in the months after my mother's execution, her demise having left him with a thirst for blood that seemed insatiable.

But Robin is better than that, better than me if it comes to it, for I am Henry's daughter as much as Anne's. God forbid that the same murderous impulses that dwelled in my father find expression in me. However much I fear a husband, no consort of mine could ever think his head secure beneath his crown.

"What of the succession?" he demands. "Have you thought of that?"

At times I could think of little else, so relentlessly have Cecil and the other members of my council dwelled upon this point. My Spirit has convinced me to name an heir in secret, but I will not speak of that. Instead, I wave a hand airily.

"There are any number of candidates. It will sort itself out in time."

Robin's face hardens. I have hurt him and he would be less than human if he did not wish to do the same to me.

"What if there is no time? What if you fall to Mordred?"

I laugh and laugh again when I see his shock. Still, the question deserves a serious answer.

"Sweet Robin, if I fall to Mordred, there will be no doubt whatsoever about the succession. As my grandfather claimed the throne when he slew King Richard III, so will Mordred seize this realm and everything in it before my body can grow cold."

While yet Robin contemplates this, I command his gaze with mine. "Promise me that if that happens, you will not hesitate but will leave this land with all speed and never return."

His lip curls in disgust. "You think me such a coward?"

"No! I think that I will take my last breath with far less fear and pain if I believe that you, my love, will be safe."

I touch my spurs to the mare but she needs no urging. As much as I, she is ready to be done with this place. Her hooves throw up clods of dirt as we race back the way we came. If I could, I would fly on and on to the ends of the world and beyond, but that is not to be.

I have passed down the length of my life across chasms that threatened one after another to entomb me—the child of tragedy, the target of conspiracy, the queen called bastard and witch borne—all to come to this moment.

The ribbon has run out and time is gone with it.

From the winter park, sere beneath frost, I ride certain of my purpose and accepting of whatever my fate may be.

I am the Slayer and I have come to kill.

*Afternoon, 22 January 1559*

---

"*Enough!*" We are in my council chamber—Cecil, Walsing-ham, Dee, Robin, and myself. We have been there for an hour and more after my return to the palace. I am still in my riding habit, my skirts swirling as I pace back and forth.

"No more advice," I declare, for I have had a bellyful of it.

Cecil, first and foremost, wants us to proceed with caution, as though that were remotely possible. Dee supports him. Neither of them seem to understand that Mordred will not wait. He will know what has happened to Blanche and will realize that I am a greater danger to him than ever. If I do not strike first, he is cer-tain to do so.

But when I point that out—again—all I get in return is more hemming and hawing, more scholarly pontificating, more talk of the alignment of the stars, the political realities, and all the rest of that nonsense that makes me want to tear my hair out by the roots and use it to strangle them.

"You heard Her Majesty." Robin finally bestirs himself. He has largely been silent since our return to the palace. While he is there in the council chamber, seemingly supporting me, I sense that he harbors his own doubts. "I remind you that we are all sworn to do Her Majesty's bidding."

Which makes it clear enough that but for his oath on the matter, he would take a very different view.

Only Walsingham looks at me foursquare and does not hesitate. "Indeed, we have heard the Queen. She makes good sense. Mordred will never be more vulnerable than he is right now."

"At last!" I exclaim. "Someone who has his head elsewhere than up his posterior." I like to think that such vulgarity is not usual for me, but I have passed the point of maintaining any decorum.

My enthusiasm does not last long before Walsingham dents it. "Even so, Majesty, you are wrong to think that you must settle this matter alone."

Cecil sucks in his breath, for not even he dares to speak to me so bluntly. Worse yet, Walsingham is his man, introduced into my service by him. Any displeasure the schoolmaster earns for himself will also accrue to my Spirit.

"I would not go that far," Cecil says quickly. "Clearly, Her Majesty is better able than any of us to deal with the inhuman foe who afflicts this realm."

"Indeed, she is." Walsingham stands, a sober figure all in black, seemingly at his ease. If he harbors any fear of my displeasure, he conceals it masterfully. "However, upon her pleasure, others of us can provide assistance."

"How?" I demand, for my patience runs thin. I count the hours until darkness and wonder how I will endure so long.

"I have continued my inquiries into the vampires' activities hereabouts," Walsingham informs me. "In the course of which, I have gleaned more about them."

"Their nature is already well-known," Dee protests. "Those of us who have made a lifelong study of them—"

"—and protected Her Majesty against them during her tender years—" Cecil adds.

"—have withheld nothing from her," Dee concludes.

"Of course you have not," Walsingham agrees. "Nothing that you know, at any rate. But there is always more to be learned. That is as great a truth in life as any ever found."

"Enough, schoolmaster," Robin says. "Tell us what you have discovered that we may stand in awe of your cleverness."

A look of honest confusion crosses Walsingham's face. "I only wish to assure that Her Majesty is in possession of all useful information before she acts."

"Of course you do," I say quickly, anything to urge him on. "What have you found?"

"By day, Southwark Manor appears deserted, except for those you call thralls, and they are in a greatly subdued state, almost quiescent as it were, neither moving nor taking note of anything that goes on around them."

"How could you possibly know this?"

"I returned there yesterday."

"You what?" The schoolmaster had gone alone into a den of vampires to ferret out such information as might prove useful to me? I can but stand in awe of his daring even as I wonder at its source. Is he so devoted to my cause as to have no care at all for his own life? Or is his devotion to something beyond myself, perhaps the England he believes I can protect and nurture? The former flatters my vanity, but the latter places him in the ranks of those whose counsel I must be wise enough to take.

"I returned there," he repeated, as though surprised that his actions should be of any note. "Someone needed to do a more complete surveillance, and I thought myself best suited to the task. I was curious to discover if the legend about vampires sleeping by day had any truth behind it. I think it must for I found no sign of them. However, neither could I find their resting place, though logic suggests that it is within the manor."

"And undefended, at least by the thralls, from what you observed." As usual, Robin has leapt to the heart of the matter. I am not far behind for all that I trip along the way.

"I told you not to enter the manor precincts," I remind Walsingham. If he intends to remain in my service—and I definitely intend to keep him there—he must learn that my instructions are not to be lightly disobeyed.

He sketches me a bow. "Your pardon, Majesty. I assumed that particular instruction applied only to the night in question and was not a general prohibition."

His parsing of my orders to his advantage rings a rueful smile from me. "In future, I will take care to be clearer."

He bows once more and scarcely has time to straighten before Cecil latches onto what has been learned.

"If this is true," my Spirit says, "we could enter the manor in full force with a contingent of men-at-arms, determine Mordred's location, and dispose of him before he can act to stop us."

"Is that what you propose?" Robin asks. "An armed attack on the manor in broad daylight? That is your best advice?"

Cecil hesitates. In matters of diplomacy and politics he has no equal, but he is astute enough to realize that he has no military experience whatsoever. Indeed, the entire direction of his life and everything he tries to persuade me to do is in service of avoiding war, which he regards as an unnecessary extravagance.

"Well . . . perhaps not," he hedges.

"A degree of subterfuge is called for," I acknowledge. "After all, we don't want the common folk alarmed any more than they already have been." Before any of them can respond, I plunge on.

"Cecil, you will remain here as before to keep the rumors to a minimum and generally deflect attention from my absence. The rest of you will come with me. At the manor, we must conduct a quick but thorough search. If Mordred can be located, I will deal with him, but every care must be taken not to alert the other vampires to danger. Should that happen, we will be hard-pressed to escape with our lives."

My plan is greeted with general acceptance, although Cecil manages to feign disappointment at being left behind again, while Dee struggles to hide his unease at being drafted to go along. Walsingham could appear no different if I had invited him to go for a pleasant stroll, whereas Robin . . .

Robin gives a wolf's smile that puts me in mind of the thirst for battle that he has shown in the past when he distinguished himself fighting for my sister, Mary, at Calais and later when he became a champion in the lists. My woman's heart would have me leave him safe at Cecil's side. But beyond the insult I would thus inflict on him, as Queen I must steel myself and do whatever is needed for my cause.

Walsingham clears his throat. "An excellent plan, having the virtue of both simplicity and clarity. If I might just add—"

"Yes, what is it?"

"To avoid undue attention, Your Majesty will require a disguise."

He is right, of course, I should have thought of that myself. It is one thing to travel secretly by night, quite another to do it by day. My appearance is sufficiently well-known to Londoners that I would be spotted before I could cross the river.

"I believe that I can help with that," Robin says. "Come with me."

My council chamber is connected to my private quarters by one of the many interior galleries that allow movement through the palace without the need to go through the public areas filled with gawkers and petitioners. Such passageways are by no means secret, but neither is anyone encouraged to loiter in them. The gallery that Robin and I enter is empty, as is my bed-chamber. From there, we move quickly to his own, emerging through the hidden door to startle one of his servants, who is putting away Robin's freshly laundered clothes.

"Out, man!" Robin bellows, and the fellow scampers off.

Throwing open the lid of a chest, Robin begins rummaging through it. His actions remind me suddenly of what passed between us after the successful search for the French gloves. I cannot help but laugh.

"If we are to disport ourselves, we will have to make haste," I say.

He straightens with an armload of clothes and eyes me narrowly. "Good enough for that, am I, but nothing more?"

In a flash, my good humor evaporates. Of course, I understand that he feels driven to air his disappointment, but the moment hangs so perilously . . . could he not have waited?

Unless he does truly believe that there may be no future opportunity and would not have me die without knowing of his anger.

"Out with it then! Tell me how ill-used you are, how vile I am. Call me cruel, unnatural, whatever you will. Heaven forfend that you think of anyone other than yourself!"

He drops the clothes and comes at me. In an instant, I am tumbled back across his bed and he is on top of me.

"You are cruel!" he exclaims. "I give you my heart and you take delight in shredding it!"

"Your heart? What of mine! I cannot even claim to own it for my people have a prior claim. I have nothing of myself, nothing! And now, with all that has happened, I do not even know who I am!"

It is the truth, plainly spoken, but it is not what he wants to hear. He wants me to tell him that I cherish his heart and that he has mine in turn. Much good that it would do him, for I fear that it is a poor, shriveled thing withered from scant use.

Not so my body, which appears to have a will entirely of its own. We tear at each other, clothes banished, flesh bared, mouths clinging, limbs entwined. He is in me and all around me; I possess him completely and I glory in it. If I die, let me die now as I soar into the heat of the sun and the infinity of the heavens. Fear falls away, the world with all its shackles does not exist. It is a masquerade, nothing more, and we the poor dupes who account it real and suffer so much trial and tribulation in it.

But false or not, inevitably, the world exerts its claim once again. I descend from bliss to rumpled sheets, pounding heart, and the certain knowledge that precious time is passing.

Robin lies beside me, gasping. When I start to rise from the bed, he clasps my arm and pulls me to him. Eye to eye, he says, "Forget my angry words, I pray you. I spoke in thoughtless haste."

His apology wrings a wistful smile. "But truthfully, all the same. I have disappointed you."

He laughs faintly. "Believe me, sweetling, right now *disappointed* is not how I would describe myself." More seriously he adds, "Think only of what must be done to end the threat to your realm. Once Mordred is sent to his hellish reward, there will be time for everything else."

I cannot bring myself to tell him that no amount of time will favorably dispose me toward matrimony. I am unalterable in my conviction that to take a husband would be to tempt the cruelest fate.

And so I smile, slip from the bed, and hold out my hand to him. "Help me to dress. I have no notion of how to put on male garb."

He hastens to oblige me and plays the willing maid until, swiftly, we are both decently clad and on our way. An awkward page boy tugging at "his" hose and not quite able to keep his feathered hat on straight follows Robin back to the council chamber.

Cecil sucks in his breath at sight of me. "Sweet heaven . . ."

Beside him, Dee colors with embarrassment and looks away. Scholar that he is, apparently the sight of a woman's legs undoes him. He says nothing.

Alone among the three, Walsingham appears unfazed by my disguise. "Well done," he decrees with a nod to Robin, who apparently gets the credit. "I believe we may now proceed."

The departure of three men—Cecil remains behind—going briskly from the council chamber would attract attention under any circumstances. In the eager speculation that accompanies their passing, no one takes any notice of the page trailing after them.

For the first time in my life, I am effectively invisible. The experience is disconcerting but not unpleasant. How refreshing not to be the focus of all eyes or the target of all tongues. How delightful not to have every aspect of my appearance and behavior dissected for the tiniest hidden meanings.

How different the world looks when one does not scan every face for signs of treachery or wonder if every shadow conceals an assassin.

The respite is too short. Quickly enough, we are across the river, and from there it is scant time before we reach Southwark Manor.

*Late afternoon, 22 January 1559*

_____

The high iron gates set within the stone walls that circle the manor grounds open once again at my touch. Before we pass through, I caution my companions.

"We have only a few hours of daylight left. We must find where Mordred sleeps quickly so that I may dispose of him. If we are still within these walls when night falls . . ."

I do not have to state the terrible danger we will face. They all know well enough that if our presence is detected, the entire court of the vampires will rise up as one to defend their king and themselves. Against such overwhelming odds, not even I with all my newfound power could hope to prevail.

We go swiftly up the path, still glistening with frost, and across the wide stone terrace to the double ironbound doors. Unlike the gates, they are securely fastened.

I turn to Walsingham. "How did you get in when you came here?"

"This way." He leads us around a corner and through an archway giving onto a broad flagstone courtyard framed by the three wings of the house. At this hour, so large a residence should be bustling with servants, retainers, and the like. Carriages, wagons, and riders should be coming and going. The kitchens should be a hive of activity as dinner is prepared. Nothing of the sort is happening here; there is only stillness eerie enough to raise the hairs on the back of my neck. Staring up toward the steeply pitched roof, I glimpse stone gargoyles, winged beasts with leering faces and cloven hooves. They crouch as though about to leap down on us.

A small wooden door set near a corner of the building sits so deep in shadow as to be all but invisible. The schoolmaster lifts the iron latch and eases the door open. On the far side is a low passage.

"The hall is this way," he says. We have gone only a short distance in that direction when we encounter the first of the thralls. He—or she—is standing motionless against the far wall. We can make out nothing but the all-encompassing brown robe that hides every feature.

Robin, who has not seen such a creature before, sucks in his breath. Knowing as I do now how they are created, I wonder who the brave soul was who dared to go against Mordred and has suffered such a dire fate for it.

We make our way past the thrall without arousing it but shortly encounter two more. Both are as unresponsive as Walsingham promised they would be. The phenomenon seems bewildering until I consider that perhaps the will of the vampires is needed to animate these helpless beings. While their masters sleep, their slaves remain insensible.

Dee may be thinking along similar lines for his color improves as he throws off the fear that has kept him stooped and anxious ever since entering the manor.

"If legend is to be our guide," the magus says, "we should consider that the sleep of vampires is said to mimic death. They are believed to favor crypts for their resting place."

"Is there a church on the grounds?" Robin asks. "If so, it is likely to have a crypt."

"Not so far as I have discovered," Walsingham replies. "However, I have examined the original plans for the manor and confirmed that there was a private chapel. I suggest we start there."

The chapel is on the far side of the entry opposite the hall. We enter through an intricately carved wooden door depicting the fall of man and the expulsion from Eden.

Robin calls my attention to the scene. "Apt, wouldn't you say?"

I recall Mordred's argument that either the vampires are as much a part of God's natural order as we are or there is no God as we conceive Him. With all that has happened so quickly, I have yet to find a cogent response to his argument, but one will undoubtedly come to me in time.

Beyond the cautionary door with its reminder of human frailty, the chapel is much as I would expect. Great houses always have some lavish space set aside to demonstrate the owner's piety. Such private chapels were spared the depredations that fell upon public churches and abbeys when my father remade the world. These enclaves remain much as they have been for centuries. This one boasts a high ceiling supported by intricately carved columns and painted to resemble a starry sky. In addition, stained-glass windows represent the Passion of Christ, and a tiled floor is laid out in a mosaic of the Greek letters alpha and omega to remind us that our Savior is the beginning and end of all things. Lastly, upon the altar gleams a gold and jeweled cross of rare beauty.

"How astonishing that Mordred and his kind left all this intact," Dee exclaims.

"Perhaps they feared to enter," Robin suggests. "We may be in the wrong place."

I walk closer to the altar, studying it. The entrance to many crypts is down steps near the altar. But I can find no trace of any such thing here.

"My father had this manor built. His architects might have included a crypt for tradition's sake, but they as easily could have omitted it. Neither would the Archbishop of York, to whom the manor passed, have had reason to add such a thing."

Walsingham looks disconcerted. "Then where could the vampires be?"

"A house of this size will have vast undercrofts for the storage of food, armaments, prisoners, and the like," Robin says. "We could spend days searching them."

Dread fills me. If we fail to find Mordred quickly, he will strike with all his might. As much as I want to believe that I can defeat him in fair battle, I would much prefer not to have to find out.

Regrettably, what Robin says makes good sense; the vampires may well retire to the undercrofts by day. But is Mordred among them?

It is a truth understood by those who hold power, but not always by those who seek it, that people yearn to believe in something greater than themselves, something set apart and above them. A wise ruler encourages that belief.

If I were Mordred, where would I seek my rest? Among my kind, as one of them, or somewhere exclusively my own?

The moment the question occurs to me, I try to root it from my mind. We are nothing alike, the vampire king and I. Fate has made us enemies for a reason; we see the world and everything in it entirely differently. But for all that, we are bound together by forces I have only just begun to sense. Like it or not, there is a link between us. Can I use that to my own ends?

If I were he, where would I go?

Walsingham looks at me intently, as though he is following the play of thoughts across my face. "Majesty . . . you have a thought?"

"Would that I did . . ." My voice trails off. I sink into memory, striving to recall every tiny fragment that I can reconstruct from each encounter I have had with Mordred, anything that might give me a hint of his whereabouts. Nothing comes to me. I drift instead to thoughts of Morgaine in her eternal home on the hill where now the Tower sits.

In fair sight of this hill rising above Southwark is Mordred's ancient home that he has reclaimed.

"This manor boasts a tower, does it not? I thought I noticed it in darkness when I came the first time and again when we entered now."

"It does," Walsingham agrees. "But I fail to see—"

"Show me the way to it."

If I am mistaken, we will waste what little time we have, yet I am gripped by a sudden conviction that will not loose hold of me: The tower would have an excellent view out over the river toward Tower Hill. Within it, Mordred would have constant sight not only of the city at the heart of the realm he aspires to rule but most particularly of the place where Morgaine dwelled. The more I think on it, the less I can imagine him anywhere else.

A tight spiral of stone steps leads upward. I insist on taking the lead, to the consternation of the gentlemen, especially Robin, who must be dissuaded from pulling out his sword and charging straight ahead.

We mount slowly and with care. Torches set at intervals along the curving wall cast twisting shadows. In their flickering light, we appear as giants even as I feel the full weight of my own doubts threatening to crush me into nothingness.

If I am not strong enough—

If I waiver in my conviction—

If fortune simply does not favor me—

Fie with fortune! And fie with all the rest as well. I will slay Mordred and take his power as I took that of Blanche. With that, no one will be able to come against me ever.

But I will keep my humanity all the same because I love and am loved.

And because I am Elizabeth, daughter of Anne, who died rather than sacrifice her soul—and mine—to evil.

The top of the winding steps gives out into a large, circular room with a high, vaulted ceiling. Fading daylight pours through high windows that look out toward the city. I can make out Tower Hill clearly, but I have scant time to notice it before I am distracted. Books and scrolls line the walls in number beyond any I have ever seen. Many are lavishly bound within embossed leather set with jewels and secured with golden clasps. Others are of such an age that the leather has worn away, revealing the wooden boards beneath, still protecting the precious pages within. What must be the oldest works are the scrolls rolled within leather and horn cases that are themselves ornately embellished.

What treasures are among them? What works long forgotten or believed lost? The scholar in me yearns to delve into their midst and not emerge again until I have plumbed at least some measure of their mystery.

But the queen I must be remembers her business. I cast a long look around the library and am disappointed. "There is no sign of him here."

Indeed, but there is another door leading . . . where?

"With me." Before I can think better of it, I plunge through the door into the room beyond. Unlike as in the library, the windows of this chamber are heavily curtained to block out all light.

Even so, such is the power of my heightened senses that I can detect the shape of a bier set in the center of the floor. It appears to be draped in velvet and lying upon it . . .

*Mordred.*

I do not hesitate but raise my arm to strike at once. The blow I loose bathes the room in incandescent white light. The air itself tears apart in a shriek that echoes across the stone walls. Dimly, I am aware of Robin thrown back by the force of it, but my attention is focused on the vampire king. To my horror, in the very instant before my blow would have struck him, he rolls to the side, drops off the bier, and in an instant is on his feet.

"Elizabeth." My name sounds to my ears like a hiss, long drawn out and evocative of the serpent I have so lately seen carved into the door of the chapel below.

A suffocating cloud of blackness hurls toward me. Behind it, I hear him clearly. "How nice of you to call. And you've brought friends."

I have no choice but to strike again before the light of my first blow has faded. The effect is blinding. When next I can see, the black cloud remains intact but at least it is no closer to me. I am managing to hold it off even as Mordred hovers above to mock me. He is, as always, beautiful in the extreme, his eyes aglow with power, his manner regal, his strength so vast as to set the very air to strumming. Every nerve in my body shivers in response. I have never been more drawn to him nor more repulsed by my weakness.

"Shall I take this as your answer to my proposal?" he asks.

Is it he I loathe or myself? He has opened a window into my soul to reveal possibilities that would tempt the purest saint. He has enticed me to reject everything I was raised to believe in and reach instead for what I simply want. Were I to do as he wishes, I would have to reject my mother's sacrifice and my father's legacy together.

What then would be left of me?

"Take it any way you wish, fiend!"

Again, I strike at him, but again he eludes my blow. The chamber cannot contain the energy we both unleash. Slowly but unmistakably, the stone walls begin to crack.

Behind me, I can hear Dee frantically muttering incantations. To the side, I catch sight of Walsingham, all the color washed from him as his lips move in prayer. Robin is upright again, his hand on the hilt of his sword.

Stone dust showers down from the ceiling of the chamber. The cracks are spreading in all directions. Through them I catch a glimpse of the sky. Day is fast fading; the first scattering of stars has appeared.

Night is almost upon us.

The light gathers in me, a wave growing in remorseless power as it races toward the shore. Everything I am, everything I can be, surges in this single breath of time.

Beyond the dark, thickening cloud, Mordred starts. He has not guessed the full extent of what I have become. I am a heartbeat away from destroying him when—

Robin—dear, foolish Robin—yanks his sword from its scabbard and darts forward, directly into the path of the blow I am about to unleash. No doubt he means to protect me or prove his valor or show himself as the worthy consort he believes himself to be. Or perhaps none of that is true and he acts purely on rash impulse. It does not matter.

With a flick of his hand, Mordred takes command of him. Before my horrified eyes, he lifts Robin free of the ground, his sword falling from fingers suddenly unable to clasp it. My sweet, infuriating love hangs suspended in the air before being yanked forward. The moment he is close enough, Mordred lashes out an arm and grasps him around the throat.

The stone walls begin to tumble. The last rays of the setting sun are too low to touch the tower; darkness swallows us. With a triumphant laugh, Mordred rises past the wreckage and soars into the sky, taking Robin with him.

In an instant, they both vanish.

*Did I know that Elizabeth would bring her dog with her? Certainly, I
had an inkling. Dudley had been left behind before and had yapped
about it. And she had taken him along to the Tower when she met
Morgaine there. I had seen the undeniable evidence of her feelings for
him. When my rage—and I admit my grief—at Blanche's demise
cooled a little, I knew what I had to do.*

*Elizabeth would seek to strike first, of that I was certain. Once in
possession of Blanche's power—second only to my own—she would
waste no time. I considered laying a trail for her to follow to find me
but thought better of it lest I raise her suspicions. I was counting on
her intelligence to determine my whereabouts and I was not disappointed.*

*Had I not been expecting her, that first blow she hurled at me
would have meant my end. Strange to think of that. After existing
for so many years, I might actually have perished. And then what?
The damnation that Elizabeth and no doubt many others believe is
my due? Nothingness? Or perhaps something far more remarkable
than any of us, mortal or otherwise, can imagine.*

*But I digress. With Dudley in my grip, I removed myself from the
manor to the secure location I had already prepared. Although it irks
me to admit it, he bore his sudden captivity with as much courage as
a man can be asked to muster. Although ashen and trembling as he
confronted me, he strove for the semblance of valor.*

*The moment I released my hold around his throat, he staggered several feet away, gasped for breath, and, having found it, lashed out at me.*

*"Foul fiend! If you think to use me to harm my beloved Queen, think again. I will happily die a thousand deaths rather than have her discomfited in the slightest!"*

*I couldn't help but roll my eyes at this bit of melodrama. Even so, I will admit to responding in like manner.*

*"Fear not, faithful hound, I have no intention of killing you. In fact, it is your continued life that interests me."*

*As he stared at me in angry bewilderment, I gave him a firm shove backward into the cell I had readied and quickly slammed the heavy door. As I secured it, I saw his white face through the narrow grill. He was consumed with the fear and helplessness that is the fate of all mortals, whether they wish to recognize it or not. I could pity them for that, but really it just confirms the essential pointlessness of their lives.*

*Except, of course, insofar as they can serve and sustain my kind. That solace, at least, I can offer them.*

*"Where are you going?" he demanded.*

*Over my shoulder, I replied, "To bargain for your life. Pray to whatever god you like that I succeed."*

*With that, I lifted into the night.*

---

*I* am in a pit, at the bottom of a well. Around me there is only darkness and despair. I cannot move or think or do anything other than cry out against what has happened.

"Robin!"

What devilish twist of fate has ripped him from me even as I stood by helplessly and did nothing?

Dee and Walsingham drag me along with them as they flee the collapsing tower. We only just descend the spiral steps before the whole gives way, sending huge blocks of masonry down all around us. Choking on clouds of stone dust, we race through and around the wreckage, along the frost-rimmed drive, and out beyond the iron gates.

Nothing stirs in the street beyond. No one has come to see what is happening. Londoners, normally the most curious of people, are nowhere in evidence.

Behind us is a different matter. The vampire court is awakening to the discovery of what has happened. Already, I can hear their howls.

"We must get you to safety, Majesty!" Walsingham exclaims.

I would laugh were my throat not so tight with shock and tears. Safety? There is no such thing. It is as much an illusion as is the world itself.

Only despair is real.

Crossing back over the river, I stare down into the pewter

water and imagine myself sinking into it. And why not? I have failed utterly. My power—not to say my vanity—proved unequal to Mordred's wiles. Because of that, Robin will die or worse yet be condemned to the living death of a thrall.

Either thought is unbearable. I suck in a sob between my teeth and struggle to find some fragment of strength in this most desperate hour.

"Where could he have taken him?" I ask.

Sitting on the plank facing me, Dee and Walsingham exchange a look. The magus says, "I will examine the skies, Majesty, and cast charts, but all that will take time and—"

Walsingham makes a dismissive sound. "The answer Your Majesty seeks is not to be found in the heavens. It is on the ground, where I will set my eyes and ears to ferret out every morsel of intelligence. But again, it will take some time—"

Time! Time! All that they propose will take precious hours if not days, and in the meantime Robin remains Mordred's hostage. What if he has already drained my love of his mortal life?

From deep within myself, past all fear and anguish, cold reason rises. It comes implacably, a ruthless warrior striding into battle. Before it, all else falls away. What is its origin? My mother's proud spirit, steadfast faith, and courage? Oh, how I would like to believe that! But it is my father I see against the landscape of my mind—the monarch bestride the world, fighting for all that he believed in no matter what the cost. Great Henry, who sacrificed friendship, love, and faith together for the sake of his kingship. Who became the monster he believed he had to be to preserve his realm.

Reason speaks above human weakness.

What good is a hostage if not to be bargained for?

While I am thinking only of finding Robin, Mordred has to

find me, if only to reveal his terms for leaving Robin unharmed. He will know exactly where to look.

"Hurry! I must reach the palace!"

At my command, the wherryman bends his back to the oars. He rows with the fury of a sober fellow with a keen instinct for trouble and the will to avoid it. Each passing moment speeds us toward the shore. I have scant time to decide how to proceed.

I have encountered Mordred in two locations in Whitehall—the gallery where the would-be assassin came at me and before that in the walled garden reached down the hidden passage from my chamber. Scarcely does the wherry bump against the water steps than I am on my feet, stepping over Dee and Walsingham before they can rise. Without pause, I race for the garden.

Over my shoulder, I call, "Do not follow me! Stay well clear!"

The winter garden is dark and still. Frost crackles beneath my feet. I take a breath and free the senses that have grown so powerful since my awakening.

He is here; I can feel him, a dark and forceful presence hovering somewhere nearby. I turn in all directions, but see only bare trees and empty flower beds, the debris of the season of death that will, please God, give way in time to spring's rebirth. But first . . . what is that there in the shadows near the wall?

Mordred steps from the darkness as naturally as another man would walk from his house into the street at the height of day. He is all in black, as ever, but the light that glows from within him is breathtaking in its beauty. He smiles as though genuinely pleased to see me.

"Dear Elizabeth, I knew that you would come. The bond we

share grows stronger by the hour. And now we share Dudley as well. I have him, you want him. What are we to do?"

My fists clench at my sides. It is all I can do not to strike at him. The smile I summon in turn threatens to crack my face. "What are your terms?"

He shrugs, as though the answer should be obvious. "What they have always been."

Indeed, why should they change? He has outplayed me. Or so he thinks. Fair Fortuna favor me that I may yet prove him wrong.

"You went to such trouble to take Robin hostage. And all for what? Because you believe that I mean to refuse you?"

"You did come to the manor to slay me." He appears more amused than concerned. His failure to take me seriously gives me hope that my plan, cobbled together in desperation, may yet have some chance of succeeding.

I wave a hand as though to brush aside his foolish misconception. "I came to negotiate. I merely sought to make you aware of my power first."

It is as bold a lie as I have ever told, and for a moment I fear that he is about to call me on it. Quickly I add, "I will not be a submissive consort. Do not ever imagine that."

Amusement gives way to surprise. He looks at me narrowly. "What are you saying?"

I force myself to take a step and then another. The distance between us shrinks. Dressed as I am as a boy, I cannot hope to be alluring, but I do snatch off my silly hat and toss it to the ground. My hair tumbles loose, fiery strands blowing on the wind.

"Do you think me such a fool that I would refuse eternal life, protection for my kingdom, all that anyone could possibly desire?"

"And yet you killed Blanche."

"Of course I killed her. She wanted to be your queen. She thought it her due."

Slowly, never taking his eyes from me, he nods. "But she understood why that could not be."

"Did she? That was not my impression. Had I not been so swift in defending myself, she would have struck first and might well have killed me. Then what of all your plans?"

Sternly I drive the point home. "Blanche betrayed you. She saw me as a rival and she was right to do so."

Vanity is a wonderful thing. It can persist despite centuries of opportunity to learn its folly. Indeed, perhaps it flourishes under such circumstances.

Something for me to think about if my new and hastily constructed plan goes horribly awry.

"Let us be frank," I continue. "As you have already said, there is a powerful attraction between us."

Mordred tilts his head to one side, observing me. I return his gaze with all the warmth that I can muster. I can claim that it is only thoughts of Robin that enable me to create the semblance of desire, but that would not be true. I think instead of my throne, of power, of my queenship, and of slaying Mordred. I stare into his eyes and smile as I imagine his death. What will he look like when he flies apart into a thousand shards of light bright enough to rival the star-draped sky?

Whatever bond he believes exists between us, it does not extend to being able to read my thoughts. Thanks be to God for that.

"Then it is settled," Mordred says though a question lingers in his tone. "You will be my queen."

My course is set; nothing in this world or beyond could persuade me to change it. Yet a treacherous flutter of temptation stirs within me. I repress it ruthlessly even as I remain aware of its presence deep within.

"It is settled," I agree, "but I need time to prepare my people. Surely, you will grant me that?"

"How much time?"

"A month . . . scant enough for the purpose, but I think it can be done—"

"That is absurd. I will give you a day, no more."

I scoff at that. "A single day to meet with all my counselors and other high lords and persuade them to accept what I must do? How can you imagine such a thing is to be accomplished?"

"What need have you to persuade them? You rule here. Announce your intent and be done with it."

"It is not that simple!"

He moves too swiftly for me to avoid him. His hands are hard on my shoulders, his grip implacable. He bends his head, his mouth brushing my neck. "Yes, Elizabeth, it is. You are Queen, act as one."

I gasp, overwhelmed with pleasure at his touch, yet desperate to deny it. "You don't understand. I wish only to smooth your way so that when you become my consort, my people will accept you. Isn't that what you want?"

He considers this. Scarcely breathing, I can only wait balanced between hope and dread until at last he nods. "A day, no more." A sardonic light darts behind his eyes. "One day to convince your people to love me as no doubt you will yourself."

"A week."

He laughs. "Be done, Elizabeth. You have wrested more concession from me than I meant to give, but my generosity comes with a condition."

My mind is racing ahead to what I must do—so swiftly!—once he is gone. Mention of condition trips me up.

"What do you want?"

"You must demonstrate that you mean what you say."

"How can I do that? I don't—"

His hand moves to the curve of my throat, his touch sending a frisson of pleasure through me.

"Do you understand the process by which you will become my queen?"

By which I will become a vampire, he means. I have been too squeamish, refusing to really think about it. But I know a little.

"You create a vampire by feeding on . . ." Horror fills me. I would shrink from him but his grip is too strong.

"Several encounters are required, one being not at all sufficient. Yet I would taste you now without further delay. Do this for me and I will grant you a day to make your preparations."

*Taste me.*

I want to cry out in revulsion, truly I do, and yet his closeness coupled with the sense of his power calling to mine is all so darkly compelling. From the depths of my being, desire such as I have never known rises, growing fiercer with each breath, until it threatens to consume me.

I tip my head to the side, pull my hair away, and bare my throat to Mordred's caress.

I thought up to the very last that Elizabeth meant to back away. When she claimed to have decided to become my queen—and to have killed Blanche only to eliminate a rival—I hesitated to believe her. She was, after all, Henry's daughter, and if ever there was a master of ruthless duplicity, it was he.

But when she bared her throat . . . that lovely slender, white throat, I confess to being all but overwhelmed. I had waited for that moment for so very long, long before Elizabeth's birth, even before I had any real hope that my dream to assume my rightful place as Britain's king could be fulfilled.

In the months after Morgaine perished in battle against me, leaving me sorely wounded, I cursed the cruel fate that condemned me to be a cheerless wanderer in a world of perpetual darkness. With virtually all the vampire clan in Britain slain, I was truly alone. Had I understood the means by which I could contrive my own death, I would gladly have used them. But for all my power, I remained ignorant in the ways of my kind. I had no choice but to endure.

That is not to say that I did not attempt to end my existence. In those as yet early days, I tried every method I could think of— poison, the knife, fire—everything, all to no avail. Yet the effort was not wasted for by it I began to discover the extent of my powers. I traveled for a time on the Continent—several centuries in all—find-ing my own kind, learning from them, and growing in strength. At length, I returned to Britain and began creating a new race of vampires to serve as my court. Eternal life breeds great patience, but at length even my forbearance threatened to run out. Anne's decision to go to the scaffold rather than accept what I offered almost undid me. Only the knowledge that Elizabeth still lived, and could be kept alive by me, preserved my resolve.

All the while I waited for the moment to arrive when I could at last assume my rightful place as Britain's king. At long last, I stood on the very precipice of all I had ever desired.

That lovely slender, white throat . . .

I wrapped an arm around her waist, holding her securely not because I thought she meant to flee, clearly she did not, but in an effort to reassure and perhaps even comfort her. I did not want her to be afraid. Fear has an unpleasant taste. At the first touch of my mouth on her, she flinched, but in the next instant dug her fingers into my arms and held on. I went carefully, sinking into her slowly, giving her time to adjust to me. She tensed and I tasted the swirl of emotions rising in her—shock, dismay, and then, to my great joy, a wave of pleasure that washed out all else and left her clinging to me.

Elizabeth, so beautiful, so passionate! Everything I had hoped for from the first moment I glimpsed her behind the ice-laced tower window. My exhilaration was boundless. I was so close, so very close, to all I have ever desired. In my eagerness, I sank a little deeper only to be drawn up quickly by her moan. Her eyes were closed, her lids blue-tinged against the paleness of her skin. A rush of tenderness swept over me. With only a small thought for my self-restraint, I withdrew from her and laid her tenderly on a stone bench.

A single day and she would be mine forever. What glories we would create! The world and all in it would never be the same. We would throw off the shackles of death and lay the foundation for a future as brilliant as the light that glows within my kind.

No shadow of doubt touched my mind as I spared her a last fond glance before soaring into the night.

## Midnight, 25 January 1559

---

*S*now melting on my cheeks wakes me. I rouse slowly, uncertain of where I am or what has happened. My memory has a dreamlike quality—the tumbling tower, the flight back to Whitehall, the winter garden.

*Mordred.*

My hand flies to the side of my throat. The instant I touch my skin, an echo of pleasure ripples through me. I gasp in shock and snatch my hand away.

Sitting bolt upright on the bench, I struggle to recover my senses. Did I really agree to Mordred's condition and allow him to "taste" me? And have I truly suffered no ill effects?

On my feet, heedless of the chill, I take the measure of myself. Arms, legs, eyes, mind, so far as I can tell, I am unharmed, yet how am I to know what he has done to me?

What he has put into me or taken from me?

What I am becoming?

A sob breaks from between my clenched lips. At the sound of it, I am hurtled back into reason. I am Elizabeth! I do not stand about in a dead garden moaning over what could not be helped.

I have a day, and by all that is holy and unholy, I intend to use it.

Striding into my chamber, I startle poor Cecil and Kat. The highest counselor in my realm and my dear nurse are keeping each other dour company while awaiting my return. Kat, bless her, smiles in relief. Cecil does not.

"Majesty," my Spirit begins, "if you would but take a moment to hear my advice . . ."

"Walsingham," I demand. "Where is he?"

Cecil hesitates, clearly struggling with such cavalier dismissal. For a moment, I regret my harshness but I have no chance to contemplate it. Kat steps past him and nods her head toward the door leading to my antechamber.

"He's out there along with that so-called magus. Shall I admit them?"

"With all speed."

They come, stumbling in their haste, clearly much relieved to see me.

"Majesty—," Dee begins, but I wave him into silence and address the schoolmaster instead.

"How quickly can you deploy these eyes and ears of which you spoke?"

"It is already done, Majesty. I should begin receiving reports by dawn."

I nod once, all he will get until he produces something I can act upon. To the magus, I ask, "Have you surveyed the skies? Cast a chart?"

He tugs hard on his beard. "I have taken the first steps to do both, Majesty. The signs are favorable thus far but require more study. However, I can tell you that I believe Lord Dudley lives still and that there will be opportunity to rescue him."

Scant comfort, but some at least. Even so, it is not remotely enough. "Work harder and faster. In a single day, Mordred expects me to announce to my people that he is my chosen consort and their king. If I do not, I have no doubt that he will kill Robin and come after me."

I ignore the gasps that follow this declaration and plunge on. "I must know before then where Lord Dudley has been taken. Once he is free, I will deal with Mordred myself. Is that clear?"

Kat's fingers are pressed against her lips. Through them, she says, "Sweetling, what are you saying?"

I take her both her hands in mine and hold them firmly. "The battle is upon us, dear one, or very nearly so. Do not be afraid for right and goodness are on our side. You have always taught me that and I know it to be true."

She appears little comforted by my brave words, but for love of me she musters a brave smile and squeezes my fingers. "You'll set him right, dear one. You'll give him just what he deserves. I've no doubt of it."

For a moment, my eyes tear over. I blink furiously to clear them and take a quick breath to steady myself.

Cecil, Walsingham, and Dee all look appropriately intent and grim. I have no doubt that they will do their utmost to help me, but I suspect their efforts will fall far short of what I need against so formidable an enemy.

Where else can I turn?

"My Spirit, I am going to the Tower. Arrange it."

Cecil opens his mouth to protest or at the very least to ask what I am about, but catches himself. With a swift nod, he hurries off to arrange an escort.

I turn to Walsingham. "I will be back before dawn. Have something for me by then."

He bows gravely.

"As for you, magus, consult the stars, cast your charts, but also turn that keen mind of yours to consider where a vampire king would go to conceal a valued hostage and himself as well."

Dee's hand falls away from his beard. He straightens his

shoulders and looks at me with clear determination. "I will do my utmost, Majesty."

"I hope so, for much may turn upon it. Now all of you save my nurse leave me. I have had enough of boy's garb and would be myself again."

I would leave them with the belief that they are important to me, as they are. But I have no illusions. The fate of my realm rests upon me, and in truth I would not have it otherwise.

Scarcely has the door closed behind them that Kat presses me most urgently, "Let me go with you."

Yanking off the doublet and shirt that are part of my disguise, I shake my head. "I cannot. It is too dangerous."

She frowns at me just as she did when I was very young and up to no good. "To visit a grave? Where is the danger in that?"

I roll down my hose and add them to the pile. Kat drops a chemise over my head but she does not relent. "That is where you are going, is it not?"

She can be pardoned for assuming that in this dark hour of need, I seek the solace of my mother's only memorial, scant though it is. And she is not entirely wrong. Even so, I try to dissuade her.

"There is more to the Tower than benighted St. Peter ad Vincula, so filled with death and pain."

"Oh, indeed, there are any number of places where poor souls lived in fear of their fate or suffered even worse."

She does not have to tell me that; I was one of those poor souls. As was Robin.

"Where I am going, you cannot come."

She steps back a pace and glares at me. "Is that a fact? And why not, if I may ask? Do you imagine that anything can shock or dismay me? That I will cry out in terror and run away?"

When I fail to answer, she shakes her head chidingly. "For

pity's sake, Elizabeth, I have been a prisoner there, too. I know what terrors that grim place holds. Let me come with you or toss me on the dust heap once and for all for truly I will believe myself of no more use to anyone."

What choice have I when I love her? "We will ride hard," I warn.

For a woman of her years, she does not spare herself. We make good time through the silent streets, our guard clattering after us. At the Tower, scarcely has the watchman thrown open the gate than I am in and riding across the green where my mother died. Kat is hard after me.

We dismount and she takes a moment to look around. Softly she says, "That last night before your coronation, I told myself that I would never come back to this place again."

"I am sorry to bring you here."

"Nonsense! I would not have it any other way. Where are we going?"

"We are there."

I see her pale for she realizes at once what has brought me. Kat has never said if she was at the Tower the day my mother died, but from her expression I glean that she knows exactly where Anne's blood was shed.

As I know, for I can feel it calling to me.

I do not kneel but fall instead upon the winter grass. It is brown and sere, with only hints of the green that will soon come. I feel the chill dampness through my skirts but scarcely notice it for an entirely different sensation, vastly more powerful, overwhelms me.

The essence of my mother's life poured out here in sacrifice. My father's effort at atonement was in truth the tribute she paid on my behalf, to preserve my soul and win for me the future she knew that I was meant to have.

"Mother!"

I am weeping and scarcely realize it. My tears fall upon the killing ground. I am within myself and not. Time and space bend, twisting out of all recognition.

Winter fades away and it is spring, but of a cruel and mocking sort in this place of death. I can smell the newly planked wood of the scaffold still redolent of the resins of the living trees from which it has been made. Except they are not trees, they are the monster's bones, a breathing skeleton, and they are about to swallow me whole.

Looking down, I, Anne Boleyn, Queen of this realm, see the black damask of my skirts sway as I walk. To either side of the gravel path, fresh grass perfumes the air. The guards move ahead and behind me, the blades of their halberds gleaming. Above me, I see the sweep of the blue sky lightly streaked by cloud and feel the blessed warmth of the sun upon my face, warmth so soon to be denied me forever.

But surely the light of Almighty God is a far greater radiance that banishes all fear, all doubt, and all longing. I must cling to that else I lose all courage.

I have prayed until I can pray no more, asked forgiveness for my sins, beseeched any I have offended in this life to pardon me. All this I have done for the well-being of my soul. But I also have made other preparations. The letter to Elizabeth is written and passed into safe hands. I have consulted with trusted men who possess the arcane knowledge necessary to protect her and who will find those best suited to continue that task until she is of age to protect herself.

I am comforted that I have done all that I can and now there remains only to die.

Four steps lead up to the scaffold. I climb them slowly, my hands clasped at my waist. My ladies follow, weeping. Truly, I wish that they would not do so for I fear the sound of their grief will weaken me at this, the moment when I need my greatest strength.

At the top of the stairs, I pause and gaze out over the sea of those who have come to witness my death. Most are of the nobility. I recognize several, malign men who conspired to turn the King against me for their own ends. They look well satisfied, but standing as I do on the brink of eternity, I know that their time will soon come. One or more of them will fail to satisfy Henry in some way and pay for it with his life. Even those who die in their beds at a great age will die all the same, as must all of us who have a claim to being human. When they do, they will face the same reckoning that I am about to confront.

This life is but the single beat of a heart carrying us into the life beyond.

With the assistance of my ladies, I remove my damask overgown. Beneath, I have dressed in bright red. The color of martyrdom proclaims my innocence and my peace with God. At sight of it, more than a few in the crowd gasp. Their countenances flicker with uncertainty.

Let their doubts take seed and grow. Let them speak of what they have seen this day in whispers, traveling ear to ear, that the Great Whore, as they have dubbed me, went to her death proclaiming that she was without stain and secure in the love of the Almighty.

I have come to the moment when it is expected that I will speak. I choose my words with the greatest care, knowing as I do that if I dare say anything of the vicious offense against God's law and man's that my royal husband is about to commit, I condemn our daughter to his vengeance. But knowing also that what I say will be remembered, chewed over through the years to come, and dissected for every shred of meaning.

On the very edge between life and death, about to face divine justice, which is the only justice that truly exists or matters in any way, it is well understood that I dare not lie. Accordingly, I say only that I am judged to die according to the law and that I yield myself to the will of the King. No one can dispute that for it is manifestly true. But I say nothing else. I confess to nothing; I admit no guilt.

In my silence is my absolution.

The malign men and their kind remain unmoved by my little speech, but here and there among the crowd I see tears begin to fall. Those who so lately condemned me now feel the thorn of doubt pierce their hearts.

Were I not already moving beyond the cares of this world, I would pity them for soon they will realize that if I am truly innocent, as they will fear, then they are ruled by a monster who killed his wife only because she failed to give him a son. What will the women of this realm make of that? What will the men who truly love their wives and daughters, and hold their lives to be of value, think of it?

With each word I speak, I am laying the road along which my daughter will walk to the throne as Queen regnant, accepted, loved, and trusted by her people.

It is time.

Henry's notion of mercy is that I shall not be burned and for that I am duly grateful. So, too, am I glad to be spared butchering by an ax that can take several strikes to end a poor victim's agony. Behind me stands a swordsman from France. I trust him to make a good job of it.

I sink to my knees and close my eyes, only to open them a moment later when I hear rustling. Here and there among the crowd, a few brave souls, openly weeping, are likewise kneeling. I am grateful for this small show of support but surprised when more follow suit. It is as though a wave rolls through the assembled mass. One by one, they fall to their knees until only a very few remain standing, held erect by their own complicity in my death. All around them the good people of this land honor the moment when my soul will take flight.

I have won! The truth will be known; my daughter, my beloved Elizabeth, will be safe. She will come into her own and she will save this realm from the one of whom I refuse to think in this my final moment.

*I am ready.*

*I throw out my arms to release my soul. My lips shape my last words:* Into Your hands. *But it is, as I have promised, of my bright-haired child that I think.*

*An instant of pressure, nothing more. No pain, no terror. But then—*

*What trick is this? I see the crowd but differently, as though I hang above them. See their faces contorted with horror and grief. See the bright sky over all and the brilliant light opening in it to receive me. And just there, on the very edge of my darkening vision, I see the poor crumbled remains of what I was, no longer of any consequence, the river of my life flowing out over the scaffold, falling onto the green grass of a new season just now being born.*

*I am free.*

*I am, now and forever, Anne.*

*Before dawn, 23 January 1559*

---

I am choking. On my knees, scrabbling in the dirt, I cannot breathe. I taste blood and for a moment fear that it is my mother's, only to realize that I have pressed my finger to my neck where Mordred bit me and sucked the traces onto my tongue.

Kat kneels beside me, her arms flung round my shoulders. "Sweetling!"

Her voice echoes down through the tunnel of time I am hurtled through to return me to my rightful moment. I feel a powerful, vibrating force coming up through the earth against which I press my hands, unlike any force I have ever known but which I recognize at once. It is the heartbeat of the earth itself, our Mother. But it is my mother as well, the sacrifice of Anne that is my strength.

In the depths of winter, I am surrounded by the scent of roses.

Kat holds me as I stumble to my feet. Grasping her hand, I turn, seeking frantically until I see it finally . . . rising in gleaming white above all else.

"Come with me!"

Please God that I have her fortitude when I attain her age. Together, we mount the steps leading up through the height of the great White Tower, built by the Conqueror when the Normans first came to this land. It is well-known that the tower stands upon far older remains that were discovered when its

foundation was dug. A watchtower has been in this place at
the bend of the river for as long as people have dwelled in this
land.

We climb, Kat puffing behind me but never lagging until at
last we come out on the walk that runs around the top of the
tower. There I pause a moment to get my bearings.

Ahead of me lies the river and, on its far bank, Southwark.
Closer still is London Bridge, crowded as it is with houses and
shops with only a narrow passage left for the vital traffic that
flows across it. Behind me the city stretches a short distance
north before giving way quickly to fields, pasturage, and wood-
land.

To the east, beyond the bridge, I see the dockyards where
vessels from all over the known world make port. To the west,
past the piers where the river whips to a fury when the tide is
high, is the City, followed by the residences of my high nobles,
and finally Westminster, with its proud Abbey and Whitehall
Palace. Somewhere in all of this Mordred waits. Dee may find
him in the stars, Walsingham may find him on the ground. But
I, Elizabeth, Queen regnant, cannot wait for either of them. I
must find my foe this night while my mother's blood sings in my
veins.

The moon is setting, bringing with its descent thickening
darkness. I gaze out over my city, over Morgaine's home, beyond
the place where my mother died, straining for any hint . . . any
clue . . .

Torches illuminate the precincts of the tower. Their reflections flicker in the river as it runs down past Whitehall and the
great mansions that glow against the night. All the houses
along the bridge show lamps burning in at least one or two windows and outside their doors. Along the wharves to the west, I
can see lanterns in the ships rocking at anchor and in the tav-

erns and brothels beyond. The warehouses that run alongside the docks are dark, as I would expect at such an hour.

Where has Mordred gone? Given his powers, he could be anywhere and Robin with him, but I know that he is somewhere nearby for I can feel his presence. After so long, he must know every lane and close in London. He could choose anywhere to conceal himself. No bolt hole then, resorted to upon the moment, but a place that he controls.

In a great house of obscure ownership? In the crypt of a church? Down an obscure alley? Behind a concealed door? In a tavern such as the one the laudanum users frequent?

Laudanum that was created on the Continent and is imported from there to our shores.

My attention returns to the docks. The wind is picking up, the ships rocking a little harder at anchor. Every manner of goods arrives on those vessels—timber and tar from the Baltics, herring and cheese from the Netherlands, wine from France and Italy, olives from all over the Mediterranean, and so much more all subject to the keen scrutiny of my tax collectors.

And laudanum?

The making of it requires opium, according to what Walsingham told me, and the poppies that produce it cannot be grown here. It must of necessity be imported.

Which means that Mordred has some connection to the sprawling dockside. I press against the stone parapet that rings the tower and stare out over the ships and warehouses. Nothing about any of them draws my particular attention . . . except . . . perhaps . . . just there, on the east side of the bridge directly next to the river. Not a large building, small really compared to some of the others, and in no way remarkable. Yet, my heightened senses catch something . . . a faint rippling in the air, an otherworldly glow from within its walls as though an unseen power is making itself at home.

It is all slight and could be credited to my desperate need to find something . . . anything. But the more I stare, the more certain I am.

Kat grabs hold of my arm as well she should for I have leaned far out over the parapet without even realizing that I did so.

"Come away, my lady," she urges.

The wind is growing stronger still. My hair whips wildly around me. The sliver of the moon dips below the horizon and it is fully night.

I smile into dear Kat's white face and murmur a word of reassurance. But I cannot be certain that she hears me for just then the stone parapet falls away and I am rising, lifting on the air, no longer a creature shackled to the earth but free to do as Mordred does. To soar.

Kat gasps and reaches out to me but I am gone, away from the tower, beyond the walls, out over my city. The hunt is on and I know exactly where to seek my prey.

———

*E*ven as I soar into the star-strewn sky, I cannot escape my horror at what I am in danger of becoming. I fear that Mordred's feeding upon me has unleashed power all too akin to his own. The distance that separates us, too small already because of the temptation he has exerted on me from the beginning, has narrowed to a perilous degree.

Yet there is a barrier against my surrender of which he knows nothing. Traveling up through the palms of my hands, along my outstretched arms and through my entire body, I can feel the power of the earth that drank my mother's blood. Anne is with me. The woman who climbed the scaffold rather than yield her humanity strengthens my courage and reconfirms my determination.

London slips beneath me. I cross over the sleeping bridge and quickly light on the riverbank near the warehouse. This close I am even more certain that an inhuman presence moves within it. The stone walls glow faintly and the very air surrounding them seems to shimmer.

All too aware that Mordred may be as able to sense me as I sense him, I go cautiously along the side of the building that faces the river. A pack of rats skitters out suddenly almost across my feet. I stifle a scream. They pause and eye me with twitching whiskers and bared yellow teeth before racing on toward the muck along the river.

When they are gone, I breathe again, but there is no time to indulge my sensibilities. My plan is to free Robin first, then deal with Mordred. To that end, I debate the wisdom of waiting for dawn in the hope that my enemy will be forced to rest. He was ready for me when I came against him at the manor; I have to expect that he will be again whether I attack by day or night.

Without Walsingham to rely on, I must find my own way into the warehouse. As I expect, the wide, arched doors fronting on the river are securely locked and bolted. With a quick glance around to be sure that none of the watch is nearby, I lift again into the air, settling behind the building in a small courtyard connected through an alley to the river road.

The windows along the back are shuttered; no hint of light escapes. Not that it matters. I make my way without difficulty, guided by the faint illumination of the stars, all that my heightened senses require.

The problem of how to enter still confounds me. I am close to wondering if I will have to pry open one of the shutters, the noise of which raises the possibility of discovery, when I notice a small flight of worn steps leading down toward a basement entrance. There, well concealed from all eyes and with my actions muffled by the surrounding walls, I find a sunken door that looks as though it has not been used in a generation and more. The door is locked but it hangs weakly on its hinges.

Is this a trap? Mordred anticipated that I would come to the manor and was prepared for me there. Has he guessed that I would be able to find him here and planned accordingly?

There is only one way to find out.

Slowly, with painstaking care, I ease up the bolts holding the hinges in place. Fortunately, the door is so old as to be eaten away by rot; I have no difficulty opening it the few inches needed for me to slip through.

The interior smells of dust and nothing more. I catch no whiff of rare spices or perfumes, no hint of timber or leather, no suggestion of exotic foodstuffs. A few crates and barrels are strewn about, but overall the warehouse appears all but empty. Save for a worktable placed almost exactly in the center of the floor, I see only a few benches, some unlit rush lamps, a large set of scales, and a wooden crate, which I discover upon examination contains small crystal vials waiting to be filled.

Reassured that I am in the right place, I take a careful look around while doing my best to stay in the shadows. The unmistakable resonance of Mordred's power that has drawn me to the warehouse tells me that he is somewhere nearby. I cannot hope to go undetected for long. I must find Robin with all speed.

Several small, ironbound doors lead off the main part of the warehouse, most likely to secure rooms used for storage. Quickly, I move from one to the other, peering through the grills. I have reached the fourth door when I am drawn up short by the sound of ragged breathing.

Grasping the grill in both hands, I boost myself up and stare into the room. There, on the floor, lies a huddled shape.

"*Robin.*" I dare no more than a whisper. The man, for I can make out that it is a man, does not stir.

"*Robin!*"

A flicker of movement, just enough to fan the flame of hope. With all my strength, I yank on the door, only to discover that unlike that through which I entered, the cell door is all too strong and unyielding.

There is only one thing to do.

"Robin, for pity's sake, hear me! Get as far away from the door as you can!"

Slowly, he turns his head to look at me. It is Robin! He is

pale and dazed but manages to crawl upright, first to his hands and knees, then hoisting himself to his feet.

"Elizabeth— My God, is it really you?"

Joy fills me but I repress it sternly. "Later, my love. There is no time to waste. Get back from the door!"

He hastens to do as I bid. When I am certain that he is at the far side of the cell, I call out, "Do not look. Turn your eyes away!"

I am afraid that the power I am about to unleash could blind him, especially coming as it will in such darkness.

The bolt I hurl illuminates the entire warehouse in incandescent light. If Mordred has not already sensed my presence, he certainly knows of it now. When the radiance subsides just a little, I can see that the door securing the cell is no more.

Robin stumbles out through the roiling dust. He looks stunned but alive and whole.

"Come," I order. "There is no time to waste." With my arm around him, I hasten back the way I came.

To give Robin full credit, he rallies with admirable speed. Having been snatched up by the vampire king, transported across London, and deposited in a dank cell, a man might be forgiven for requiring a little time to recover himself. Not so my dear love, who within minutes is expressing far more concern for my welfare than his own, if in the petulant way that men have when they feel put upon.

"For God's sake, Elizabeth, what are you doing here? Don't think me ungrateful, but tell me that you are not alone? And you didn't come with only those idiots Dee and Walsingham, did you? There's a squadron of men-at-arms outside, isn't there?"

Remarkably even to my own ears, a ripple of laughter escapes me. I attribute it to nerves and sheer giddy relief that he is safe, at least for the moment.

"I'm afraid there is only me, but never mind that. Thank Heaven I found you. We must make all haste—"

A ripple of movement, a sense of deeper, more impenetrable darkness, and I know at once that we are not alone.

"Run!" I scream, and push Robin toward the low stone steps through which I entered.

Infuriating, disobedient man, not only does he not heed my orders, he flings himself directly between me and Mordred, who strides from the shadows like the avenging fury I have no doubt he intends to be.

Yet he speaks calmly enough. "Really, Elizabeth, just when it seemed that you and I were making genuine progress."

Before I can reply, Robin thrusts me back and brandishes his sword.

"Stand and fight like a man! Or do you lack all courage and honor?"

Mordred stares at him in blank amazement, as I admit I do as well. What can Robin possibly be thinking? A mortal man against the full might and fury of the vampire king? If Robin is trying to prove that he is entirely daft, he is doing a damn fine job of it.

"For pity's sake," Mordred says.

"Robin, get out of the way!"

"I will not! Damn you, too, for thinking so low of me. You won't marry me because you think I would actually hurt you when all I've ever wanted to do is love and care for you. You think you have to do everything for yourself because you can't trust anyone else. Don't you see, he"—Robin raises his sword to point at Mordred—"he's taking advantage of all that, making you think that he's the only one who can help you or, if you won't agree to what he wants, that you have to fight him alone, which means that he will kill you and take what he wants anyway."

Generally speaking, Robin is not given to speeches, being more a man of action than words. This is more than I've heard from him at any one time since . . . I can't actually remember when.

"I'll just dispose of this and then we'll talk." Mordred raises a hand.

"No!" The blast I hurl should have done him severe damage, at the least, and no doubt would have if he hadn't been too fast for me. An enemy who can slow time has a grossly unfair advantage. Mordred uses it to both evade my blow and at the same instant snatch up Robin. I have only a moment to glimpse my dearest's strained, white face before they disappear.

When time returns to its accustomed flow, I am alone.

And infuriated with myself. Why did I not anticipate that Mordred would use every weapon in his arsenal, including his ability to bend space and time, to defeat me and make me a helpless supplicant to his wishes?

But he has made a mistake, perhaps a fatal one, for in feeding upon me, he has truly awakened latent powers I have not previously possessed. Not only the power of flight, as I have discovered, but also to do as he does and walk in the gaps that fall between the moments we know as reality, strung as they are like pearls on a string.

I leave the warehouse, noticing as I go that a rat, skittering between barrels, stands frozen, one paw lifted in the air, whiskers braced. Outside, the smoke rising from banked fires all over my city hangs motionless. The vessels moored at the quays do not rock. The few lamps lit here and there do not flicker but burn with an unnaturally steady light.

Swiftly, I seek some sign to tell me where Mordred has taken Robin. At first, I can find no hint of him. Only when my gaze travels to the bridge, heaped as it is with multistory dwellings clustered tightly together and hanging out over the water, do I sense the emanations of his otherworldly presence. When I realize where they are coming from, my heart sinks.

At the very center of the bridge lies the ruined chapel built four centuries ago to the memory of Thomas Becket, the Archbishop of Canterbury, who dared to challenge the authority of the great king Henry II. Becket died, supposedly at Henry's order, and was promptly declared a saint by the Roman Church grateful for the opportunity to put down an upstart ruler considered insufficiently respectful of its holy privileges.

My father, for reasons that should be obvious, had the chapel rededicated to Saint Thomas the Apostle, but that subterfuge had little effect and the chapel remained a focus for those objecting to reform of the Church. In the final months of my brother Edward's rule, his supporters, perhaps sensing what would happen once Catholic Mary assumed the throne, destroyed the chapel utterly. She left its ruins as a silent rebuke of the Reformers. It falls to me to do something about the blight on an otherwise prosperous and happy stretch of commerce, but, as of yet, I have been unable to give it my attention.

I will certainly need to do so now for there is no doubt where Mordred has gone. With all speed, I make for the ruins. As time resumes its flow, the wind off the river picks up. My hair streams out behind me. Small prickles of ice strike my face. A frozen mist rising from the water obscures the scene. I climb past the shut-up shops and slumbering residences, along the empty road that runs between them, barred now at the south side until morning comes and the tax collectors once again awake, for nothing enters my city without me being paid my due.

Mordred is waiting at the chapel ruins. He perches on the very edge of the tumbled stones, closest to the river. Robin is with him, choking in the grasp of the hand around his throat. His body dangles out over the water that, with the turning of the tide, is running at a fury through the piers of the bridge directly below.

"What will it be, Elizabeth?" Mordred calls. "Shall we have this out now or go our separate ways and cogitate upon the matter?"

Why would he give me such a choice? And why would he imagine that I would agree? Does he want more time to take the measure of my newfound powers and perhaps increase his own? Or does he still harbor the misbegotten belief that I can be persuaded to his side?

"What is to be gained by delay? We cannot both exist in this realm."

Mordred stretches his arm out farther. Robin, clawing at his hand, is now fully suspended over the deepest point of the river.

"Let him go," I call, "and face me in fair battle."

Mordred appears to consider it, his gaze luminous by starlight. His cloak whips around him. Even now, his beauty catches at my heart. I have never seen a more magnificent creature, but it is his malignancy that I must remember.

"The winner to take all?" he asks.

"Hasn't it ever been so? When Richard fell to my grandfather, his throne, his crown, his realm, all fell into Henry's hands. Would you have it differently?"

Instead of answering directly, Mordred looks amused. "Are you so confident of victory over me that you are willing to risk everything you hold dear?"

"I have no choice!"

"But you do, Elizabeth. The choice has always been yours.

You could have gone to Mary and asked her to find you a fine Catholic husband. She would have been overjoyed to do so. By now, you could be a mother several times over. Or you could have become a nun; your royal sister would have accepted that even more eagerly. You could have devoted your life to the scholarship of which you are so fond. You did neither. Instead, you risked your life to stay the course and become Queen. Why?"

"Because it is what I am meant to be. Only I—Queen and Slayer both—can protect this realm from you!"

"From me? What about from the Spanish, the Pope, and everyone else? Or have you forgotten about them?"

He shakes his head at my incomprehension. "Don't you see? To protect this realm from its mortal enemies requires that we work together. Believe me, I'm not happy to admit it, but the truth is that neither one of us can succeed alone. That is why I have waited for you so long and why I wait still."

His admission that his own powers have limits surprises me, but I cannot be deflected by it. Drawing on all my nerve, I say, "Well . . . that truly is a shame because tonight one of us is going to die."

Valiant words, but I tell myself that I mean them. Mordred's claim threatens to undermine my will at this most crucial point. Even as I raise my arm to strike at him, a small seed of doubt begins to blossom. Before my resolve can weaken, I must act.

To my surprise, Mordred makes no move to defend himself. Instead, he looks at me with what gives every appearance of regret.

"I cannot let you do this, Elizabeth. Both of us are far too important to this realm to sacrifice either on the altar of your misconceptions. You are young yet and in time you will come to understand that."

"You cannot stop me—"

"Oh, but I can."

He opens his hand.

Robin plummets toward the raging river. I hear myself scream as though from a great distance.

For a fragment of time I do indeed have a choice—strike at Mordred as he stands exposed on the crumbled stone of the destroyed chapel making no effort to defend himself. If my aim is true and my blow strikes home, I will slay him.

I then risk that he is right and that only the two of us together can preserve this realm.

I can do that or I can save Robin.

For Morgaine, love was the most powerful force of all. I thought the notion frivolous and congratulated myself that I could not be prey to any such weakness. Yet love has come upon me and with the same results: I am its hostage. Without it, all that I fight for will be no more than a dry, empty husk.

Mordred knows this in some way. He knows me better than myself.

"No!"

I leap from the side of the bridge down toward the stygian water, which hurtles up to meet me. Frantically I stretch out my hands, straining for Robin. Time bends to my will but it is not enough. My fingers scarcely brush his doublet. He strikes the surface and at once sinks beneath it.

The moment hangs suspended. My heart does not beat, my blood does not flow. Only desperation exists and it drives me on. I plunge into the river that is the lifeblood of my city and my realm, fumbling in the darkness for any sign of hope.

And find none, only emptiness that sinks my soul. Robin—bold, daring, stalwart Robin—must not end this way, not because of me.

My mother died a monarch's sacrifice; I cannot let a flawed but well-meaning man who loves me do the same.

*Robin!*

My hand brushes . . . something. A bit of flotsam such as clogs the river in all seasons? Or vastly more precious than that?

Desperately, I tighten my grip and rise up, erupting out of the water toward the bankside. Whatever I have grasped goes with me. On the shingle shore, I collapse, gasping for breath, and scarcely dare to look up until I hear the blessed sound of gagging and see a spew of foul river water erupt.

"Robin!"

More gagging, more spewing. Then, when he is finally done: "Lawd, Elizabeth, you let him go!"

Incredulity fills me. He cannot possibly be serious. I gaze into his strained, white face and shake my head in disbelief.

"Should I have let you drown instead?"

"I'm glad you didn't. But *he* still lives." Robin drags himself upright and stares toward the bridge. There is no sign of Mordred. The vampire king is gone on the night.

"I had to make a choice." Weak words even to my own ears, yet true enough although the life I chose to preserve is not the one Robin will assume.

"I know and I am grateful but—"

He does not know. When a little time has passed and he thinks of this moment, he will believe that I leapt into the water for love of him. He will preen in the light of that imagined love and his ambitions will swell. It will be the undoing of us in the end, but what other course is there?

Am I to tell him that I acted for love not of a man but for this blessed isle, to which I, its anointed ruler, am consecrated? That I did not try to slay the vampire king because I may have need of him?

Robin turns and looks at me from behind those dark, liquid eyes of the sort the Italians paint so well. "I heard what he said. Mordred really believes that it will take the two of you together to preserve this realm. Is he right?"

Without replying, I scramble to my feet and start up toward the river road. I am fleeing from myself as much as from Robin, but I can escape neither. He hurries after me. I hear him calling.

"Is he right, Elizabeth? Do you believe that this realm will perish without you both?"

The going is littered with sharp shingles but I scarcely notice. After all, if I had not been born with a light step and the instinct for when and how to stretch out my arms to embrace what I need most, I would long since have perished. Let no one condemn me for being what I must be unless they think to wrest the crown from my head, and then, by God, they will have such a struggle as the world has never seen.

The wind is picking up again. Toward the east, a rim of gray appears. A new day is being born. I walk into it, uncertain as yet what I must become in order to preserve my realm, but resolved that while I yet draw breath, no enemy mortal or immortal shall prevail against me.

I am the Slayer awaited for a thousand years but I am more.

I am, and I shall ever be,

Elizabeth, the Queen.

# POSTSCRIPT

―――――

FROM THE DESK OF LUCY WESTON

I first became aware of the existence of *The Secret History* some years ago in London when I overheard a discussion in a private club hidden away down a narrow lane that has changed little in centuries and is known to few. There Mordred was holding court before an audience of his acolytes, regaling them with episodes of his long, eventful career. In doing so, he mentioned *The Secret History*. I have done my best to faithfully record his remarks here.

I confess that my interest was piqued. For too long, the highest echelons of the British government have concealed the deadly peril posed by vampires. The discovery of Elizabeth Tudor's journals, written in her own hand and recording her battles with the vampires of the British Isles, would forever shatter this cruel deception.

I was mulling over how best to proceed when, on the afternoon of 20 November 1992, everything changed. The first reports of a massive fire at Windsor Castle began to come in around noon. By midafternoon, it was clear that a significant part of the castle was burning. At about six o'clock, my phone rang. The caller was an antiquarian aware of both my interest in all things Elizabethan and my lack of scruples in acquiring them. He told me that he was at the scene of the fire, watching the items being removed, among them a small chest containing a collection of journals bound in embossed leather and bearing the initials *ER*. For the right price, he would arrange for the chest to slip unseen from the pile of salvaged items. Less than half an hour after receiving the call, I was en route to Windsor.

I will not dwell on the excitement that accompanied my smuggling of the chest back to London. My hands shook when I opened it. There they were—the leatherbound personal journals of Elizabeth Tudor, who identified herself as "Vampire Slayer."

I was terrified that the pages would crumble to dust before I could read a single word. But time—and the dry, cool environment within the walls of Windsor Castle—had proved kind. Quickly, I started to read the elaborate script. The story that unfolded before my eyes was startling in the extreme and unlike any I could have predicted. By the time I finished it, I knew that I had exactly the weapon I needed to rouse public rage against the vampires that threatened the land still, and bring them down. But I also knew that it would be of no use to me if I was not able to deploy it correctly.

In the time since then, I have employed experts to confirm that the paper, ink, and bindings of the journals are all consistent with their creation during the Elizabethan Age. Other experts have matched the calligraphy to known samples of the Queen's hand. Still more have confirmed that the small details occurring throughout—a mention, for example, of the presence of a particular ambassador at court on such and such a date or a particular gown worn by the Queen at an event—conform to what is described in numerous authenticated sources.

This task has been complicated by the need for me to avoid detection by both the vampire clan and British intelligence, each of which remains determined to deny the public any awareness of the great peril humanity faces. I have been forced to keep on the move and use all my wits to avoid capture.

Now at last, after a silence of centuries, Elizabeth Tudor may once again speak for herself.

*Lucy Weston*
*January 2011*

www.lucywestonvampire.com

*The*
SECRET HISTORY
*of*
ELIZABETH TUDOR,
*Vampire Slayer*

# LUCY WESTON

# Introduction

On the eve of her coronation, Elizabeth Tudor discovers that she is heir to more than just the throne of England. In an arcane ritual performed at the Tower of London, her powers as a vampire slayer are awakened. Plunged into a deadly struggle for the future of her realm, she is caught between her human yearnings and the temptation presented by Mordred, king of the vampires, who offers her eternal life as his queen. In her own words, Elizabeth reveals to us her greatest fears, her most intimate longings, and ultimately the choice she makes that will change her world forever.

## Questions for Discussion

1. *The Secret History of Elizabeth Tudor, Vampire Slayer* reveals the hitherto hidden connections between the worlds of the Tudors and the Vampires. Were you surprised to discover that such connections exist? Does the involvement of paranormal forces help to explain how Elizabeth was able to reign so long and so successfully in a time of such danger?

2. If, like Elizabeth, you discovered that you had a secret destiny upon which the fate of a nation rested, how would you feel? Would you be (a) thrilled and excited; (b) terrified and apprehensive; (c) stunned but resolved to do your best?

3. Elizabeth's awakening as a vampire slayer happens beside the grave of her mother, Anne Boleyn. Beyond Elizabeth's determination never to marry, what do you think was the effect on her of her mother's death? How did Anne's tragic fate influence Elizabeth's behavior as a woman? As a monarch?

4. Elizabeth found a surrogate mother in Kat Ashley, a woman from a very different background than Elizabeth's own. How do you think the largely self-made Kat, who defied so many of the conventions of her time, influenced Elizabeth's character?

5. In her journal, Elizabeth reveals intimate details of her relationship with Robert Dudley that have previously only been speculation. What do her feelings for him say about her as a woman? As a monarch? Do you believe that he truly loves her or is he, as Mordred claims, only using her to regain his family's wealth and power? Dudley comes from a long line of traitors. Is Elizabeth foolish to trust him?

6. In bringing *The Secret History* to light, Lucy Weston also reveals the vampire Mordred's version of these events. What do you think of Mordred? Is he, as society would claim, entirely evil or are there positive forces at work within him?

7. When Mordred proposes to Elizabeth that they work together to protect England, do you think she should agree? Are the worldly enemies she faces actually more dangerous than the vampires?

8. Elizabeth is frank about her attraction to Mordred and the temptation he presents. In her position, would you be as attracted to him as she is? If you had to choose, which would you pick: eternal life as Queen of the Vampires or life as a mortal?

9. What do you think is Lucy Weston's motivation for revealing *The Secret History*? How closely connected do you think she is to Mordred and the vampire clan?

10. Lucy tells us that the British government has concealed the existence of the vampires and their role in British history. How do you think Her Majesty's government is likely to respond to the release of *The Secret History*? Is Lucy in danger?

## ENHANCE YOUR BOOK CLUB

1. This book is composed of the journals of Elizabeth Tudor, found in the Windsor Castle after a fire and brought to the public by one Lucy Weston. Learn more about Lucy and the journals online at www.lucywestonvampire.com. And follow Lucy's ongoing adventures on Facebook and Twitter.

2. Have a vampire- and/or Tudor-themed costume party! Serve beverages and snacks that match the theme (e.g., Bloody Marys, red velvet cupcakes, high tea).

3. Many great movies and shows include vampires or the Elizabethan era. Encourage group members to bring their favorite vampire and/or Tudor show or movie to a viewing party. Some suggestions: *Bram Stoker's Dracula, True Blood, Twilight, Dracula: Dead and Loving It, The Tudors, Elizabeth, Shakespeare in Love, Buffy the Vampire Slayer.*

# AN INTERVIEW WITH THE AUTHOR, LUCY WESTON

In the months preceding release of *The Secret History* to the public, the publisher made repeated efforts to contact Ms. Weston. As her whereabouts remain unknown and communication with her is difficult, we had almost given up when she re-appeared and agreed to sit for a short interview. Here are the results.

**Q: There has been some confusion over whether you yourself are a fictional character or an actual person. Would you like to take this opportunity to clear that up?**

A: Not really. My decision to rescue the secret journals of Elizabeth Tudor, revealing her life as a vampire slayer, from the concealment in which they have languished for centuries has put me at odds with both the vampire clan itself and elements of the British government. Anything I can do to obscure my identity, my whereabouts, or my future plans helps to assure my safety.

Q: **That sounds as though you believe you really are in danger. Do you?**

A: I have been in danger since the day I was ripped from my human life and turned into a creature I never wanted to be.

Q: **On that subject, your transformation into a vampire is depicted in Bram Stoker's *Dracula*. He changed your name to Lucy Westenra and obviously, his claim that you were subsequently slain was false. What reason did he have for obscuring what actually happened?**

A: You would have to ask Mister Stoker. But, of course, being dead, he can't be called to account for his actions. I will say only that he had his reasons for promoting the notion that vampires are fictional. At another time, I may reveal his motivations more fully.

Q: **In among Elizabeth's recounting of events, you include commentary by the vampire king, Mordred that provides a very different perspective. How did you come into possession of such information and why did you decide to share it?**

A: Mordred has no hesitation about discussing his exploits. Anyone familiar with the vampire world in London and elsewhere can gain access to him and hear what he has to say. I decided to make known his version of events in order to help the public understand the danger he presents.

Q: **You refer to "journals" as in more than one. Should we conclude that there are more volumes of *The Secret History* to come?**

A: Only if I survive long enough to bring them to public notice.

At this point in the interview, Ms. Weston received a text. Upon reading it, she indicated her need to depart immediately. Further efforts to contact her have been unsuccessful.